An excerpt from
Beard (Ironclad Bodyguards 3)

Jenna stared at the door. She shouldn't have slammed it, but she felt a little intimidated by the new bodyguard. He was bigger than she expected. Taller, more intent.

Handsomer.

No, he wasn't that handsome. He wasn't Nathaniel-handsome. He was too wholesome or something, too sincere. Vivid blue eyes, square jawline, hair that was buzzed on the bottom and golden-brown spikes on top. He had a goatee, discreet and closely trimmed, that looked like he spent time on it. She'd thought her personal bodyguard would be more like the scowling, retired Marines who roved the compound, protecting the perimeter without speaking to her or meeting her gaze. Caleb Winchell had looked directly into her eyes like he was trying to take her measure. It'd been forever since someone dared to do that.

She made a face, even though no one could see it, and flopped on her deep, soft bed. She didn't know when Gladys would take him touring, or how soon he'd be back in her part of the house. She hoped he didn't expect to scope out her bedroom, at least not while she was in it.

He's going to be wherever you are. Get used to it.

This was all that fucker Tom's fault, and Nate's, for being obsessed with the maniac. She closed her eyes, trying not to think about them, but that made her start thinking about the bodyguard instead. *He's going to be where you are. He's going to be around you all the time.*

He wasn't handsome. No. She'd already forgotten the specifics of his face. Well, she kind of remembered his full, attractive lips set off by his goatee, and the symmetry of his cheekbones, and his blue, blue eyes. Okay, he was actually pretty handsome in a simple, classic way, not that it mattered. He was so *young*.

She wondered if he was staying over tonight, since he was starting tomorrow. He'd brought luggage, but he might just be leaving it and unpacking in the morning.

She kind of hoped he was going to stay…

Copyright 2018 Annabel Joseph/Molly Joseph/Scarlet Rose Press

* * * * *

This book is a work of fiction. Names, characters, places, and incidents are products of the author's imagination or are used fictitiously. Any resemblance to actual events, locales, or persons living or dead, is entirely coincidental.

All characters depicted in this work of fiction are 18 years of age or older.

BEARD

Ironclad Bodyguards #3

Molly Joseph

Other books by Molly Joseph
Pawn
Diva
The Edge of the Earth

Books by Annabel Joseph
Mercy
Cait and the Devil
Firebird
Owning Wednesday
Lily Mine
Disciplining the Duchess

Fortune series:
Deep in the Woods
Fortune

Comfort series:
Comfort Object
Caressa's Knees
Odalisque
Command Performance

Cirque Masters series:
Cirque de Minuit
Bound in Blue
Master's Flame

Mephisto series:
Club Mephisto
Molly's Lips: Club Mephisto Retold
Burn For You

BDSM Ballet series:
Waking Kiss
Fever Dream

Properly Spanked series:
Training Lady Townsend
To Tame A Countess
My Naughty Minette
Under A Duke's Hand

1.
APPEARANCES

Caleb took a couple deep breaths before he stepped off the elevator. He wasn't normally one to experience anxiety or nervous tics, but when the big boss and the big boss's boss called you in for a private meeting, there was a reason. Possibly a bad reason. When he reached Ironclad's suite of offices, the receptionist smiled from her desk. "Hi, Caleb. Hector and Michelle are waiting for you in the conference room."

"Thanks."

Bea's smile meant nothing. She smiled at everyone, even though she was one of the most lethal model-gorgeous blonde women he knew. When she unlocked the door, he proceeded down the hall to the conference room, catching a glimpse of his reflection in the corridor's glass walls. He looked put together in his company's required dark suit, with his high-and-tight buzz cut and trimmed goatee. Appearances were everything in Hollywood, even for bodyguards.

When he reached the conference room, the door was open. He tapped it anyway, and his boss, Hector, stood to beckon him in. "Good afternoon, Caleb. Coffee?"

"No, thank you."

"You remember Michelle from Ironclad's corporate headquarters?"

Caleb's gaze moved from his solid, dark-haired boss to Michelle Fawkes, the willowy district manager. Her playful afro and easy smile hid a will of steel, and her dark eyes struck fear into the heart of more hardened security agents than him. He shook her hand when she offered it and seated himself at the mahogany conference table.

"Thanks for coming in on such short notice," said Hector. "We were just looking over your file."

Daunting words, but Caleb had nothing to hide. Since he'd started as a Hollywood bodyguard eight months ago, he'd done several assignments: taken starlets shopping, shepherded actors to awards parties, even shadowed a young rave performer on a close-security detail for a while.

Michelle cleared her throat, her fingertips sliding over her tablet's screen. "I see from your resume that you came to Ironclad from Special Forces." She arched a brow, glancing up at him. "You're only twenty-five now. You must have joined the military early."

"Yes, ma'am. I joined as soon as I graduated high school."

Caleb had actually been recruited out of high school after earning state titles in Tae Kwon Do and shooting. His Army supervisor had funneled him into Delta Force soon after he graduated basic training, the youngest candidate ever admitted to the organization. He'd been so proud. He'd never imagined then that a Texas boy could end up in the places he'd been, doing the things he'd done.

"Did you enjoy your time in the military?" she pressed. "What kind of action did you see?"

"Smaller operations," he said. "Close combat situations, mostly. My unit traveled a lot."

"Where?"

Caleb bit his lip, knowing how much he was allowed to reveal, which was basically nothing.

"He can't give us the details," Hector broke in. "You know how it is with those Special Forces guys. Top secret missions."

Caleb tilted his head, neither confirming nor denying. "Special Forces" was a fiction the Army let him use on his resume, when in fact he'd been placed with a CIA Special Ops Group by his twenty-first birthday. They'd taught him the noncommittal head tilt, among other useful things.

"I enjoyed my work in the military," Caleb said. "I'm able to use a lot of those skills in personal security."

"Well, we appreciate your skill set and hard work," said Michelle, "and in light of your glowing reviews, we're ending your probationary period early and promoting you to a fully vested bodyguard here at Ironclad Solutions. Clients describe you as trustworthy, dependable, and easy to work with. In this city, with the types of people we service, that's pretty high praise."

An early promotion for good performance. Like the military, they were pushing him ahead, past the average Joes. It triggered an uneasy feeling, a sense of caution. *This is different. Bodyguarding is different.* He smiled and thanked them for the honor.

"While you're here, Caleb, we have a new assignment we're thinking about for you," said Hector, glancing at Michelle. Since the district manager had traveled here to talk about it, there was more to this prospective assignment than the typical A-lister needing a ride to some charity ball.

"We had a big celebrity visit the office yesterday, along with his manager and an entourage of guards." Hector cleared his throat. "Nathaniel York is growing his security team. You wouldn't think someone with that many bodyguards would need more bodyguards, but Mr. York wants a specialized detail for his wife. Close security and management, a full-time thing."

Nathaniel York? He was the biggest celebrity in Hollywood, an A-list king. He was arguably the most famous actor in the world, with his face and production company attached to all the biggest films. "His wife doesn't already have a bodyguard?"

"They have an operations team for general security and public appearances, but they've decided they want Mrs. York to have a personal agent close at hand, both at home and on the outside. If you take the assignment, you'll be given a private suite in the household to stay proximate with your client. You can expect to have all mornings off, and one full day a week without duty, sometimes more, depending on scheduling."

For close security, it was a decent deal.

"I know you recently came off the Lady Paradise assignment, which was similar in scope," said his boss. "She spoke highly of your discretion and professionalism."

Caleb's discretion had been tested on that job, because Lola, aka Lady Paradise, was a bundle of trouble, but Caleb was from Spur, Texas, where people were discreet to a fault. You noticed trouble, sure, but you didn't make a fuss about it, because that embarrassed everyone. If a friend was in deep trouble…say, if their arm was dangling from their body by a couple of tendons, you might offer to do something to improve the situation. Otherwise, you erred on the side of discretion and kept your mouth shut.

Same thing with the CIA. You did your secret missions and didn't ask questions, and didn't talk about them when they were over. If you had too much of a mouth, you'd find yourself demoted or kicked out. Caleb only mouthed off once, but he'd been kicked out of the military altogether. Honorably discharged on paper, but kicked out by his command leader all the same.

Now he'd been working out of Ironclad's largest U.S. office for the better part of a year. When he signed on, they'd warned him about the industry craziness, but stars and their nonsense was a craziness Caleb could control. Nothing here was as bad as it had been in Russia, Yemen, or Afghanistan. He pushed those thoughts from his head and refocused on what his boss was saying.

"The Yorks have a sizable estate in Hollywood Hills. It's close to your apartment if you want to stay there while you're off duty, but they'll want you available at short notice if needed."

"That won't be a problem."

"And there will be some long-haul travel involved. Mr. York has a movie coming out this summer, with some international premieres he'll attend with his wife."

As if Caleb didn't know. Trailers for *Fire and Fury* had been showing in theaters and online since December. "Travel's fine," he said. "What other information should I know?"

Michelle gave an amused snort. "You're right, Hector. He's a seasoned agent. He knows there's always more information."

Hector smiled, but it didn't quite reach his eyes. "Okay. The nitty-gritty on the Yorks. Our friends in law enforcement tell us the compound is heavily guarded because of overzealous fans. As you know, not all of them are mentally stable, and Nate York makes the high-octane action flicks that get the crazies wound up. The grounds security team intercepts trespassers several times a week. You'll be given detailed information about the most frequent offenders, and have an opportunity to look over the various restraining orders on file."

"Sounds good."

"In addition to trespassers at home, your client, Jenna York, has to deal with crowds and paparazzi while she's out, as well as the occasional jealous female fan."

"I imagine so."

"There've been a few kidnap attempts over the years," added Michelle, pointing out a file titled INTERPOL. "We call them attempts, but none of the assailants got close enough to the Yorks to pull anything off."

"Kidnapping?" Caleb raised a brow. "And Mrs. York is just now agreeing to close protection?"

Hector put down his tablet and slid his fingertips across the smooth tabletop, stopping them with a tap. "There's a lot going on in that household, as you'd expect considering Mr. York's worldwide stardom and recognition. Your military experience and availability to travel makes you the perfect candidate for this assignment, if you're interested."

"I'm definitely interested."

"Good. Pay is top of scale. End date of duty is not defined. Let me know within the next couple days."

He didn't have to think about it. "I'm in." What else did he have to do with his time? He'd recently ended a two-year relationship that wasn't healthy for either of them, and moved to an apartment he didn't like very much. "If you think I'm a good fit for the assignment, I'm willing to start whenever Mrs. York needs me."

"Perfect. I'm glad to hear that." Hector studied him a moment. "There's one more thing you should know going into this assignment, so you aren't caught off guard."

Caleb suppressed a chuckle. There was more? The two managers exchanged a glance, then Michelle cleared her throat.

"This is delicate," she said. "What I'm about to tell you must not be repeated outside this room, ever."

"Of course."

"There's been some speculation about the nature of the York's' marriage," she continued after a heavy pause. "Maybe you've heard the rumors?"

He shook his head. He didn't keep up with celebrity gossip. "Is there a divorce brewing?"

"No, no divorce." Michelle looked uncomfortable.

"Just spit it out," Hector said. He turned to Caleb. "There's a full-time bodyguard in the household, Thomas Maxon, who accompanies Nathaniel York everywhere."

"Is he with Ironclad?" Caleb asked.

"No. York uses LSS Security for most of his teams, but Maxon doesn't work for any agency." He brought up a photo on his tablet to show Caleb the bodyguard. He was built like an old-school bouncer. Tight suit, big muscles, alert gaze. "As far as we know, Maxon has never been certified by any security agency. His last known job was acting in some B-films about ten years ago."

"I see."

"Speculation is that he's not really Mr. York's bodyguard." Michelle's expression was inscrutable. "A trusted source connected to our company believes Tom Maxon has a more...intimate relationship with his employer."

"With Jenna?" Caleb asked.

"No. With Nathaniel York."

He tried to digest that theory. Nathaniel York, buff, hyper-masculine, lady-killer action star, in a gay relationship with his bodyguard?

"To be honest, it's not speculation," said Michelle. "According to our source, Tom and Nathaniel are in a long-time romantic relationship. Jenna York willingly married Nathaniel ten years ago to keep up appearances, as they say."

"In other words," Hector said, "your client is Nathaniel York's 'beard,' and the three of them live together in their mansion on the hill."

They watched him, expecting a comment perhaps, an observation, but he was still stuck on the idea that Nathaniel York was secretly gay. Of course, there was nothing wrong with being gay. But if your career depended on playing superheroes and ladykillers...

There was only one thing Caleb could think to say about that situation. "That's sad." He looked up at his bosses. "I guess it would be detrimental to his career if that kind of information got out."

"Yes, which is why discretion is so important in this assignment."

Caleb narrowed his eyes. "So...when the Yorks came in to set up this protection detail, they didn't say anything about...?"

"Nate York came in with his manager, and they didn't say anything, so you'll need to act like you don't know anything," said Hector. "Like you don't notice anything unusual in the course of your duties. As I said, these are only 'rumors' that have not been 'confirmed.'"

"Got it." Caleb glanced down at the table's smooth grain, wondering what kind of situation he was getting into. "Is that the assignment, then? They want a live-in bodyguard for purposes of beard protection?"

"It seems so." His boss shrugged. "Shouldn't be that difficult. I looked into Jenna York, but there's not a big imprint. She's not a troublemaker or public nuisance. She hangs on Nate's arm and looks pretty, keeps herself up and walks well in heels."

That, too, seemed sad to Caleb. "She's never had another job?"

"Like Maxon, she tried acting, but never even made it to B-films."

Michelle showed him some photos, early headshots of Jenna with bright, deep brown eyes and a wide smile. Jenna Carpenter, unknown actress. He flipped past those to more recent event photos of Mrs. Jenna York, with a very different smile. A cooler, more guarded smile. He remembered seeing her with Nathaniel York at a couple red carpet assignments. He'd found her pretty in the brittle, elegant way of Hollywood wives. Dark bangs, wavy long hair, a petite build, and an unreadable expression.

Amazing to be unreadable, when she seemed to have so much to hide.

"Any kids?" he asked.

"No," said Hector, while Michelle muttered, "Thank God for that. Not that I'm judging," she added. "It just seems like things are already complicated enough in that household. Anyway, if you're up for the assignment, we'll let the Yorks know to expect you. Can you report in a couple days?"

"Sure. I'll throw some things in a suitcase."

"Hector told me you were a minimalist," she said, her serious expression warming to a smile.

He nodded. "It's good for living on the run."

"That rave gal had him on the run," Hector joked. "Flying back and forth across the country, dealing with parties and drama, and emotional breakdowns."

"And loud, irritating music," Caleb added. "Well, she was young."

They both laughed. "You're young, too," said Michelle. "Or had you forgotten?"

Caleb hadn't forgotten. He just didn't feel very young most days. In that way, he and the "rave gal" had had a lot in common, which made that assignment somewhat easier. He wondered how things would go with Mrs. Jenna York. Did she have emotional breakdowns when the cameras weren't flashing? What lurked behind that brittle, beautiful facade?

He'd just accepted a close security assignment to protect her, so he was about to find out.

* * * * *

Jenna jerked awake at the knock and swung her knees down from the sofa. Her knitting project had turned into a tangle in her lap. She moved it to the side and went to peer through the peephole that separated her from the rest of the York mansion. "I was sleeping," she said through the door.

"C'mon, Jen, let me in."

She unlocked the door and stood back to let Nate pass into her private living space. This was her sanctuary, so he didn't look comfortable as he crossed to sit on her couch. She chose to stand.

"How're you?" he asked, crossing one leg over the other.

She reached to touch her jaw, tracing the spot where a bruise had faded, leaving behind a faint ache that flared when she pressed too hard. "I'm okay."

"Has Gladys gotten with you about the charity dinner next week? Everything's set?"

"You know Gladys. She has everything under control."

He looked up at her, then at the sofa beside him. "Don't you want to sit down?"

She regarded her handsome, famous husband, thinking how many women would swoon at the chance to sit beside him. He was just Nate to her, the guy who'd invited her into a bogus marriage, charming her into believing everything would work. Oh, back then she'd had stars in her eyes, or she wouldn't have gone along with it. Nate could seduce a block of wood with one smoky look.

She sighed and sat beside him. He pulled her closer, gathering her in his arms. "How many times do I have to apologize?" he asked.

"An infinite number of times."

He pressed his cheek to hers, then gave her a kiss that was as gentle as it was chaste. "Tom feels terrible about what happened. He's so sorry he lost it."

"He says he is." Her throat went dry, as it often did when they discussed Nate's lover.

"He really is sorry, babes. He can't help his temper, that's just how he's wired. I'm sorry he came after you. I never, ever thought he'd do something like that. I never thought he'd cross that line."

Jenna rubbed her eyes, pulling away from him as far as he'd let her. Honestly, she wished Tom would die. She wished Nate loved anyone else. She wasn't jealous of Tom, no. She wasn't deluded enough to hope Nate would ever love her, or any woman, no matter how accurately he played a dashing hetero out in the real world. She was just tired of taking abuse from Nate's love. Recently, verbal and emotional abuse had escalated to an actual physical altercation. He'd attacked her, landing a punch as the three of them raged.

Nate had defended her right away, pushing Tom away from her. His lover had sobbed, melted down, and apologized endlessly, but it was only to protect himself. Nate said they wouldn't go to the police, not yet, not this time, because of the "optics."

As for her, she still felt numb.

"You okay, babes?" Nate asked, tilting up her head.

"I'm fine."

"You've been so reclusive. You never come out of your rooms anymore. Are you still staying honest with all the...?"

"You can say it. My drinking problem."

"It wasn't that big a problem," he said.

But to her it was, which was why she'd stopped before it got any worse. It would have been so easy to let everything go, to sink into an alcoholic stupor and stay there, allowing Nate's many security agents and minders to guide her dumbly where she needed to be. She could smile just as well when she was drunk as when she was sober. But looking down into that abyss had terrified her. Yes...so easy...

He touched her arm, drawing her from the darkness that dogged her days. "I wanted to let you know that I hired a bodyguard for you today, the way I promised. Well, Gladys picked him out. Sorry it took a few days. I was busy with the *Fire and Fury* promo."

And you needed the bruise on my jaw to go away.

"We decided to go with Ironclad Solutions," he said. "Gladys heard their agents were best at close protection. With our upcoming travel, it'll be good to have someone next to you in case of crowd control issues."

And in case your secret fucktoy decides to attack me when he's had too much to drink.

She stared at her hands, accustomed to Nate's fakeness, his awful disingenuous bullshit and her inability to call him on it. She was so used to it by now, so inured to the false stories and manufactured scenarios that had nothing to do with reality. Crowd control issues? Crowds were the same everywhere, but it was easier for Nate to hire a bodyguard for that, than to admit his lover was a psycho maniac who enjoyed tormenting his fake wife.

"When does he start?" asked Jenna, looking at the half-open door. Tom might come storming in at any moment, and that scared her. She'd given Nate an ultimatum—personal bodyguard or divorce. They'd had a terrible fight about it, with Tom pounding crazily on the door from outside. Nate had reminded her—again—that their prenuptial document provided nothing, no support or payout, if she elected to end their marriage. He, of course, could end it at any time, but he never would.

Jenna thought she might be able to fight the prenup based on Tom's escalating attacks, or at least threaten her way out of it, but she wasn't sure. Whenever she talked about things like that, Nate's rage was as terrifying as Tom's, and she, the weak, friendless pseudo-wife, retreated into her hidey hole and doubted if she'd ever be happy again.

The bodyguard was an olive branch. She knew that, so she tried to muster up a smile as Nate went on about his visit to Ironclad, the contract's terms of service, and the fact that the bodyguard would be showing up in a couple days to move into the spare room in her suite.

"He's going to live in my suite?" she asked. "Like, in my guest room?"

"That's close protection, babes." For a moment, Nate looked tired. "If I put him on our side of the house, Tom would probably try to hook him into a threesome."

"Why do you stay with him?" She couldn't keep the words inside. Sometimes they burst out despite all her intentions. "I mean, really, Nate, why?"

Nate's large hazel eyes took on a cinematic glint. "You know why. Tom makes me feel alive. I'm an artist, Jen, an actor, a performer. I need inspiration, even if he drives both of us crazy. I'm sorry, but I need him. I depend on him."

He started into his pitiful act. Tears glistened in his eyes. She knew they weren't real.

"I know. I *know*, babes. I'm sorry you have to put up with me and my craziness." He touched her hand, then clasped it with an overblown sigh. "I try to make you happy. I give you money, clothes, vacations, a glamorous lifestyle."

"You won't get me an assistant."

"Why would you need an assistant? You don't do anything. What's on your schedule? Nada. Alcoholics Anonymous meetings you probably don't attend anymore, and charity work where you don't get paid."

"That's kind of the point of charity work, isn't it? Are we hurting for money? Anything you aren't telling me about?"

"When you get back into acting, we'll talk about an assistant," he said. "Or if we try for another baby…"

His voice drifted off when she glared at him, stricken. He shrugged and used a couple fingers to tousle his million-dollar hair. "Well, you know how I feel about having a bunch of people in the house. There are already my assistants and the security team, and now your bodyguard…"

Her bodyguard, so she'd be safe in her own home. What had become of her life? She used to enjoy acting, had desperately wanted to do it as a career, but they both knew it would never happen now. She was disgusted with acting at this point, because she did it every day for no money and no recognition. He made the money, he basked in the fame. She was the useless wife who didn't even merit an assistant.

Marrying Nate had seemed like a spectacular opportunity at the time, a stepping-stone to more roles and unlimited contacts within the industry. Who needed a straight husband when you had fame and money, and all the opportunity in the world? He'd been honest with her about what he needed—a beard. He'd never lied or tried to hide his orientation from her, not from the beginning of their negotiations. He'd promised a life of luxury and security, the world at her feet, a glittering existence where she would want for nothing.

And she wanted for nothing, except actual marital love and a shot at some heterosexual sex.

"You can blow off steam with outside people," he'd promised her. "People I trust." That had been the bargain, that she could satisfy her sexual appetites with men he approved, who could be depended on to keep the York's unconventional marriage a secret. But those men turned out to be Nate's bisexual friends, or expensive, blank-eyed gigolos who were too slick and practiced, and gave her the creeps.

She glanced at Nate, handsome and dashing. At least someone in their marriage got regular, satisfying sex.

"I hate when we bicker," he said. "I love you, Jenna. I hope the bodyguard helps you feel better, and safer. I hope it shows that I want to make this work, even if we have our problems."

"We're all about making it work, aren't we?"

She glanced around her comfortable, lonely space as he hugged her again. She'd been born in squalor, and risen to something her parents would consider paradise. She'd made her life work. Maybe it wasn't the life she'd envisioned, but she was warm and pampered, she had books to get lost in, and yarn to knit into baby hats when books didn't work. She had people who fed her, cleaned her rooms, did her laundry. Her husband was considerate, if confused, and he smelled good. He did try to make things work, even if he was in love with a train wreck of a man.

She wondered what the bodyguard would be like, and an important question came to mind.

"Will he know?" she asked. "About us?"

Nate's warm embrace tensed, and he pulled away. "No one knows about us. Ever. Of course he won't know, and you can't tell him. You know what happens if you ever tell. You'll never get out from the financial penalty when I sue you. Your life will be over."

"Down, boy." She held up a hand to silence him. "I just thought, since he's going to be living here…"

"You'll tell him the story we agreed on, regarding the separate living spaces: I snore, and I get antsy having you around when I'm trying to learn my lines."

"I remember the story, Nate. I helped you come up with it." She needed to wrap up this conversation. Her fake husband made her so tired. "Thanks for hiring someone to look out for me." She laid a hand on his leg, appreciating his exemplary body even though it wasn't for her. "I'm sure he'll be too busy being a bodyguard to worry about our weird marriage. Hollywood's weird all around. We're par for the course."

"Kind of par for the course," joked Nate, flashing his megawatt smile. "Well, we'll see what the guy's like when he shows up. He's on the young side. Hopefully he's hot."

"Keep your hands off him," she said, and she wasn't joking. Everyone in this house was on Nate's side, always, and everything in the house belonged to him.

If she had her way, this bodyguard would be on her side. Hers, and only hers.

2.
THE NEW BODYGUARD

Caleb looked over the contract one more time before he loaded his two suitcases and wardrobe bag into his sensible steel-gray sedan. Why invest in a flashy car when he barely used it? Maybe he'd get something sportier when he saved a little more cash, something to make his friends back home in Spur jealous.

According to the contract, he was guaranteed one parking spot at his new client's compound. He was also allowed full access to the gym and sauna when he was off duty, as well as the swimming pool, hot tub, tennis courts, and basketball courts—but only when they weren't in use by Nathaniel York. He wondered how many lawyers had worked on this very detailed contract, considering the intense confidentiality rider he'd had to sign yesterday with two witnesses, a legal advisor, and a notary at the Ironclad offices.

The more secrets, the longer the confidentiality papers. This time around, the non-disclosure docs had been fifteen pages long.

Caleb's duties and work hours had been described in similar detail, with a suspiciously high salary and generous bonuses for travel and overtime. If he stayed at this close-protection job for six months, he'd have enough extra cash to blow on the fancy car. He wasn't even guarding the movie star, just the movie star's wife, Mrs. Jenna York. Contractually, he wasn't required to perform any other security tasks.

Good. One protectee would be easy, even if she was a high-maintenance Hollywood wife. He loaded the trunk and slung his suit jacket onto the passenger seat. It was damn hot for May in Los Angeles, but a micro car meant the interior would cool down quickly. He folded his tall frame into the driver's seat and tuned the satellite radio to a country-rock station. You could take the boy out of Texas, but you couldn't take the Texas out of the boy.

As he drove the short distance from his apartment to Nathaniel York's compound, he shrugged off nerves. There was nothing to worry about, no need to get star struck, even if he was going to be working around the most famous action movie star in the world. He wasn't expecting to befriend either Jenna or her husband. He was just going to do his job—guard the wife from harm and act as a protective presence when she went out.

Nathaniel and Jenna York were used to being guarded, if the size of their home-security team was any indication. They kept a twelve-man rotating detail around the compound's perimeter, as well as six at the door, and two more inside, not including Nathaniel's personal bodyguard, who apparently wasn't really a bodyguard. For all those security positions, there would be two to three more men on call.

With all that in place, he didn't expect Jenna to be a wild client, like the rave star he'd guarded last. His new protectee was thirty-five, with no PR scandals or public meltdowns in the course of her ten-year marriage. She supported children's charities when she wasn't supporting her husband's career. The Yorks had no children, and Ironclad hadn't turned up any information on troublesome friends or family members. It would likely be a calm, straightforward assignment; he wouldn't even have to deal with the fake marriage issue, since it was such a closely guarded secret.

It wasn't long before he pulled up at the gates just off the circuitous main road far up in the Hills. The mansion sat back from the road, sprawling in all directions behind seven-foot stone fencing. Now, in late afternoon, the sun glanced off glass walls and chrome siding interspersed with slabs of marble brick. Since moving to Hollywood, he'd grown used to these types of showplaces, but he couldn't help admiring the house's massiveness as one of the two guards at the gate checked his credentials.

When they were convinced he was Caleb Winchell, the new bodyguard, they had him pop his trunk and open the back seat so they could go through his car for drugs and contraband. They checked his firearms—the one he carried and the one he kept close at hand—recorded their serial numbers, and handed them back. Thank God for the car's air conditioning, because by the time they let him proceed through the gates, fifteen minutes had passed.

He followed the driveway around to a multi-car garage, where another guard guided him to his assigned spot. He parked amidst customized SUVs and sporty Italian marvels, and wondered how Nate York had time to amass so many cars, much less drive them. Caleb's shoddy sedan looked even shoddier now.

A middle-aged woman approached the car as he got out to unload his luggage. She was short and stocky, with red hair and weirdly intent blue eyes, a lighter blue than his. She exuded energy as she thrust out a hand.

"Mr. Winchell, welcome to Casa Del York. We're so glad you're here. I'm Gladys, and I manage most of the York's day-to-day affairs."

"Pleased to meet you." His voice held a little more twang than he liked, and it came out the most when he greeted people. "I'm happy to be here. This looks like a really nice place."

Her wide, instant smile was at least ninety-eight percent fake. "Oh, I'd say so, and it's a marvelous place to work. Kendall, can you help with the bags?" She beckoned one of the guards, then turned back to him with another fervent smile. "Why don't we get you moved into your new quarters so you can meet Mrs. York?"

"Sounds great."

He took his wardrobe bag and one of the suitcases, and they made their way from the garage to an entryway that soared two stories above their heads. The door was opened for them by one of the guards on duty. In five minutes time, he'd seen almost a dozen uniformed men.

The inside looked even more spacious than the exterior, with corridors leading in three different directions from the sprawling entry room. It was designed like an upscale hotel lobby, with paintings and sculptures, huge potted plants, club chairs, and three large, deep, shockingly white sofas. Water careened down the far stone wall with a soothing murmur of sound before disappearing into the floor.

Caleb followed Gladys through the glistening space, his eyes on the corridors ahead. She took him toward the one on the right, deeper into the compound. There was nothing comparable to this home in Spur.

People owned big plots of land, but thirty-thousand-square-foot homes? No.

"Mr. York resides over there, in the leftmost wing," Gladys said, gesturing like a flight attendant. "He and Mrs. York decided soon after they married that his snoring was too disruptive to her sleep. Anyway, he's often up late studying lines, so separate bedrooms work out well for everyone, especially when he's doing his acting exercises or learning a new script."

"Does the staff live in the center wing?" he asked.

"No. The middle wing is for guests, and the occasional party or event, so it's closed most of the time. You'll be staying in the same wing as Mrs. York, and the rest of the staff doesn't sleep over. Well, Mr. York's personal bodyguard does, but his rooms are in the left wing near his boss."

A nice little setup for everyone, especially the movie star and his "personal bodyguard."

Kendall followed Caleb and Gladys as she keyed them through a door and into another foyer. The walls opened up with glass and sunshine. This room was as grand as the main entry room, just on a smaller, less-intimidating scale. Outside, Caleb could see an expansive, infinity-edge pool stretching in all directions, with views of wooded hills and faraway cliffs. They walked through that silent room to a pair of carved double doors on the far wall.

"Jenna York's suite is through here," said Gladys with a smile. "Let's knock."

Yes, let's. Gladys' chipper personality was starting to grate on him. He accepted his other bag from Kendall and stood back as Gladys knocked briskly. She turned back to him.

"As you can see, everything here is very secure. These doors are lined with bulletproof steel." Her brows rose, as if she were gossiping about a delightful new movie or TV show she'd seen. "Of course, all the doors are kept locked around the clock. You'll be given a key card later today."

"Great," he said aloud, but in his head, he thought, *what a fucked up way to live.* Locked and separated all the time, and surrounded by strangers. Then the lock clicked and the door swung open. A woman looked out at him, past Gladys and her smiling face. Jenna York's large, brown eyes were cool and hard.

"Good morning, Jenna. This is Caleb Winchell," Gladys said brightly. "Your new bodyguard."

Despite Gladys' bubbly intro, Jenna didn't offer a hand to shake, so he didn't offer his. All Ironclad recruits spent the first three days of training having etiquette lessons drilled into them. *Never initiate physical contact with a client unless duty demands it. Don't hover during phone calls or conversations. Don't try to befriend clients or their children.*

Jenna York's eyes were as dark as her gaze. He didn't attempt to guess her ethnicity, but she was some interesting blend, with warm-toned skin and sweeping, shoulder length wavy black hair. She was dressed in leggings and a casual dress, with very little makeup. She looked tired.

"Come in," she said, standing back. Her lips were pressed in a line, whether from anxiety or irritation, he didn't know. Few people liked having bodyguards. Close security, especially in the beginning, could be an awkward thing to get used to.

He smiled, hoping to put her at ease as he intruded into her sanctuary. It didn't work. She moved away from him, crossing her arms and taking up a position beside the sofa. Okay, so they wouldn't get friendly. That was for the best.

He focused on security concerns instead, his eyes sweeping the space from force of habit. There was an open kitchen straight ahead, with a long, wide granite counter, and an adjacent living area with an overstuffed, dark leather sofa facing a large TV. He noted the windows on the opposite wall, how they opened, how they locked, and then he located the exits. There was one door to the left that opened to the pool area, and a hallway to the right.

"Jenna can give you the full tour later," Gladys said, as if the woman wasn't standing a few feet away from them. "For now, I'll show you where you'll stay."

She led him down the hallway to the first door, and gestured him into his room, which was more like a small apartment. The main space was bright and comfortable, with a dark blue sofa, a coffee table, television, desk, and plants arranged near the window, leaning toward the sun. From there, she led him back to a luxuriously appointed bedroom, done in traditional gray and navy, and then into the adjoining private bathroom, where he found more glistening marble and chrome, along with a jetted tub and open shower. He had a walk-in closet for clothes and shoes, along with a storage closet that was bigger than the bedroom he'd shared with his brothers in his childhood home.

"You'll find everything you need here to be comfortable," she assured him. "And if there's anything else you need, just ask."

He couldn't imagine anything else he'd need. In fact, he couldn't wait to see what the rest of the mansion looked like. He'd need to walk it soon for security purposes, all of it, including Nathaniel's private wing and the center wing that was only for parties and guests. There had to be another, larger kitchen somewhere, and a dining room, maybe a game room and home theater, and the gym and sauna he'd be allowed to use.

"I'll need to learn my way around the place," he said to Gladys. "I'd like to see the whole property."

"But you'll mostly be working in this suite." The older woman led him back into the sitting room, her smile so forced it hurt his eyes.

"I'd like to know the whole layout, if you don't mind. A map would help, if it exists."

"There's no map," said Jenna, not quite managing to look at him.

The red-haired assistant made a bright, excited sound. "Hmm. Maybe we can have one made."

From her pinched expression, he could see that Jenna was about as fond of Gladys' overbearing energy as he was.

"After Gladys shows you around, you can use the pool, get moved in, whatever," Jenna said to him. "From what I understand, you don't officially start until tomorrow. I'd just like to ask..." She paused, her gaze darting past his shoulder. "I'd like you to stay out in the other room while you're working." She indicated the room we'd entered through, outside her carved double doors. "This room is kind of my private area. I mean, of course you can pass through to your rooms whenever you need to."

"I'll be happy to remain in the outer room as much as I can, Mrs. York," Caleb said. "But you'll need to leave the doors between us open, so I can hear if there's a problem. With that said, I'll do my best to preserve your privacy at all times."

She stared at him a moment, then said "Thanks," turned on her heel, and strode down the hall to the last door.

"That's Mrs. York's room down there," Gladys told him, just as the door slammed. "Hmm." Another scintillating smile. "Why don't we go on that tour?"

* * * * *

Jenna stared at the door. She shouldn't have slammed it, but she felt a little intimidated by the new bodyguard. He was bigger than she expected. Taller, more intent.

Handsomer.

No, he wasn't that handsome. He wasn't Nathaniel-handsome. He was too wholesome or something, too sincere. Vivid blue eyes, square jawline, hair that was buzzed on the bottom and golden-brown spikes on top. He had a goatee, discreet and closely trimmed, that looked like he spent time on it. She'd thought her personal bodyguard would be more like the scowling, retired Marines who roved the compound, protecting the perimeter without speaking to her or meeting her gaze. Caleb Winchell had looked directly into her eyes like he was trying to take her measure. It'd been forever since someone dared to do that.

She made a face, even though no one could see it, and flopped on her deep, soft bed. She didn't know when Gladys would take him touring, or how soon he'd be back in her part of the house. She hoped he didn't expect to scope out her bedroom, at least not while she was in it.

He's going to be wherever you are. Get used to it.

This was all that fucker Tom's fault, and Nate's, for being obsessed with the maniac. She closed her eyes, trying not to think about them, but that made her start thinking about the bodyguard instead. *He's going to be where you are. He's going to be around you all the time.*

He wasn't handsome. No. She'd already forgotten the specifics of his face. Well, she kind of remembered his full, attractive lips set off by his goatee, and the symmetry of his cheekbones, and his blue, blue eyes. Okay, he was actually pretty handsome in a simple, classic way, not that it mattered. He was so *young*.

She wondered if he was staying over tonight, since he was starting tomorrow. He'd brought luggage, but he might just be leaving it and unpacking in the morning. She kind of hoped he was going to stay.

She understood the ridiculousness of both not wanting him around, and desperately wanting him around. It was no crazier than anything else going on in her brain.

* * * * *

"So, how bad is the everyday threat?" Caleb asked as Gladys chaperoned him around the compound.

She shrugged. "There are four or five certified loonies to watch out for, and a hundred or so that I'd call 'problematically invested fans.' Then there are the gawkers, the paparazzi, and the autograph hounds that follow them around town." She fell silent, blinking nervously and smiling at the same time. "It's high time Mrs. York had more dedicated protection."

"It sounds that way."

Caleb caught a glance of Nathaniel and his bodyguard steaming in the sauna. Gladys guided him in the other direction, toward the gym and tennis courts. "Your only duties will be to look after Mrs. York during the afternoon and evening, with the occasional outing. We have a driver if she wants to take an impromptu trip somewhere, but I'm not going to lie to you. You'll do a lot of sitting around."

"Who's on duty in the mornings?" he asked.

"Door security, unless Mrs. York needs to go out during those hours—and she rarely does. She stays in, she reads or swims, and knits baby hats."

"Baby hats?"

"She does a lot of work with children's charities, and she has a soft spot for infants. Or knitting." She made an amused sound, opening a door to show him the pool, complete with a slide, a gushing waterfall, and a colorful swim-up bar. "You'll find Mrs. York is introverted. If you can tempt her out in the sun now and again, it would probably be good for her soul."

Caleb gave her a look. "Is her soul troubled?" He wondered if the woman would come clean to him about the fake marriage. Did *she* know?

"She's about as troubled as any fame-burdened Hollywood wife would be," she said instead.

He didn't know what to make of that comment, or the shrug that accompanied it. Well, it didn't matter. The bogus marriage wasn't his concern. His client's safety was. "Can you show me the home's security features?" he asked. "Doors, windows, cameras, phones, security system, control room?"

"Security Central is last on the list, but we'll get there," she promised. "Just a few more places to go."

They did a quick tour through Nathaniel York's living space. There was no obvious evidence he shared it with someone other than his wife. His area of the house had another large kitchen, as well as two extra rooms set up as an office and studio. Gladys opened the door to a bedroom of spa-like luxury. There was a window with a panoramic view of the valley, heavy wood furniture and chairs, and a king-size mahogany bed covered in an espresso-colored counterpane. "Mr. York's bedroom. You shouldn't ever have cause to come here. If there's a problem, contact security, and they can contact him."

"Got it."

"As I explained, he and his wife sleep apart because of his snoring. He snores like a thunder cloud." She forced a laugh. "I've heard it myself, when I've had to wake him for an early call time. Mrs. York prefers to sleep in."

Next, she led him into the center wing, which not only housed spare rooms, but a ballroom, indoor basketball court, and museum full of Nathaniel's film memorabilia, including posters, photographs, and a glass case of statuettes and awards. "He's great, huh?" Gladys sighed, lingering in front of the gold and silver trophies. "Have you seen any of his movies?"

"I think everyone's seen his movies." Caleb wouldn't categorize himself as a huge fan, but he respected the man's career. Numerous awards, millions of dollars, a mansion in the Hills, and a beautiful wife. Jenna York was a stunner, dark and curvy and somewhat of a mystery. Why would she waste that sumptuous body, that striking beauty, on a man who couldn't appreciate them?

None of your business. Not your concern.

As they headed back toward Jenna's side of the house, he refocused on the job at hand. "If you don't mind, Gladys, I'd like you to send me everything you have on the crazies, especially the most immediate threats. Email's fine. Ironclad has its own secure server."

She nodded, her eyes sparkling too bright again. "I'll get right on it." She shook Caleb's hand. "Honestly, we'll do whatever it takes to help Jenna feel comfortable and safe. We're glad to have you on the team."

3.
Fucking Lucky

Caleb opened his daily morning email from Gladys, outlining notable events for the day. He was a week into protecting Jenna York, and so far, everything was going well. Not that he'd seen her, aside from awkward encounters in the kitchen, or the hallway between their rooms. This evening, he'd have his first outing with the movie star couple. Jenna was going to a charity dinner with her husband, a big event downtown.

She started getting ready hours in advance, and Caleb settled himself in her living room in case she needed help. That was the rule. If "outside" people were around, so was he. He tried to stay out of the way as her stylist Malik stalked in and out, accompanied by various helpers and deliveries. The security guys brought sushi while Malik was still laboring over Jenna's "look," but no one stopped for a break. After dinner, a makeup artist arrived, and the housekeeper came by to collect the takeout dishes. She tsked, shook her head over Jenna's untouched cartons, and stowed them in the fridge.

"Mr. Bodyguard," she said, "see if you can get her to eat something later."

"Will do, Wilma. My name's Caleb, by the way."

"I'll try to remember." She bustled out of the room, definitely forgetting. He'd already told her his name several times. He sat back on Jenna's sofa and stretched his legs. This was such a bizarre household.

People didn't know each other, or want to know each other. None of them wanted to know him, especially the woman he was supposed to protect.

He heard her door open and sat up straighter, so she wouldn't find him lounging. She and Malik spoke in low, irritated voices.

"Just one more minute," the stylist said in his sharp eastern accent. "Don't dare leave before I set your makeup."

Caleb heard a muffled curse, a couple spritzes, and Jenna complaining that she was going to be late.

"So what if you're late?" Malik scoffed. "What's he going to do?"

"Whine. Complain. Make me feel bad."

Jenna emerged looking fragile and exasperated, and so gorgeous that Caleb stared. She noticed his shocked expression before he could hide it, and blew a nonexistent stray hair from her face, rolling her eyes at the same time.

Caleb knew to be professional. He couldn't comment on her transformation from yoga-couch-surfer to glamorous charity queen, but he marveled at it all the same. She wore a pale silver sheath dress, fitted at the top and flaring into a skirt adorned with embroidered and beaded flowers in pale pink and sage. One shoulder was bare, while an asymmetrical silver strap crossed her chest and draped over her shoulder. Her dark hair was swept to one side, embellished with a tiny row of matching silver flowers. The effect was both sexy and ethereal.

Malik followed behind her, noting Caleb's appreciation, and sent him a cheeky smile. "She's beautiful, yes?"

Jenna stared at Caleb, and he tried to read what was going on behind those dark, guarded eyes. He thought she wanted to be complimented, but she also seemed embarrassed and uncomfortable. She tugged at one side of her shimmering skirt. Of course, Caleb couldn't respond to Malik's question. He couldn't agree that she was beautiful, as well as gorgeous, stunning, mysterious, luminous, tragic. It wouldn't be appropriate.

But she was all those things.

Instead he pretended Malik's question was only rhetorical. Why would the man even ask, when the answer was obvious to them both? He looked at his watch and stood.

"The car should be here, Mrs. York, if you're ready to go."

She slid a look over Caleb's tuxedo. He knew it was quality, both in brand and fit, because Ironclad made sure its high profile agents were appropriately dressed. Of course, he wouldn't be going into the actual dinner. He'd wait in the lobby with the other close-security agents, all of them standing stiffly and looking taciturn so they wouldn't be mistaken for waiters, and asked for champagne or canapes. He wore the tux for the arrival photos, so if he was photographed behind or beside Jenna York, he'd look worthy of being in her company.

Not that he was ever in her company. As they walked to the car, she stayed a step ahead of him, gliding across the glossy floors until they reached the main area of the house. Nathaniel stood by the front door with his bodyguard, hands clasped in front of him.

Caleb had only seen Jenna's husband a handful of times since he'd started protecting her. Truth was, he avoided him, for fear his expression might show that he knew *the big secret*. As for the bodyguard, he'd only seen glimpses. Tom Maxon was the same height as Caleb, but broader. Swarthier, darker, hairier. A bear. Was that the term the gay community used? He made Nathaniel look like a slight man, even though he was famous for doing most of the stunts in his action movies, and was pretty swarthy on his own.

"Oh, Jen," Nathaniel said, holding out a hand as they approached them. "I love that dress."

"Thanks."

According to Gladys' memo, Nathaniel was going to speak at the dinner, and the whole event was expected to take under three hours. He pulled his wife close and pressed a kiss against her cheek, apparently for Caleb's benefit, since he was the only one here who wasn't in on the charade. A faint smile curved the corners of Jenna's lips.

"Thanks for coming tonight, Nate," she said.

"Of course. Thanks for caring about the kids. You know I'll do as many of these charity things as you want. Well, as many as I can."

Caleb tried to understand the vibe between the couple. It was friendlier than "cordial," but not anything approaching "comfortable." Maxon glowered in the background, adding a dissonant note to the proceedings.

"Have you met Jen's new bodyguard?" Nathaniel turned to Maxon with a forced smile. "This is Caleb Winchell from Ironclad Solutions. He'll also be accompanying us on our upcoming trips."

"Great to meet you," said Maxon in exactly the brusque, gravelly voice Caleb expected from his appearance. They had a grip battle while they shook hands. Ah, the hand-crush, that classic male posturing game. *Give it up, dude. I know you're not a real bodyguard. Not only that, you're banging your boss.*

Once they entered the limo, he and Maxon settled into the backward facing seats so the married couple could sit together. No one spoke, and no one made eye contact. Caleb directed his gaze out the window, but he could see Jenna reflected in the glass, sitting very straight with her hands in her lap. When he turned to look at her, she was looking back at him, and she quickly turned her eyes away.

"Want something to drink?" Nathaniel asked his wife. There were a couple bottles of champagne in the limo's ice cooler.

She shook her head. The champagne remained untouched as the driver maneuvered them up steep hills and around curves. Soon they'd reach more level ground and make their way into the city, and Caleb would be ready to work, to crowd out pushy spectators and clear a place for Jenna to walk and feel safe. He'd scan the surroundings for hands moving under coats, for strange expressions or intense eye contact, all the things they'd been trained to notice in a crowd. By now, he'd studied and committed to memory the photos of known threats to the York family.

Jenna bit a nail, just for a moment, then lowered her hand to her lap. As she wiggled her glittering wedding rings, a surge of protective emotion washed through him. She seemed reclusive at home, shy and quiet; out here, in the limo, in her designer finery, she looked exposed and vulnerable as hell. Her hairstyle bared her neck and her gown revealed her shoulders. He wanted to put his hands on those shoulders, to knead and caress that bare expanse of skin...

What? No. He wanted to protect and support her. That was all. He wanted to explore the texture of her body, run his fingertips over it. Would she feel as velvety and cool as she looked?

No. Jesus. Fuck no. He tore his gaze from her décolletage and stared at her knees, delicate and hidden beneath her gown. No, he shouldn't think of things that were delicate and hidden beneath her gown. He averted his gaze from her altogether, staring at Nathaniel's shoes instead. He hadn't developed a physical attraction to a client before, and he didn't intend to now. He needed to keep his mind on the job.

They arrived at the charity dinner venue after a twenty-five minute ride that felt like an hour. The only conversation had been quiet exchanges between Jenna and Nathaniel, while Maxon sat like a statue. Since Caleb was curbside, he exited first, offering a hand to Jenna. She took it, and he was so preoccupied helping her navigate the exit in her high-heeled shoes and ornate gown, he forgot to notice the way her hand felt in his.

Maxon emerged next, and Nathaniel came last. His appearance caused an eruption of cheers and screaming from the crowds across the barricade. He flashed his movie star smile, waving, greeting them, then he turned to Jenna. They went hand in hand to face the cameras while Caleb and Maxon trailed behind, scanning the crowds for possible threats. If Maxon wasn't really a bodyguard, he was good at acting like one. Still, Caleb checked everyone for himself, not trusting his pseudo-professional counterpart.

After a full minute of flashing cameras and bellowing photographers, Nathaniel and Jenna moved down the carpeted entryway toward the door. With one last wave, the two went inside. Security at the door was tight. The head agent scrutinized Caleb's credentials even though he knew the guy from a previous job. The charity's guests were corralled into one area for screening before being allowed in the event space. Nathaniel and Jenna sailed through the VIP line, and he and Maxon were allowed as far as the entrance to the ballroom before event security took over, motioning them toward the other bodyguards congregating in the hallway.

Caleb parked himself in an alcove near the door. He nodded at a couple of fellow Ironclad agents, wondering which other celebrities were attending this thing. A dozen more A-listers breezed by over the next fifteen minutes, along with their high profile agents and producers. As the event got under way, he could hear music, speeches, applause, but nothing very clearly. Waiters buzzed around like flies, carrying trays of drinks and food. All of them were probably frustrated actors. They carried themselves like performers, veering out of one another's way with theatrical flair.

"She met him at one of these, you know," said Maxon.

Caleb turned, not even realizing he was standing near him. "They met at a charity dinner?"

Maxon nodded, gesturing toward a clutch of waiters Caleb had been watching. "She was one of those. She got fucking lucky that day."

Caleb wondered at the vitriol behind the expletive, and the man's expression. "I thought she used to be an actress."

Maxon scoffed. "She was an actress like all these chicks here are actresses. She was waiting tables to make ends meet, and doing events when she wasn't auditioning. Just goes to show, anything's possible. Look where she is now. Guest of honor."

He slid a sideways look at Caleb, monitoring his reaction, but he kept his expression neutral.

"She's a nice girl though." Maxon shrugged. "Mr. York adores her."

"She's not really a girl, is she?" He tried to sound conversational. Light. He hated Maxon without knowing the depth of that vitriol either. "She's his wife, right?"

"Yeah, of course." He tensed, frowned, and threw back his shoulders. "Just a professional word of warning, since you're working so close with her. She can be really immature and whiny about shit."

"I haven't noticed that, but I'll be on my guard." Again, he softened the words with the Texas accent he could turn on and off. It made his dislike for Maxon a little less pronounced. "Any other advice about the York household?" he pressed, mainly to see what else Maxon would say.

The older man shrugged, his fitted tuxedo pulling across his muscular shoulders. "Just watch out for crazies." His biceps bunched under the fabric as he held Caleb's gaze. "A lot of people idolize Mr. York, and the Mrs. has her own admirers. They're a good family. They love each other a lot." He looked back out at the bevy of busy waiters, aprons tied smooth around their hips. A corner of his lip turned down. *She was one of those*, he'd sneered. *She got fucking lucky that day.*

Caleb imagined it was hard for Maxon to see the man he loved attending public events with a woman on his arm. But it was Nathaniel, surely, who'd engineered the fake-marriage arrangement, choosing a pretty, struggling waitress to play his wife. Jenna had been around almost as long as Maxon. Did he feel threatened by her?

The celebrity lifestyle was weird. All the pseudo marriages, the jockeying for stardom, the abuses visited on those who weren't protected by money or connections. He'd heard stories about the "casting couch" that turned his stomach. Aspiring actors flocked to Hollywood, seeking stardom at any price, but those who found stardom lost the safety and privacy they had as normal people. All of it seemed schizophrenic and depressing, but Hollywood was the busiest Ironclad office in the U.S., so he was determined to hang in there and make it work.

When Jenna left the ballroom on Nathaniel's arm a couple hours later, they passed the row of photographers again, their smiles and body language as fresh and convincing as when they'd entered, even though her shine faded when she turned away from the bank of cameras. While Nathaniel lingered for solo photos, Caleb fell into step beside Jenna, guiding her to the waiting car.

He touched her back, telling himself it was accidental contact, but he'd brushed his fingers across her bare skin, so how accidental was it? She glanced over at him, meeting his gaze as if relieved to find him there. It was all he could do not to touch her again, to take her elbow, or, God, take her face between his hands and tell her everything was going to be okay.

Instead, he put on his most reassuring expression and indicated that she should enter the car. She did, sliding across the seat. When he settled across from her, she looked out the window, the corners of her lips drawn down in a frown.

"Everything okay?" he asked.

"Everything's great." She graced him with a fleeting look. "Just tired of smiling. How are you?"

"I'm doing well."

That was the end of their conversation, although it was polite enough. She put her head back against the seat, not stirring when Nathaniel and Maxon entered the limo a few minutes later. Nathaniel seemed energized, smiling even though his adoring fans weren't around, but Jenna drew into herself. Nathaniel put his hand on her leg, patting it through her gauzy silver dress, an affectionate gesture she didn't respond to.

"Charity corpse," he joked. "You look dead."

"I am."

"But the disadvantaged kids are a million dollars richer. It was a successful event."

She roused herself enough to smile at him. "Thanks for speaking tonight."

Maxon shifted on the seat across from them, and her smile faded. She stiffened and cut her eyes toward the window, and tension filled the car.

"I'm thinking about going to LouLou's to meet some friends," Nathaniel told Jenna, his voice loud in the limousine. "Feel up to a party?"

"I don't know. It's been a long day."

Nate's phone buzzed and he pulled up the screen, then flicked his finger across it a few times. "Photos are already online. They're nice, babes. You looked so gorgeous tonight."

He took her hand, squeezed it affectionately, then let it go so he could flick through more of the photos. He didn't show her any of them, even though she was seated right next to him. Her expression said she was done for the evening. She'd dressed up and played her part as his elegant, doting wife, fulfilling her side of their bargain, but now the charade was over, and she was clearly tired of acting.

No, you can't step in to comfort her, Caleb. You can't try to soothe away the tension lines on her forehead. You definitely can't try to kiss them away.

Well, he could, but then he'd be fired, and he'd have to find another job or go home to Spur, where there wasn't a lot of work for guys with his skill set. He rested his hands on his knees, tensing them to keep them still, pressing his fingertips against the tuxedo pants to wipe away the lingering feel of her bare skin.

Today was the most time he'd ever spent around her, which explained why he was so aware of her nearness, and her shadowed expressions. He'd never had so long to look at her, or had the opportunity to sit so near, even though they lived just a few steps apart. It was the novelty of her presence, he assured himself. This inappropriate fascination with his client would wear off soon enough.

4.
THE STORM

Jenna jerked awake from a jolt of thunder at one-thirty in the morning, her body seized by fear. She hated storms, a holdover from her Florida childhood, but she thought she'd probably been having a nightmare too. She hated the nighttime and the dreams that came with it. She hated waking in the dark with her breath stuck in her throat.

She rolled onto her back and tried to do some of the relaxation techniques she'd learned from her sobriety coach. *Envision a place of peace. Let your face go soft. Unclench your jaw. Feel your brain cradled gently by your skull.* But it was hard for her to envision a place of peace when her life was so screwed up, and her brain didn't want to be cradled by her skull. Her brain wanted to think about the charity dinner and all the eyes that had stared at her and Nate.

Why was she still so bothered by the scrutiny? She'd dealt with it forever, and hell, she'd asked for this life. She'd been one hundred percent thrilled when Nate had asked her to be his wife in the public eye.

But there were so many *eyes* all the time, so much pretending to keep up appearances. There were always cameras, interviews, appearances, and Tom hovering at Nate's shoulder. Ugh.

She thought of the two of them at LouLou's, playing client and bodyguard. She hoped professional appearances kept Tom from drinking, because when he got drunk he came home ranting and angry, eager to cause drama. The only time he was safe to be around was when he got so high that he forgot how much he hated her, and these days, it seemed like there wasn't enough coke in the world for that.

Let your face go soft. Unclench your jaw.

She didn't have to stress as much now, with Caleb sleeping in the next room. Even on his day off, he stayed here to sleep, which she appreciated more than he knew. She knew her new bodyguard could beat up Tom, easily. Tom wasn't as tough as he looked, and Caleb had a no-nonsense face and a particular way of holding his hands, like he could use them at any moment to strangle someone to death.

Tonight was the first night he'd taken her out of the compound as a personal bodyguard, and she'd felt his presence, not in an obtrusive, annoying way, but in the way that he was *there*. He'd stayed near her all the way into the ballroom, an arm's length away, serious and alert. She wished he could have come inside and sat next to her during dinner, and stared at all the people who stared at her. Maybe they would have stopped staring.

She shivered, hugging herself under the sheets. He'd touched her once on the way back to the car. It had been such a fleeting, gentle touch, not like Nate's possessive touches or Tom's angry ones. She'd thought about that touch all the way home.

Another boom of thunder sounded, rattling the windows. She sat up in bed, rubbing her eyes. No, she wasn't going to fall for the damn bodyguard and his kind, protective shit. He was only kind and protective because he was doing his job, and anyway, she was married and he was too young and the whole thing was stupid and dangerous to think about.

With the storm gathering strength, she gave up trying to relax her brain back to sleep, and pushed open the sheer curtains around her bed. She needed something to drink. Not alcohol, no, but something sweet and soothing, like tea with honey. She'd make herself some chamomile tea and curl up on the sofa to read until the storm passed. She could fall asleep there and be just as comfortable as she was in her bedroom. Maybe she'd put on the TV for some background noise, quietly enough that it wouldn't wake Caleb.

She slipped a robe over her nightshirt and moved to the door, opened it and fumbled for the hall light. Even when she was little, she hated walking around in the dark. Back then it was bugs and monsters that scared her. Now it was Tom, or trespassers. She left a small lamp burning in her room all night, even though she knew she had a constant web of security around her. Cameras, a security gate, deadbolts, steel doors, alarms, her own bodyguard. None of it was enough to help her feel comfortable in the dark.

She walked down the silent hallway, yawning and adjusting her robe. Her bare feet sank into the carpet as the air conditioning's cool flow drifted over her skin. Lightning flashed, lighting up the hall. She stopped just before the bodyguard's room and held her breath, listening. The door was slightly ajar, but she couldn't hear anything.

She went the rest of the way into the living room, and turned into the kitchen to make some tea. She clicked the light on over the stove so she could find the pod she wanted and drop it into the machine. Moments later, it spit hot, fragrant chamomile into her mug, which she doctored with a healthy dose of honey. She stirred it, turning toward the counter. Then she saw the hulking figure in the doorway to her living room, threw the mug onto the counter, and screamed.

Well, in her head, she screamed, but in reality, nothing came out, only a choked yelp that probably wasn't loud enough to be heard over the mug breaking against the granite. It took a moment for her to realize the figure was Caleb. He looked apologetic, and crossed to the kitchen with purposeful strides.

"Sorry I startled you, Mrs. York."

He was beside her before she could collect herself, righting the mug and pushing the jagged pieces away from her hand. Jenna sagged against the counter, staring at him in a haze of indignation. Why was he lurking around at one-thirty in the morning? Why was he dressed in a damned suit at this time of night? "Jesus," she said. "You scared the shit out of me."

"I'm sorry." He took her hands, inspecting them briefly. "You dropped your mug."

"Because you scared me."

"Are you burned? Cut?"

"No."

He tried to pull her from the counter, his grip careful, but she wanted to stay there for the support. Finally, he released her, looking apologetic. "You scared me," she said for the third time. "Why are you sneaking around in the dark?"

"I was doing one last security check before I turned in for the night."

"I thought you were already asleep." She felt a flush spread across her cheeks. Now that the terror had abated, embarrassment took its place.

"I didn't mean to scare you, Mrs. York."

"Stop calling me Mrs. York. It's Jenna."

Even though she'd snapped at him, he replied politely. "I'm sorry, Jenna. Would you like help cleaning up the counter?"

He didn't wait for her to answer, just made a neat pile of the broken cup shards and threw them in the trash. He grabbed a handful of paper towels and mopped up the cooling liquid, pushing it toward the lip of the sink.

She studied him as he did these simple tasks, his big hands taking care of things with ease. She realized then that she'd dreamed of those hands in her restless sleep, dreamed of blond-gold hair and the muscles at his neck, and the warmth of his large, strong body against hers. He looked impassive, made of stone, but deep inside her, some desperate urge cried out for him to hold her. *Protect me. Please.*

She mashed her lips together, terrified that some kind of plea or begging sound would leak out. To distract herself from her confusing feelings, she grabbed her own handful of paper towels and crouched down to mop up the tea that had trickled onto the floor.

"Watch for glass," he said.

"There isn't any glass down here." Her ceramic mug had broken into large, manageable pieces, unlike her brain, which still felt scattered in a million shards. His soft, kind warning—*Watch for glass*—made her want to cry, and she didn't understand why he had that effect on her.

She stood to throw away the paper towels, and looked at his earnest face, his untroubled features. How long had it been since someone had looked at her with honesty, with no veneer of fakeness or mockery? As she thought it, another flash of lightning illuminated the space between them.

"Are you feeling steadier?" he asked. "Can I help you with anything else?"

Yes, she needed help getting used to the presence of a normal, well-adjusted human being in her life. In her kitchen. She took a deep breath and forced a smile now that her heartbeat was almost back to normal.

"I'm fine. I think I'm going to make more tea. Would you like some?"

He paused a moment, then nodded. "Sure. That'd be great."

While she took out a couple more mugs, he regarded her from a few feet away, briefly brushing his palm over the left side of his suit. *He has a gun under there*, Jenna realized. *He's armed, right now.*

She focused on making their tea, and offered him cream and sugar, which he declined.

"It's chamomile," she said. "It won't keep you awake." She stopped, realizing the hour. "Am I keeping you awake?"

"It's fine. Want to sit for a while? I can go in the other room if you prefer."

The flush on her cheeks intensified as she remembered telling him to stay out there as much as he could.

"Oh, no." She shook her head. "You can sit in here. I mean, I'm more used to you now. Let's..." She heaved another deep breath. "Let's sit and drink tea."

"Sure. I'd enjoy that."

His conversation was so easy, so comfortable. She led him to the sofa, gesturing with her mug. "Sit anywhere."

He wisely chose to sit on the end that wasn't crowded with her books and knitting projects. She watched as he took a sip of the tea. She couldn't tell if he liked it or not. She had the feeling he would have hidden any negative reaction to its taste.

"Sorry it's not wine," she joked. "It would have been better before bed, but I'm not allowed to have it now that I'm sober."

"It's fine. This is good." Even seated, his posture screamed alertness. She felt like a slouch. Well, she deserved to be a slouch. She'd had a long evening in an uncomfortable dress and layers of makeup.

"I'm sorry I freaked out at you earlier," she said. "I've been a little on edge lately. And I'm sorry if I seemed standoffish or snotty when I met you. Well, I'm sure I came off like a bitch, but the thing is..."

"There's no need to apologize."

"There probably is, but honestly, I'm not like that. Well, I don't mean to be like that." She let it go, as he had, and squeezed her hands in her lap as thunder rumbled. "This storm has me on edge."

"You don't like storms?" She could see him filing the fact away in his bodyguard brain. "Is it the noise, or..."

"It's the fact that I grew up in a trailer park in south Florida. Do you know Florida has the highest number of lightning strikes in the U.S.? They have a lot of tornadoes too."

"I guess that's not fun when you live in a trailer."

"No. And we had nowhere to go when the worst storms came. We lived in this no man's land between Miami and Naples so my mom could clean rooms at the casino hotels."

He made a sympathetic noise. "You couldn't go to one of those hotels when the weather got bad?"

"We didn't have a car. When the weather got bad in the middle of the night, my mom and I would hide behind the couch and pray we didn't get blown away. And there was this big lake nearby that would flood and strand us in the trailer, which would have been okay, but we only ever had food to last a couple of days." She stopped, embarrassed by her whining, her self-pity. "I don't know why I'm telling you all this."

"It's okay. Everything you tell me is confidential."

His earnest words unmanned her. No sarcasm, no insincerity. She laughed and turned away. "You're so weird, Caleb. So pure."

He didn't respond to her comment. Was he insulted? His expression was unreadable. Outside, she could hear the rain lashing across the pool deck.

"So, how do you like living here so far?" she asked to change the subject. "Has everything been okay?"

"Yes. It's a beautiful house, and you seem very secure here. Makes my job easier to do well."

"Where do you come from?" She felt the flush rising again. "I mean, your accent..."

"Texas," he said with a smile. "Try not to hold it against me."

"I won't. I mean..." *Jenna, you dumbass, he was joking.* "I didn't mean to say you were weird just now. You seem like a great guy." She took a sip of tea, and rolled her eyes. "Sorry I'm so awkward. This is just...difficult for me."

He listened patiently, his silence prompting her to say more.

"I'm used to being by myself, at least when I'm not out there." She gestured, indicating the big, loud, rude outside world that followed her whenever she left the safety of her home. "And when I'm out there, I'll probably seem like a rude bitch to you, because I hate making appearances. I hate everything to do with the Hollywood scene." She didn't say *I hate my life*, not out loud, but it was implied.

"I can't imagine the stress you deal with," he said when she couldn't continue. There was that gentle note in his voice again. She liked that about him, that he wasn't hard all over. That maybe, despite his gun and his stone jaw and his muscular body, he had a softer side.

"Anyway, Caleb, if I act like a bitch, don't take it personally."

"I never take anything personally. That's part of my job."

She believed him. He didn't sound the least bit annoyed or insulted by her words. He took a drink of his tea. Not a sip, a drink, like a capable, unflappable Texan. If someone broke in this minute and tried to attack her, she felt like he could handle the situation without the slightest change in his calm expression. "You're good at this, aren't you?" she asked. "Personal protection?"

"Yes, I'm good at it." Total matter-of-fact, not bragging. "Ironclad only hires the best."

"And you carry a gun, don't you? Under your suit jacket?"

He hesitated a moment. "Yes. You require armed protection. You have more crazies and stalkers on your tail than a dozen other celebrities put together."

She appreciated his candor, even if it made her think of all the lunatics revolving around her like planets around a sun, getting crazier and more numerous with each successful film Nate produced. "I don't do anything to attract them," she said. "It's because of Nate."

"I wasn't blaming you or your husband, just explaining the gun. I'm sure you're well aware of the threats around you."

She went from admiring to hating him a little, hating his cold, practical sizing up of her day-to-day battle with the movie star life. She wondered if he'd ask what everyone else always asked. *Is it worth it, being married to him? Is it worth looking over your shoulder and having security agents around you all day?* She hated that question because she'd realized soon after she married Nate that no, it wasn't worth it. But he didn't ask.

"Have you ever shot anyone?" She wondered why she couldn't move on from the gun. "I mean, have you ever had to use your weapon while you were protecting someone?"

"Bodyguarding? No. Not yet."

She took a sip of tea, thinking over that statement. "You haven't always been a bodyguard?"

"No, I was in the military for a few years after I graduated high school."

The military. That explained the capability, the respectful way he spoke, his earnestness. It didn't explain the way he could sound so kind. That must have been his own natural thing. Southern hospitality.

"How long have you been doing the bodyguard thing, then?"

"A little less than a year," he replied. "Most of it close security."

"Like, shadowing someone? Living in their house, like you do here?"

"Yes, ma'am. Or in hotels with them, or vacation resorts. Wherever their job takes them."

He was supposed to go to Europe and Asia with their entourage after *Fire and Fury* came out. She wondered if he'd be staying in her actual hotel room, or in an adjoining room. Would they have a suite? How close was close security? She was too embarrassed to ask.

"It's kind of hard to work in close security, isn't it?" She was talking too much, but she couldn't seem to stop. "It doesn't give you much time to have your own life. I mean, what about your friends? Your family?"

"My friends are all busy with their own jobs, and my family's in Texas. I don't have my own family yet. I guess when I get married and have kids, I'll do other kinds of assignments." He shrugged, resting his mug against one of his knees. "I don't know. This works for me, for now." His smile transformed to more of a grin. "And close security pays the most. It's good money."

He looked so young when he smiled that way. He said he didn't have his own family yet. That sounded like he wanted to have a family someday. A wife, a real one, and kids. She'd given up on all of that by now. She'd given up on anything real. With a sigh, she sipped the last of her tea.

"Sorry to ask so many questions," she said. "I'm sure you're tired."

"I'm fine. How are you feeling?"

At first she thought he was asking how she was feeling, like, emotion wise. *Oh, I don't know. I'm pretty miserable. I'm married to a gay man, his lover hates me, I'm surrounded by freaks and stalkers, and I haven't had real sex in years.* Then she realized he was referring to her earlier jump scare, when he'd materialized out of the dark.

"I'm good now," she said. "The tea relaxed me."

"Me too. Thanks for making it." He looked down at his watch and back at her. "Well, it's two, and everything seems quiet. If you don't need anything, I'll head to my room for the night."

Jenna tried not to think about what she might "need" from her strong, handsome bodyguard at two in the morning. Wow, she had to get off this sex thing. It was just that physical pleasure wasn't easy for her to find, the way her life was set up. Her husband was gay, his boyfriend was gay, her stylist was gay, her yoga instructor was gay, pretty much every male in her life was gay, and sometimes a vibrator wasn't enough.

"I hope you sleep well." She tried to give Caleb a polite, sincere look, but she was afraid she looked flirty.

He looked back at her with no flirtation at all. "I always sleep well, but if you need me, all you have to do is call. I wake from the smallest sounds, if they're not usual background sounds. I've always operated that way."

"I might stay up a little longer," she said, taking their mugs to the kitchen.

"That's fine. If you need anything, don't hesitate to wake me."

She imagined doing that—going right into his bedroom and waking him from sleep. It seemed shocking, horrible, exciting. When she finally fell asleep, she dreamed of him, of the low rumble of his voice and his steady gaze. In her dream, he was naked, sitting in a chair out in her living room. She walked behind him and put her hands on his shoulders, taking in a deep breath. He smelled like musky, woodsy cologne.

She pressed her lips to the back of his neck, to his warm, tan skin. He didn't turn, but she could feel his muscles tense in response. With a sigh, she leaned closer and kissed the curve of his shoulder, running her fingers down his biceps. When she glanced down, she could see he was hard, his cock jutting up from a thatch of gold-blond hair.

Just like that, she was naked too, walking around to the front of him, letting him gaze at her. For once, he didn't look kind and gentle. He looked hungry, his sensual lips pursed with lust. When he reached out, she drew in an excited breath and straddled him, settling down on his lap, his hot, hard cock prodding at her entrance—

She came awake with a start. She couldn't go down that road. She couldn't get obsessed with her bodyguard, or wonder what his imposing body looked like under his tailored suit. She couldn't daydream about climbing onto his cock, no matter her circumstances, no matter if she was in a sham marriage that was slowly killing her soul.

He was respectful— and respectable. She'd have to offer him the same courtesy and hide her fantasies away.

* * * * *

Caleb lay awake longer than he wanted to, thinking about guns and killing people, and waking up at the slightest sound. When she'd questioned him about his experience, he'd fed her the usual lie, that he'd been in the military, but the missions he'd done had been only quasi-official. Quasi-moral.

You're going to fret about morality, man? When you chose to live and work in Hollywood? He was finally drifting off to sleep when he heard the sound of angry male voices and a scuffle at the door. Not the door to the outer room, either. Someone was arguing outside the double doors to Jenna's living room.

He jumped out of bed in his boxers, not even stopping to put on a shirt. When he opened the door to the hall, Jenna was standing outside her room, her face pale. He waved her back inside. "Lock the door," he said. "I'll handle this."

"It's Nate and Tom. His bodyguard."

Now that she said it, he recognized their voices. He didn't recognize the mask of terror eclipsing Jenna's features. "I guess you don't care to see them tonight?"

"No. They've been partying."

"Go back to sleep then. I'll send them away."

He strode out to the living room. He didn't have a gun, but he didn't need a gun to handle inebriated people, and from the sounds of their voices, Nathaniel and his boyfriend were definitely drunk, or strung out on something. He ignored the rattling knob—if they had a key they would have already used it—and listened to Nate's slurred words as the two men argued on the other side.

"You can't go in. I changed the locks."

"I live here, too," said Maxon.

"Why do you want to see her? She's not your punching bag," Nathaniel whispered in a pleading voice. "You have to leave her alone."

"This is her fault," the other man said, not being quiet at all. He was forceful drunk, his words tumbling over each other. "Fucking bitch. She's trying to tear us apart."

A fist connected with the door, followed by more angry whispers that were so slurred and frantic, Caleb could hardly understand. Maxon's voice rose again. "She wants me to go," he moaned. "You want me to go. Everyone h-hates me. I can't stand it if you hate m-me."

"Come to bed. Shh. Tommy. Come on."

"Don't touch me," the bodyguard cried with a loud groan. Caleb could have opened the door to help, but Nate probably wouldn't have appreciated him interfering in this moment. Caleb wasn't going to get involved unless Maxon made it through the door into Jenna's territory.

"Stop it," Nate said, just before a crashing sound. Someone had fallen and knocked something over in the outer room. Caleb listened, imagining a scuffle as Nate hauled Maxon upright. The man's ranting intensified, even as their voices moved away.

"You pansy-ass faggot," Maxon yelled, presumably at his employer. "Traitor. You care about her more than me." A pause, and then, "You're unfaith—unfaithful. I saw you looking at that fuckboy at LouLou's. You asshole! Don't you know that's what she wants, for us to break up? She hates me. She hates you. She wants me gone, and you—" Another crash, this one more dramatic than before. "You don't give a shit that she hates me. You fucking coward. You asshole. You'll be just fine with your fugly beard wife to protect you."

Another door slammed, and Caleb opened the double doors to inspect the outer room. Nothing was broken, but a crystal vase had been knocked off an end table, ejecting a cascade of lilies onto the floor. He checked that the outer door was locked, then turned to find Jenna righting the vase and replacing the flowers.

"Wilma will clean the carpet tomorrow," she said. "She knows the best way to do it. There's not that much water."

He watched her, amazed that she was worried about water on the carpet after what had just gone on. But then he remembered how some men in his unit used to react to trauma, the way they'd obsess over small, inconsequential things to clear their minds of what they'd just experienced. He remembered something else too. *Punching bag.* His brain fixated on those words as he studied her. *I changed the locks. She's not your punching bag.*

Had he meant it metaphorically, or did Maxon abuse Jenna? He found himself striding to Jenna, clicking on a lamp. He tilted her face up to his.

She shied away, and he realized his abrupt inspection was adding to the trauma she felt. She'd say something, wouldn't she, if she was the victim of abuse? All the security people around her... He didn't see any bruises, just her dark, slightly tearful eyes. She pushed his hand away.

"Nate and Tom party together sometimes when he's off the clock, and they get crazy when they're wound up," she said. "Lord knows what they got into at LouLou's. That's why I sleep with the doors locked."

He took a step back, because he knew she needed him to, but his heart still raced with adrenaline, and his mind raced with questions. "If the doors weren't locked, what would happen?"

She answered his question with a question. "What were they saying out there? What did you hear?"

"I heard two guys arguing," he said. "Your husband and his bodyguard. They both sounded pretty messed up."

She snorted. "Tom's so unprofessional. Nate keeps him around because he's really good at making him feel...feel comfortable, but, yeah, sometimes he doesn't do his job well, and sometimes...well...they don't get along."

He could see her trying to spin a story, to cover for her husband. He wished he could reassure her that he already knew the truth—but he wasn't supposed to know the truth. Instead he asked, "Has Maxon—Tom—ever behaved unprofessionally toward you? Has he ever harassed you when he was high or drunk?"

She shook her head with a little too much insistence, then manufactured a carefree expression. "I mean, people act out when they're fucked up. I used to drink too. Tom and I have had some scuffles."

"You've had scuffles with your husband's bodyguard, and he wasn't fired?"

"Not scuffles," she said, backtracking. "Like, you know, drunk arguments. I'm glad I don't drink anymore, because that's what you act like." She pointed toward the door.

He studied her, trying to glean the facts from the made-up stories. So much bullshit in this house. *Confide in me, Jenna. Tell me what's really going on here. Tell me the truth.* But she didn't. She fed him some story about how her husband didn't fire the bodyguard because they were longtime friends, that they'd known each other before Nate and Jenna got married, and Nate just "accepted the way Tom is."

"I think Tom might have some secret crush on Nate or something," she finished with a weak laugh. "But it only comes out when they've both been partying a little too hard."

Caleb frowned. "I'm surprised your husband puts up with that, considering the image he has to maintain."

Confide in me. Now would be a great time.

But she didn't confide in him, maybe because she was so wrought up, or because he was bare chested in boxers. Maybe it was too late at night, and too quiet after the yelling and the capsized vase. He glanced at the lilies, only slightly bent and bruised. She'd ask for help if her husband's lover was hurting her, wouldn't she?

Or would the husband hire a bodyguard so the "scuffles" would stop happening whenever his lover was drunk or high?

He let out a sigh, too quiet for Jenna to hear, and guided her back into the living room. He locked those doors and turned to his client. "I'm sorry your sleep was disturbed. Is there anything else I can do for you tonight? Would you like me to check to make sure your husband and his bodyguard made it safely back to their rooms?"

"No, it's okay." She flicked her fingers toward the other part of the house. "They'll sleep it off, and be all apologies tomorrow when they realize they came to my door, trying to wake me up."

Trying to beat you up, Caleb thought. It would have given him the greatest pleasure to go after Thomas Maxon to "check" on him with some expertly landed kicks to the throat, but then he'd be leaving Jenna unprotected, and he couldn't do that. He wasn't here to pick fights. He was here to prevent them, if tonight was any indication. Jenna seemed tough, but she wouldn't be a match for a man of Maxon's size.

As for Nathaniel York, what the hell was he doing? What was wrong with him? Even if Jenna was a beard and not a wife, he needed her goodwill and her goddamn safety to keep his cover story in place. His grandma would have said Nathaniel York was one twist short of a Slinky, but that didn't do justice to how messed up he was.

He escorted Jenna to her bedroom, offering solace and security to the extent his job allowed. "If they come back," he said, "don't even get up. Stay in bed. Let me handle it."

She blinked at him, said "Thank you," and slowly shut her door.

5.
THE ACT

The next morning, Nate tried to get rid of her new bodyguard.

He came to her room before Caleb was on duty and said it was "disruptive" having a full-time person living on her side of the house. He said the locked doors were working fine, that he was paying money to Ironclad Solutions for nothing. Jenna knew he was just worried about last night's drunken display, and Caleb finding out.

She was terrified Caleb had already been fired, that Nate had already made the call, and this was his roundabout way of breaking the news. She couldn't bear not to see him again. In Caleb, Jenna had found a tenuous lifeline to sincerity and the real world, and she couldn't deal with the thought of being on her own again.

She panicked as Nate laid out his reasons, then she cried. She hated to cry in front of him, to show weakness when he and his lawyers already held her in such a weak position, but she worried that nothing else would work. She begged and cried, and appealed to Nate's ego. *It means so much to me that you care about protecting me.* She appealed to his guilt. *I don't want to go back to worrying about Tom. It's not fair to make me live in fear.*

In the end, Nate backed down, and Jenna was so torn up by the conversation she could only come out of her room to see that Caleb was really there, sitting in the outer room in his dark suit and tie.

"Good afternoon," he said when he saw her.

"Hi." She stood beside the door, staring at him, wanting to ask if he'd heard anything about Nate wanting to fire him. "Is everything okay?"

He blinked at her. "Yes. Is everything okay with you? Can I help you with anything?"

He really would help her with anything. He offered those words constantly, and they meant so much to her, because without him, there was no one to help her with anything. There was no one who really gave a shit if she was okay.

She should use his services more, so Nate would see that he was a necessary expenditure. She thought about asking Caleb if they could go out, go somewhere where she could breathe fresh air and be away from this house, but she didn't know any place that wouldn't result in paparazzi and intrusion.

She was so trapped here, so fucking *trapped*. She fought the familiar feeling of claustrophobia, of panic, but at least he was here with her. "I'm okay," she said, forcing a smile for his benefit. "I guess Gladys told you that the stylist is coming by later this afternoon to talk about looks for the *Fire and Fury* premieres."

"That's great. I was hoping he could do something with my hair," he said, stroking his military-grade high-and-tight buzz cut.

"No, it's for me." She'd been so tense all morning, his joke flew right over her head. She covered her face. "Ha. Sorry. I didn't get enough sleep."

His gaze was kind, not mocking, even though she blushed at her stupidity. "I really do wish someone would do something with my hair," he said.

"I like your hair." There, she'd admitted it. She loved his meticulously groomed goatee, she loved his blue eyes, she loved his patient, non-mocking smile. "You look really great when you dress up," she said, trying to sound casual. "You should be an actor, not a bodyguard."

"I don't think I'd like the exposure, and acting is probably harder than it looks."

It is, she thought. *It's so hard.*

"Well, it's good to see you," she said, retreating back into her living room. "Let me know when Malik and the others arrive."

* * * * *

A couple weeks later, Jenna sat in the limousine with Nate, staring out the window at walls of screaming fans. It was the first week of June, time for the L.A. premiere of *Fire and Fury*, the first big blockbuster of the summer. Nate hummed with energy and anticipation, a movie-star wonder in his slick Armani suit.

As for her, she drew in the last precious, peaceful breaths, the last seconds of privacy she'd have for the next few hours. Once the door opened, there would be only mania and scrutiny, screaming fans and jostling cameras.

Their limo waited in line to crawl up to the red carpet entrance, where she'd emerge on Nate's arm, the beautiful, doting Hollywood wife. She tried to get her doting face ready—the authentic smile, the shining eyes, the feminine pride for her straight, sexy husband.

Her glance strayed to her husband's lover, and she wondered if, in private, Tom ever looked at Nate that way, with doting pride. Did Tom's eyes ever shine? She tried not to imagine their private moments too much. She tried not to think about what went on in the privacy of their bedroom, in their own secluded wing of the house. There was a time, a cursed, horrible time when their worlds crossed over, but that time was past and buried. Everything buried.

She closed her eyes, took another deep breath. When she opened them, she was looking at Caleb, and he was looking back at her, an undercurrent of concern in his features. His blue eyes could be so fathomless, yet so direct. When his features changed, it was slight, but she noticed. She'd been looking at him for almost a month now, and she was starting to learn real things about him, beyond her private, aching fantasies.

It was so embarrassing, her feelings for her bodyguard. What a cliché. He was young, vital, handsome, and she was...what was that awful term? Thirsty. Was she old enough to be a cougar? She needed a drink.

No, she couldn't have a drink.

She smiled at Caleb instead, so he'd know she was all right. Well, as all right as someone in her position could be. She reached down to adjust one of her shoe's straps, then realized she was sending him an open shot of cleavage. *You thirsty cougar.* She straightened, and Nate took her hand.

"Ready, babes?"

"Yeah."

He slid an approving look over her gown's plunging bodice. "Jesus, you look like a billion bucks. No one's going to be watching the movie with you sitting there."

"Stop," she said, flirting, putting on an act because Caleb wasn't supposed to know. "Are we watching the whole movie?"

"Tonight, yes. The studio guys are here, and we've got the big party afterwards."

It was all she could do not to groan. Doing the happy wife thing during red carpets was a pain, but it was over in a relatively short time. The studio party for a mega-blockbuster like *Fire and Fury* might go on all night, with so many people to lie to, so many people who held her husband's career in their hands. Worst of all, alcohol everywhere.

But Caleb would be there with her, nearby, since it'd be an open party environment. When she had to stay out late, he stayed out late too, no complaints. When the limo pulled up and Nate's public relations team descended on them with directions, Caleb was the one who helped her from the car, his large, strong hand rough from real work, not smooth like Nate's manicured fingers. When her cleavage was in danger of spilling out, he looked at her eyes instead of her boobs, then lifted his gaze to the delicate jeweled clip the stylist had put in her hair.

"Thanks," she murmured as he steadied her on her feet. "Thank you."

"Yes, ma'am."

Whenever he called her *ma'am*, she felt like the thirstiest cougar of all time, but she knew that was the Texas boy in him. Kids from rural Florida were the same, *yes ma'am, no ma'am* to any female who was older than they were. Nate took her hand and she forced herself to stop thinking about Caleb, and focus on the man she was supposed to love.

Well, she did love him, somehow. She loved him in the way co-conspirators grew close. She loved him for rescuing her from herself, but she hated him too, and she hated Tom, and all of these were really hard feelings to process on a red carpet. She shut down those thoughts as they posed for photos, close, in love, the glamorous, happy couple.

Smile, no matter what. Just get through this.

After a blinding barrage of photos, the publicist's assistant pulled her to the side so Nate could pose for his solo moments in the spotlight. She waited, studying the spectators. Any crazies out there? Nate's hardcore fans were jealous of her life, jealous of her proximity to their object of obsession, and told her so in angry letters. No one ever wanted to kill Nate. They only wanted to kill her.

Maybe today was the day. She wondered if her painfully cinched shaper was strong enough to repel bullets. Black humor had become her life, because it was easier to laugh than try to solve her problems.

Nate's publicist turned and beckoned her back to him. She couldn't remember this one's name. He had an army of them, and she'd long since ceased trying to keep them straight. She went to stand at her husband's side, doing her Queen Jenna wave. *Ah yes, I'm so happy to see you. So happy to be here.*

Bullshit. Such bullshit.

She looked over at Nate, making sure she'd appear appropriately worshipful in the photos. He took her hand and placed it over his arm, ever the old-fashioned gentleman. They'd done red carpet walks enough times that the mechanics weren't that difficult. *Stand up straight, pause every few seconds, look happy, pretend you live a dream life.* All the big stars did this. It was part of the job, part of the game.

The crowd was a swirling, popping wave of movement as Nate passed. People screamed, not just women, but men too. They waved and begged for photos and autographs, and sometimes shouted rude things because they thought it might get that one moment of eye contact or an actual response, even if it was angry. She'd long ago learned not to look or respond, but she heard them. She understood why people shouted mean things about her and not Nate. He was their idol. *Whatever. Smile. Get through this.*

It would be easier if she didn't know they had six of these looming ahead of them. London, Paris, Berlin, Tokyo, Seoul, and Sydney, and any other place that might be added at the last minute, based on *Fire and Fury*'s ticket sales and reviews.

Her heel caught a wrinkle in the carpet. Even though he was a few steps behind them, Caleb had a hand on her elbow before she could stumble, before Nate's body even reacted to the hitch. Her husband bantered with fans, never getting too close, as Tom stood like a gargoyle beside him. Nate's actorly, energized speech translated well on screen, but hurt her ears in close proximity. She opened her eyes wide and relaxed her features, trying to be the picture of contented, docile wifeliness. The layers of makeup helped.

After twenty minutes or so, they reached the end of the media barrage. Only two of the reporters had spoken to her directly, and her answers to their question—*How are you feeling tonight?*—had been the same in both cases. "I'm so proud."

Now they were in the quieter lobby, surrounded by security and film people. Tom and Caleb accompanied them to their row near the middle of the theater, and took the seats on either side of them. People milled around them, chatting, staring, until the movie quieted everyone.

Great. Time for the show to begin.

* * * * *

The party afterward was harder than the premiere, because it lasted longer, and everyone was drunk.

God, when had it gotten so hard for her? People tripped over each other to fawn over Nate and shake his hand. They never talked to her, even though she turned to them and smiled. She was nothing. A tool, a PR concoction, a begowned and bejeweled supportive wife. In private, people told jokes about her. She'd overheard comments through the years, seen people whispering behind their hands. Fuck, did they think she didn't know her husband was in love with his bodyguard? She lived with them. She had to listen to their flirting and their fights. Hell, she'd been in bed with both of them...

Now was not the time to think about that.

Nate got up and left, drawn away by an Oscar-winning producer. He was still chasing that Oscar, would do just about anything to win one, including living a secret life. For all its talk of progressive politics, for all its Democratic fundraisers, the film business was a bigoted, misogynistic cabal. They professed to welcome gays—and they did, tons of gays worked behind the scenes, in writing, marketing, directing, costume and makeup. But once you were openly gay, you didn't get very many leading man roles, especially in action flicks.

That was the simple, sad reality, and why Jenna had agreed to a fake marriage. She understood Nate's conundrum, and she felt his pain. He'd cried in her arms more than once. That was back when they weren't so contemptuous of each other, back when they'd been friends.

Now he barely looked at her when the cameras weren't around. Jenna moved toward the outskirts of the room, avoiding the bar, and took up a position beside a high top table. A glance to the side told her Caleb was there, always there, even if he acted invisible as he shadowed her around the room. At her other side was an aging actress who turned her back, declining to acknowledge her. She stared at the woman's nape, at dyed blonde hair swept into a chignon, and the glitter of more jewels. The woman's earrings were too heavy for her lobes. The stretched, distorted cartilage made Jenna's skin crawl.

Across the room, Tom shadowed Nate, acting as the alert, stone-faced bodyguard, for what it was worth. It occurred to her that everything in her life was pretend, gloss, a lie. A sham. Not just her marriage, but every fucking thing. Her existence was as fake as the film industry, as fake as the movies Nate rolled out every year. Whoever was writing the screenplay of her life was an asshole.

You wrote it, she reminded herself. *You chose this. Your choices brought you here, your desperate hunger for fame.*

Now she had to slog through four solid hours of debauchery and self-congratulation. A few blocks away, people didn't have money to feed their children, but why should that dampen the celebration of how rich and talented they all were?

Just stop thinking, Jen. Just stop.

If only she could have a drink, or ten. In the heady flush of alcoholism, it had been easy to stop thinking. Each day had floated by in a haze of rum and cokes. That had worked great for her sanity until the tabloids picked up on her problem. *Let's have a baby*, Nate had said. He thought a baby would fix her alcoholism, her smothering unhappiness. *Oh, Jesus. Stop, stop, stop thinking about that.*

Her husband returned to her, ambling through the other tables in leading-man glory and sliding into the seat beside hers. Tom stood behind him, and Jenna hated that she could see him but not Caleb. She stared at her lap and dug her nails into her wrist, because then she could think about that pain, not all the other pain.

"What are you doing?" Nate whispered, looking down at her hands. "Stop it. Stop moping and looking so sad."

"I can't survive this." She mouthed the words. He still heard them.

"Don't be a fuckhead. I only ask you to come to these things a few times a year. Anyone else would be happy to—"

A camera swung by them and they both smiled, a reflex by now, a reaction from her lizard brain. *Camera equals smile. Nate equals happy wife. Mockery equals ignore. Life equals pain.* As soon as the camera moved away, he leaned closer, squeezing her hand. She could smell the sharp tang of alcohol on his breath.

"Anyone else would be happy to be here," he said in a low voice. "Do you know how many women would give any fucking thing on earth to be in this room with me right now, talking to me, getting attention from Nathaniel York? So please stop being a brooding, complaining bitch."

"Please stop being an asshole."

He gave her a warning look, even though she'd spoken too softly for anyone to hear. She knew the rules. A tension headache started to form at each of her temples, probing into her brain. She looked longingly at the bar, and at the flutes of top-notch champagne offered by waiters to every guest, then caught sight of Caleb in her peripheral vision.

They only glanced at one another. That was all she dared with Nate around, but there was such understanding, such sympathetic humanity in his expression that she almost broke down.

Wow, she was a mess. She wished she could go to her bodyguard and collapse into his arms. What would the other guests make of that? His stance was protective. Pure. His hands were clasped in front of him, ready to assist her or pull a gun if it came to that. He was young and virile and so fucking sexy it slayed her, but still, incredibly, a nice guy. She wanted to scribble a note on one of the cocktail napkins, *I love you and you are everything to me right now*, and slip it to him even though they were at a party surrounded by Nate's contemporaries.

No, too risky, and she didn't have a goddamn pen. Instead she let herself imagine, just for a moment, *what if...* She'd been subsisting on masturbation for so many years now, on massage wands and books and porn. Tears welled in her eyes, tears she knew she couldn't shed because of 'optics' and makeup. What if she cried here? What if she screamed out all the sadness and regret that haunted her? What would Nate do? What would the Hollywood establishment do?

Her head started hurting worse. She turned to Nate and took his arm. "I need to leave. I stayed for an hour. Is that enough? Can you tell everyone I'm not feeling well?"

"Damn it, Jenna."

"Why do you even need me here? This party's about you."

"I need you here because you're my wife."

He looked irritated, but he also seemed to recognize she was about to snap. He stroked a hand down her arm, pretending to love her even when he was pissed at her. "If you have to go, then go. Take the car and have them come back for me."

"Okay."

"And go out the back with that guy."

"What guy?"

"Your bodyguard. I don't want you getting photographed together when I'm not around."

"He's my bodyguard. Pretty sure people would know that from the suit and his ID."

"Just do what I fucking say without all the talkback." He hissed the words as he pretended to hug her.

She stepped back, unable to deal with the fake, clutching embrace. "Okay. Enjoy the rest of your premiere."

He persisted in kissing and hugging her goodbye long enough for everyone around them to see. It made her burn with humiliation. It was time to draw this public farce to a close, and retreat into what privacy she could find. She forced one last smile and said "I'll see you later" in the way she thought a loving wife might. By the time Caleb stepped forward, Nate had already been drawn into another conversation.

She watched him another couple seconds before she turned away. He glowed from inside, that was just a fact. Everyone adored him. Hell, she'd adored him once, to an embarrassing degree. He deserved all this fame and adulation. He'd worked for it.

He deserved it, just like she deserved the misery of her fake, pathetic life.

"Is everything okay?" Caleb asked, leaning to check in.

"Yes." Her eyes held his for a fleeting moment. "I'm fine, just really tired. Do you mind taking me home?"

"That's what I'm here for."

He guided Jenna out the back, then led her to the longest limo parked beside the curb. "Okay?" he asked, as she crawled into the backseat. She could hardly breathe in her stupid, tight dress. "Have everything you need?"

"Yes."

"I'll ride up front with the driver, if that's all right?"

"Sure," she said, resting her head back against the seat. Of course he wouldn't want to ride in the back with her. Why would anyone want to ride with her? She was washed up, an aging, fake Hollywood wife. She felt so tired, so awfully vulnerable that if he'd ridden in the back with her, she would have broken down and told him all kinds of inappropriate things, like how awesome he was, how sexy and desirable. He wouldn't want to hear it, and she didn't want to say all that lovelorn crap anyway.

She just wanted to go home.

6.
A Jagged, Distorted Picture

When they got to the house, Caleb asked again if she was okay. Did he know she was hanging on by a thread, or did personal bodyguards just check in a lot to monitor their client's mental health?

He didn't want to know about her mental health. She said good night as casually as she could and retreated to her room. She had to get out of her flashy clothes and shaper, had to wash the Hollywood grit off her. She hung up the loaner gown and took off her jewelry, securing the jewels in their boxes the way she'd been taught by her original stylist a decade ago. The shoes came off next, arranged into their velvet-lined receptacle. She wished she could just toss it all on the floor and let Nate pay for whatever was wrinkled or damaged, but the poor country trash inside her wouldn't let her.

She turned the shower water up high and stood under the scalding stream, trying to wash away the humiliation, the makeup, the damn body shaper lines etched into her skin.

It was all so ridiculous. Her life was ridiculous.

As she showered, she thought back over the past few hours, the excitement of Nate's new movie, which was great, and the pleasure he'd found in a job well done. Her own job was so much less satisfying, and to have Caleb witness it all...

She shut off the water and wiped away the tears that still ran down her face. Fuck Caleb. Fuck his honesty and his open expressions, and his constant vigilance for her safety. He'd never go so far as to express a mean opinion in that southern accent of his, but he probably thought she was stupid and crazy.

Because you are stupid and crazy.

She pulled on a cami and sleep shorts, and then a satin robe Nate had given her, cinching the sash tight around her waist. She looked in the mirror and rubbed her eyes, trying to buff away the lingering smudges of eyeliner that streaked her face. Stupid Caleb. He couldn't stand to ride in the back of the limo with her, but sat in front with the driver so she had to ride home alone with her thoughts.

It was getting too hard for her to be alone with her thoughts. One drink would take the edge off. One tiny drink, just a few sips. Maybe a sleeping pill or two. She picked up a brush and dragged it through her hair, digging the bristles into her scalp. If only she wasn't too chicken shit to stab herself the way the bristles stabbed into her head. Peace at last.

But there wasn't going to be any peace for a while. Six more premieres, at least, then a few months down the line, the same parade of bullshit all over again. *Smile, you fucking idiot*, she thought as she stared at herself in the mirror. *That's all you're fucking good for.*

A wave of rage rose within her, rage at herself, rage at Nate, rage at Tom, rage at Caleb, rage at the glistening marble bathroom around her, the red designer dress hanging in the closet, the goddamned shoes that cost more than all the shoes her mother had owned in her life. She stabbed the person in the mirror with her brush, banged it against the glass so it made a thudding, clanging sound. She did it over and over, until her wrist ached. It hurt, but it felt so good.

She saw the towel rack out of the corner of her eye, the heavy, freestanding metal rack, made to warm her five-hundred-dollar Turkish towels. That would feel better. She lifted it and swung it like a bat right at the mirror. The sound was so much better, so much louder. The glass shattered into a spider web, and every time she hit it with the towel rack, she created more spider webs streaking outward. Now she couldn't see herself, only a jagged, distorted picture.

Good.

She swung the towel rack again. It was heavy and it was hard, but she'd started this destruction and she didn't want to stop until she finished the job. She hit the left side of the mirror, *bang, shatter*, and the right side, *bang, shatter, clink clink clink* as glass shards backed with silver hit the bathroom floor and collected in the sink.

"Jenna!"

The sharp, concerned voice stopped her mid swing.

"Don't move," he said. "There's glass."

She wanted to laugh at that observation. Yeah, there was glass. Everywhere. Instead of laughing, though, she was crying. Caleb pulled her back from the sink and the shattered mirror, taking the towel rack from her. He gave a tug when she wouldn't release it, and set it against the wall. It was bent. Broken, like the mirror.

"I don't know why I did that." She blinked at him through tears. "I didn't mean to."

He said nothing, only looked her over with his intent blue eyes, checking her for injury. He lifted her hands and opened them, turning them back and forth, then leaned down and lifted her in his arms, carrying her out through her bedroom and down the hall to the living room. He set her on the couch, kneeling beside her on the floor.

"Do you hurt anywhere?"

"No. I just broke the mirror."

"There was glass everywhere, Jenna. Let me look at your feet."

She noted the tension in his voice, an edge to his normally unflappable calm. "I'm sorry," she said as he ran his hands over her soles and ankles, and up her calves. "I don't know what happened."

He stopped touching her and sat back on his heels. He was in sleep pants and a tee shirt. She wondered if his tux was hanging up as neatly as her gown. The gravity in his expression made her eyes tear up again.

"Why did you break the mirror?" he asked.

Such a difficult question. Had she been angry? Disgusted? Exhausted? "I don't know. I—I liked the sound it made." No, that wasn't the whole truth. "I wanted to break something." There, that was the truth.

"You definitely broke something." One of his hands rested on the couch beside her. He looked right into her eyes. "Should I call someone for you right now?"

"Like who?"

"A doctor. A counselor. Do you want to hurt yourself?"

She thought a moment. "No. I just wanted to break the mirror." If he'd had little respect for her before, he must have none at all now. "It was a long night," she said, hating the whine in her voice.

"Did someone say something that upset you?"

"I just hated everyone there. I hate Hollywood parties. I hate premieres."

His brows drew together in a frown, and he moved his hand from the sofa to her knee, exerting light pressure. "Stay here. Sit right here while I go clean up the glass."

Wilma would clean it up. She started to tell him that, but then she realized it was probably around two in the morning, and Wilma was at home, asleep like normal, healthy people. "You don't have to." She felt bad now that she'd emerged from her adrenalized meltdown. "I'll clean it up. I did it."

"Sit right there, and don't move until I come back."

That was the most authority she'd ever heard in his voice. She sat and watched him go to the kitchen for a dustpan and some towels. When he strode down the hall, she felt alone and exposed, and wanted him back. She strained her ears to hear him picking up the glass, but he was too careful, or agile, to make any noise at what he was doing. Five minutes later, he returned, leaving a trash bag in the kitchen and washing his hands.

"I did what I could," he said. "I picked up the bigger pieces, but you'll have to stay out of there for now. You can use my bathroom if you need one." His normally placid gaze was darker as he crossed the room to sit beside her.

"I'm sorry," she said again. "I'm so sorry you had to clean up my mess."

He shook his head. "I'm not angry about the mess. I'm worried about you. I understand you had a stressful night, but you kind of lost it. Really lost it."

"I know. I guess I've been holding things in, and it all built up…"

She leaned toward him, toward his strength and calm, and like a miracle, one of his arms came around her. She rested her forehead against his shoulder and he pulled her closer, angling his body so she had a secure place to fall into him, with all her angst and wet hair and secrets.

"I want to tell you something," she whispered. "But I don't know if I should."

Telling him Nate's secrets would break the prenuptial agreement she'd signed, and put her in legal peril. Baring her soul would cause so many problems if he didn't keep his mouth shut.

"Jenna..." His fingers moved against her arm, not quite a caress, but soft enough to feel kind. "I'm your bodyguard. I don't know if I'm qualified to help with your...more personal problems. But if you need to tell me something to get it off your chest, you can trust my discretion."

He spoke so carefully, with such measured consideration. She blurted out her words with no grace at all. Well, she didn't blurt them, she whispered them.

"Nothing in my life is real," she said close to his ear. "Nate isn't really my husband. We're not really husband and wife."

"Why are you whispering?"

"Because I'm not supposed to talk about this. I'm not allowed. If Nate found out I told you about our fake marriage thing, he'd take me to court. He'd take everything away from me and bankrupt me and get me shut out of every friendship and connection I have in this town, and even if I could find a safe place to tell my side of the story to the public, he'd pay off the papers to silence it and sue me for breach of contract. Cause we have a contract, not a marriage."

"I see."

He didn't sound shocked or surprised. He just held her, ready to listen to more. And God, there was more.

"Tom is Nate's lover," she said in a quieter whisper. The big, huge secret, and she'd just let it out. "He has been for ten years, ever since I was hired to keep up appearances." Now that she'd started talking, she couldn't seem to stop. "I mean, Nate and I are really married, legally, but this isn't a real marriage. I'm his cover. His beard."

She couldn't see Caleb's facial reactions because she was huddled so close to him, but he breathed slowly, in and out. "A lot of Hollywood marriages are strange," he murmured after a moment. "Hollywood's a crazy place. My brother was Jeremy Gray's assistant for years, and the stories he told me..."

"I believe it. And the thing is, the craziness never ends. I'm stuck in it now, and I get so tired of acting, pretending, fawning over him when I know it's not real." Her whisper broke. "I wanted to be an actress when I came to L.A. Did you know I was almost an actress, Caleb? I had talent. People who worked with me said there was something about me. My publicist busted her ass to get me discovered, then I met Nate at a charity event. He got me into a screen test for one of his movies. That was supposed to be my big break, but I didn't get the part. Well, I got the part of his wife."

"It must have seemed a good idea at the time."

She let out a bitter laugh. "I thought it was the best idea ever, that my life would be never-ending luxury and security, that I'd never be poor again. And Nate was so kind, so engaged with me in the beginning. He offered to help my whole family, gave them money hand over fist. It was great for a few years, then just okay..." She brushed away a tear before it could fall. "But it's getting really hard now. I'm in my mid-thirties. I'm realizing this is going to be my life, my legacy. I'm stuck here. I'm never going to be...real."

"You are real." His voice rumbled in her ear. Somewhere between them, his hand found hers and his fingers wrapped around her clenched fist. "You're real to me, to a lot of people. You do things in the community. You have your children's charities. You knit those hats for the babies at Mercy Hospital."

She stared at the pile of baby hats beside him. He didn't even know that story, didn't know that she, Nate, and Tom had tried to conceive their own baby. She shook her head, shook those thoughts away, and opened her hand to grip his fingers. They weren't quite holding hands.

"Have you talked to Nate about how hard things have gotten for you?" Caleb asked. "What if you got out of the house more? What if you tried to get into acting again? Would that help?"

"I don't want to act anymore." Her voice rose above a whisper in her distress. "The things I've learned about Hollywood through the years, watching Nate and his big time directors and producers... I don't want to be in this world anymore. I hate everything about it, everything about them. Everything is fake and shitty and everyone only cares for themselves. I mean, there are people who care, but they aren't the ones who get ahead. I wish I could get the hell out of this place, but I'm stuck behind these walls with a fake husband and his boyfriend who despises me."

"Couldn't you go home?"

"I don't have a home anymore. When I married Nate, he gave my relatives tons of money, but trash doesn't do well with money." She choked on a sob as it rose in her throat, unexpected. She'd thought she was over all that. "My mom and her boyfriend started using drugs. My brother overdosed. Nate cut them off and my mom ended up in jail. She died there a couple years ago."

"I'm sorry."

"That's how it goes in that world. She was trailer trash, like her parents before her. Everything about my childhood and my family was trash, so, you know, I thought Nate was the answer for me. I thought I'd be happy forever. I thought we could all just coexist."

"You, Nate, and Tom?" His voice was soft. "But you don't get along with Tom."

"No. Tom wants me to get lost. He wants to live openly as Nate's lover, as his husband, but Nate says no."

"Unsurprisingly."

"I know, right? Nate has the money and power in their relationship, and he insists on keeping up this 'arrangement.' Nate will never come out. I don't know why Tom can't understand that. Nate will never, ever, ever come out as his true self. His whole identity is tied up in his mega-stardom and tough guy action star heroism. The people who work with him would never let him come out, even if he wanted to. Do you know how much his last movie made worldwide?"

He let go of her hand as she sat back. Her wet hair had left a damp spot on his shirt.

"How much?" he asked.

"Half a billion dollars. When you think about it that way..." She rubbed her eyes. "I probably wouldn't come out either."

"So your contract's pretty tight, huh? You can't get out of it?" He thought a moment, his lips turning down. "How about a fake divorce? Then Nate can marry someone else."

"I've asked. He refuses. When celebrities get divorced, everyone wants to know why, why, why, and he doesn't want to expose himself to any whys." She touched his hand, still lying beside hers. "I don't need you to help me with this. There's no way to help me. It was just a relief to...to get it out."

"Jenna—"

"No, honestly, I just needed to tell someone sympathetic. I'm sorry it had to be you, and that I got your shirt wet, and you're saddled with this secret—"

He leaned closer and made her meet his gaze. "Jenna, when my boss at Ironclad gave me this assignment, he told me your marriage was probably not legit. In the security community, word is that it's not legit. You're a great actress in public, but people who work in this house..." He shrugged. "Well, they see things. They figure things out."

"The security guys have been talking?" She felt frozen in shock. "How many people know?"

"No one *knows* anything, because we work in Hollywood. We keep our mouths shut and collect our checks."

"Oh. But they told you?"

"My boss told me he'd heard it from a reliable source," he said. "It's none of my business, but now that you've confided in me, I'll keep your secret. Maybe it'll help to have someone so close to you know the truth."

"You can't tell Nate that I told you."

"I won't tell anyone about anything. I promise you that."

She let out a long, slow breath. It did feel a little better to have told someone, someone who was safe. He was still worried about her. She could see it in his expression, in the way he was wide-awake even though it was the middle of the night.

"I'm glad they chose you for my bodyguard," she said. "I feel so protected when you're around."

"Good. That means I'm doing my job."

She bit her lip, heat rising in her cheeks. "I feel stupid asking this, but could you...would you mind... Since your shirt's already wet, would you mind putting your arm around me again, just for a little bit?"

He only hesitated a moment, but in that hesitation, she knew they were breaking the rules. She was used to living outside the lines, but he was a full-on integrity bomb who preferred, always, to do the right thing. Bodyguards weren't supposed to get cozy with their clients. She'd lived in Hollywood long enough to know that. There were certain bodyguards who were known to provide "services," but you didn't hire them from the legitimate security companies.

When she huddled against him, she was doubly appreciative of his warm acceptance. His arms came around her, holding her close, and she relaxed, letting this young, kind bodyguard break the rules on her behalf. She'd soak up his kindness for ten minutes, fifteen at most, and let the poor guy go to bed already.

God, he felt so strong, so solid. So amazingly true and real.

* * * * *

She was asleep within a couple minutes. He could feel her breathing soften, her heartbeat slow. Her muscles relaxed into slumber in the space of a few seconds. She was that tired.

Or that much in need of an edifying embrace.

He wasn't supposed to hold her this way. In bodyguard school, they were taught about maintaining boundaries, about appropriate and inappropriate ways to interact. "Reassurance contact" was okay, but that generally meant offering an arm for support, or a soothing pat on the shoulder. He was cradling his client as she slept, hugging her close, his cheek inching ever closer to the top of her dark, freshly showered hair. If Hector walked in on them right now, or Liam Wilder, the Ironclad CEO, Caleb was pretty sure they'd have something negative to say.

But they weren't here, and Caleb wasn't going to worry about that right now. There was training, official rules, and then there was having sympathy for someone in pain. His client had had a difficult night, and this was a form of protection, a shelter he could put up to guard her from the hectic craziness that drove her to screaming and breaking mirrors.

Not that he could ever be enough. Little by little, she'd opened up to him, and he saw the pain and frustration she lived with. He wanted to help her, but could he take on her problems without creating more problems for them both? The security guys outside...all they had to worry about were the cameras and door locks. He was the close protector. He'd chosen to be a close protector. He just hadn't realized it could feel this close.

Damn. He was getting feelings. Not just physical feelings. All guys had those when they were around an attractive protectee. No, he was getting feelings for Jenna's quiet voice, her expressive eyes, her rare, exasperated smiles. He was getting feelings for the way she knitted those baby hats, and the way she stared out at the mountains when she swam in the pool. He was getting feelings for the way she tried to be so strong, when she was crumbling inside.

She took a deep breath, falling into a deeper slumber, going limper still. She was so tired, a rag doll in his arms. He should carry her to her bed, but there was glass in her bathroom, so that didn't seem safe.

There was another bed he could take her to. His.

For a short, pleasurable moment, he allowed himself to imagine carrying her to his bed, bringing her under the sheets with him and holding her close. The closest of close protection. He wouldn't do anything sexual, wouldn't take things that far. Having sex with clients was definitely forbidden, but he could stroke her back and shoulders, kiss her forehead, and if she lifted her face, he could kiss her lips.

He stared down at her lips, half open in sleep, and knew this was a dangerous, slippery slope. He should request reassignment tomorrow, let someone else take over with Jenna before he slipped even further.

But he wouldn't.

He lifted her carefully so she wouldn't wake, slipping one arm under her knees to cradle her against his chest. Her head rested on his shoulder, her features utterly relaxed in sleep. He carried her to his bed, easing her under the covers, feeling oddly touched as she snuggled into his pillow with a soft sigh. He'd get another blanket and lie beside her, just in case. Close protection. It was a king size bed, plenty big enough for both of them. If she woke in the middle of the night, he'd be there to reassure her, tell her where she was.

He'd brought her to his bed because of the glass in her bathroom. That was the only reason.

And nobody had to know.

7.
AN ATTACK

Jenna woke in a strange bed. The sheets were lighter and the blanket felt different. When she opened her eyes, the wall was muted gray rather than pale yellow. It took a moment for her to realize she was in Caleb's room, in his bed.

It took a moment more to remember the previous night's meltdown. Towel rack vs. mirror. She turned on her side and there he was, her bodyguard, lying beside her. Not asleep, oh no. He was awake, typing on his phone, fully dressed in his suit-and-tie uniform, lying on top of the covers as far from her as he could.

"Did you sleep like that last night?" she asked.

"Not in the suit, no."

"Why am I in your bed?"

"Because I didn't want you wandering into your bathroom in the middle of the night. Do you remember last night?"

She rubbed her forehead. "Unfortunately."

"How are you feeling today?"

Something in the way he looked at her had changed. A little of the calm in his eyes was gone. "I'm fine," she said, wanting that calm back. "You don't have to worry about me."

"Worrying about you is my job." He turned away from her, stood from the bed and straightened his jacket. "I apologize for bringing you here last night. You fell asleep on my shoulder, and I didn't want to leave you alone out on the couch after everything that went down."

Everything that went down. Namely her batshit freakout. "Shit. I'm sorry I lost it so badly last night."

"Wilma came by early and had a look at your bathroom. She told me to tell you breaking mirrors brings seven years of bad luck. She also said you need more vitamins."

"If only vitamins would solve the problem."

He smiled at that, and she smiled back, because after a storm it was a relief to see a sliver of sunlight. Their smiles faded when someone started knocking on the living room door.

"Jenna! It's Gladys. Is everything okay?" *Knock, knock, knock.* "Jenna, please open this door."

"Crap." She was still in her robe and pajamas, and it was eleven. She crawled out of Caleb's bed, straightening the sheets as she gave him a pleading look. "Can you send her away? Wait. That's not your job. I'll go talk to her."

"Tell her you haven't had breakfast yet."

She shook her head. "That won't work."

"Well, I'll wait in the outer room if you need me."

"Okay." Of course there would be fallout from what she'd done. She might as well face it now. "Oh, and Caleb..." He turned back, focusing the full force of his gaze on her. "Thanks for sharing your bed, and watching over me last night." She fiddled with her robe, blushing. "I promise I'm better today."

"Good. I'm glad to hear it."

He let Gladys into the living room and then passed into the outer room with a final glance of sympathy. The manager's eyes were sparking even harder than usual. Her concerned expression looked brittle.

"Jenna." She reached out and took her arms. "What happened? Show me what happened."

"Everything's fine. I broke the mirror in my bathroom when I had a little meltdown. I guess I didn't have the best time last night."

"What do you mean, you *didn't have the best time last night*? That's no reason to destroy things."

Gladys moved past her and went down the hall to her bedroom. When she stepped into the bathroom, she gave a dramatic gasp. It did look worse than Jenna remembered. A few clinging mirror shards were all that remained on the wall over the sink. The drywall was dented where she'd hit it with the towel rack. The twisted, broken tool of destruction was propped against the edge of the bathtub.

"My goodness." Her initial assessment was followed by a low, disapproving noise. "I wouldn't call this a *little meltdown*. This is a disaster. We'll have to fix this."

"You don't have to. I don't need a mirror."

Gladys turned on her with her creepy laser eyes. "It will definitely need to be fixed. How did this happen? Have you been drinking again?"

"No." She sounded defensive, like she was lying, because she wanted nothing more than a big, strong drink. "I was just—" *Just tired of pretending. Tired of this bullshit.* "I was tired last night from the premiere and the party."

"You don't break mirrors when you're tired, Jenna. You break them when you're angry. Or crazy." She studied her a long moment, like she was waiting for her to confess. *Yes, it's true. I am crazy.*

"I don't know what to tell you, Gladys," she said instead. "You've never lost it? Nothing ever set you off?"

"Not to this extent." She gestured to the bare, pocked wall with a frown. "What happened to make you do this? Did you and Nate argue last night?"

"No. We barely exchanged words, between the time he spent with his movie people and his fans."

"Well, that's his job, right?" *Blink, blink, frown.* "I've never known you to do something like this. Maybe things aren't working out with the bodyguard?"

Already thinking of appropriate punishments, as usual. Jenna stuck out her chin. "It has nothing to do with the bodyguard."

"You've seemed more on edge since he's come to stay here. Isn't it intrusive, always having him around?"

They weren't taking Caleb away from her, even though they clearly wanted him gone. Everything in this household had become so transparent over the years. *I already told him everything,* she wanted to scream. *And you can't fucking take him away or I'll lose it for real.*

"We could get a part-time bodyguard, you know, just for when you go out."

"It's not the bodyguard that upsets me," she insisted. "His name is Caleb, by the way. My meltdown had nothing to do with him, and everything to do with me being tired last night and losing my shit."

Her lips tightened. "Well, I'll have to ask you not to 'lose your shit' in such a manner again. What will Caleb and Wilma make of this incident, and the workers who have to repair this bathroom? What will they say when they return home?"

"Nothing, because everyone who works here signs privacy agreements."

"Hmm." So much passive aggressive hatred in her *hmm*. "Maybe we'll have them install safety glass in case you 'lose your shit' again."

Gladys was super uptight, and said "shit" like it pained her to use the expletive. She turned and walked out into the bedroom, and scrutinized it for more destruction. Jenna flushed. The woman had no way of knowing she'd slept in Caleb's bed last night, but if she did know, that would be all they needed to fire him and send him away. She'd be powerless to stop them. She had so little leverage in this game. Maybe if she managed to anger Tom enough to throw a punch at her again...

Gladys turned back to Jenna, affecting a look of motherly concern. "This is a worrisome development, this violence. What can I do to help you feel better?"

"I already feel better. I'm really fine. It was a momentary lapse."

"Do you still want to visit the children's hospital tomorrow? I can cancel your appearance."

"No. I'm going."

"Maybe you should rest. Will you be ready to travel next week?"

She took a deep breath and prayed for patience. Gladys drove her nuts, but Caleb was there, right out in the other room. He'd be traveling with them, she'd made sure of that. Everything would be okay.

Except that she was coming to depend on him too much.

"I'll be ready for the foreign premieres. I've already started packing. I guess they can fix up my bathroom while we're away?"

"That would probably be best."

To her relief, Gladys headed out of her room and down the hall. When they got to the living room, she stopped one more time. "Jenna, you know I have to tell Nate about this. I don't think he'll be happy."

"Probably not."

Gladys' voice lowered in a caricature of authority that was undone by her perpetually blinking eyes. "I think you know how important it is that we all play our roles in this household, especially at a time like this. Truly, if there's anything I can do to help..." She gave a manic, manufactured laugh. "There are things in my medicine cabinet I could lend you that could get you through a rough patch, but we probably shouldn't go there, considering how you were with the..." She mimed taking a drink.

You're such an asshole. Gladys never missed an opportunity to point out Jenna's weaknesses, her unsuitability to be the great Nathaniel York's wife. Never mind that Nate himself got wasted whenever it suited him.

"I don't need any help from you," she said in a hard voice. "Just make sure the car's here at four o'clock tomorrow so I can get to Mercy General and have dinner with the kids."

* * * * *

Caleb didn't hear the conversation between Gladys and Jenna, but his client was frazzled with anger the rest of the afternoon. He could feel it coming off her in waves, like electrical sparks might shoot from her hair. She knitted baby hats with barely suppressed rage, then snapped off the TV, telling him she couldn't stand the news anymore. He suggested music. Calming country music.

She said she was going to her room to lie down. He would have liked to follow her there to try to make her feel better. Using sex, maybe. Yes, lots of sex.

She was so lonely, so troubled, and so goddamn attractive to him for reasons he couldn't name. Oh, she was beautiful, Hollywood beautiful, especially when she was all turned out to make one of her appearances, but to him, she was even more beautiful when she was in yoga pants on her couch, her knees drawn to the side as she read or did one of her crafty pastimes. He wondered if she would teach him how to knit. That would be a way to really be close to her, their heads bowed together.

Bodyguards don't knit, jackass. Get a grip.

She'd scared him last night, really scared him. When he'd heard the noise, he'd run to her room without even grabbing a weapon, and found her alone. No intruder, no fight for life, just her flailing away at her shattered mirror. So much glass, all of it sharp and deadly, and her out of control. He couldn't remember if he'd yelled at her. He tended to go calm and quiet in crisis situations, which made him a desirable military asset, so he probably hadn't yelled at her, but he'd definitely entered adrenaline mode, more so than he had in a long time.

But for all the trauma, there'd been something good about last night too. Something great, which was holding her in his arms and feeling her tense, shivery body relax against his. He'd been able to soothe her, which felt good. Also strange. Her body had melted against his in quiet trust, and he felt almost fatherly, although his thoughts were a hundred percent not fatherly. He wanted to kiss her, caress her, seduce her and make her tremble, not in fear or frustration but in pleasure. After ten years as a Hollywood beard, that part of her was frozen; he fantasized about bringing it back to life.

But they were just fantasies. He had a job to do, reports to write, outings to arrange. The next day, they headed out with the security team to Mercy Children's Hospital. She wore a calm, pleasant expression, any angst she still felt pushed down to fulfill this monthly pilgrimage. Between them lay bags of baby hats, stuffed animals, toys, and art supplies to give the young patients she called "my kids."

Jesus, someone that strong and good deserved a few orgasms. A few hundred orgasms or so might turn her life around. He wondered what her face would look like if all the pressure and tension in her features transformed to bliss. He could wonder all he wanted, but he couldn't act on the fantasies.

He sighed a little too loud, and she turned from her place on the seat beside him. He had to watch his sounds and body language, or he'd give away all the inappropriate fantasies roiling in his brain.

"We're almost there," she said. "I'm excited to see the little ones. Not excited about the hospital food, but..."

"Maybe we can stop to pick up some dinner on the way home."

"Yeah, I'd like that."

They ate together a lot, more than he'd expected after the cool reception he'd received in the beginning, but never in public. Bodyguard or not, Nate didn't like the optics of his fake wife hanging out at restaurants with a younger man. So much of Jenna's life was about optics, but Nate never saw his wife at the hospitals and shelters doing her grunt work. She was so beautiful there, almost as beautiful as she was sprawled out on the couch.

When they got to the hospital, there was the usual smattering of paparazzi waiting for her. The security ground team got out first to ensure the hospital staff had everything under control. When they waved to Caleb, he opened Jenna's door and helped her from the car. The paparazzi ducked around the security line to get their usual shots.

"Oh, wait." She leaned back into the car for the bags of baby hats and toys. As he turned to help her, he saw movement from the corner of his eye, someone moving too fast, someone coming toward them. He took in the details—middle aged male, atypical gaze, belligerent stance. Within a millisecond, he triangulated the glint of a jagged knife.

He planted himself between the assailant and Jenna, disarming him with a sharp blow to the wrist. The knife flew to the side, but the man's angry, intent eyes were still fixed on Jenna as he pulled another hunting knife from under his coat. He lunged for her just as she emerged from the car.

There was no sound to any of this. When he thought back on what had happened, why none of the security detail or paps had responded during these seconds, he thought it was because no one noticed what was happening, so no one made any sound. The attacker didn't yell, Jenna didn't scream, and Caleb was too stuck in his head to shout or gesture to anyone else. There was one thought in his mind: defend and protect. There was a yard's width between the knife and his client.

He didn't reach for his gun. The man was too close; there was no time. He grabbed his hand and tried to twist the knife from his grasp, but the man was ready this time, and persisted with the strength of someone bent on a task. Caleb drew back and punched him in the throat. The attacker reeled backward and lost hold of the knife for a moment before redoubling his efforts. How many seconds had passed now? One, two? A thousand?

That was the first time Caleb heard Jenna make a sound from her place behind him. She understood now what was happening. If she screamed, other people would react, but all she did was gasp. The other knife was in the gutter next to the car. Caleb stared at it as he twisted the man's wrist. When the bone snapped, he grabbed the knife.

That was all he really had to do, secure the knife. Even if the man had another weapon, his wrist was broken, and the security guys had come out of the hospital to help, yelling for the others to get back. Jenna had climbed back into the car, so things were under control, but the attacker was still surging toward her. Propelled by adrenaline and instinct, Caleb drove the knife into the man's abdomen, past a cotton jacket and hunting vest, and wrenched it in a way he knew would be fatal.

Now. Now the threat was gone.

It had been five seconds, maybe ten, since the attacker had lunged at Jenna. It felt like a lifetime. The screams finally erupted, and the panic. There was blood everywhere, but Caleb felt calm, because the danger was finally over.

"You're bleeding," Jenna cried, clutching at his jacket. "Caleb. You're bleeding. You're hurt."

"Not me," he said. "Just him."

He tried to reassure her that the blood wasn't his, but security guys and cameras were everywhere now, yelling and pushing, and the guy was seizing on the pavement beside the car, dying with a crazed, angry look.

"Take her home," Caleb said to the security team. "Get her out of here."

"No, I want to stay with you." He'd never heard her voice sound that way, so shrill and panicked. She reached to touch him but he shied away. There was blood on his hands, blood on his suit.

"Go with them, Jenna. You need to go home where you'll be safe."

"You're hurt, Caleb."

"I'm going to shut the door now." The baby hats and toys had fallen in the gutter next to the knife. He wanted her out of here, he wanted her safe, but he couldn't leave. The police were there, and he'd killed the man who was turning cold at his feet.

"You're hurt," she said again. "Your eye and your nose."

He touched his nose, felt warm blood and a sharp ache. He must have taken a fist or elbow from Jenna's attacker. He'd been so wrapped up in the moment he hadn't felt a thing. "I'll be fine," he told her. "I'll get it fixed up. I'll be back to the house soon."

He said that because he needed to make the panic on her face go away. He needed to close the door. She finally allowed him to do it, and he tapped the top of the car so the driver would go. He had to stay. He had to talk to the police because he'd killed a man. It was self-defense, but it was a little more than that too. It was the look in the man's eyes that said he'd try again and again, he'd try his whole life to kill Jenna York for whatever reason.

No, you won't, Caleb had thought. That was when he'd fatally twisted the knife.

"Hey man, look at me. You all right?"

One of the security guys stood in front of him. He should know the man's name by now, but it didn't come to him. He accompanied them on all their outings, with his expertise in crowd control.

"Sorry that guy got through, man. Good work taking him out of commission, but he got a slice of you too. Let's take you inside. They're gonna fix you up in the ER."

"The police..."

"They'll be working here for a while. I told them where to find you."

"Ironclad...my office..."

"Yeah, we'll call them, too. Let's get some stitches in you first, though. Damn, man, you almost lost an eye. Crazy hopped-up motherfucker swinging those knives." He was talking about the assailant, not him. He scowled at the body on the sidewalk with the knife sticking out of it, and led Caleb away from the police and yellow tape. Oh, he remembered now, the security guy's name was Jason. They walked into Mercy together, so he could get fixed up and back to Jenna. She'd be really worried.

He tried not to think about the fact that he'd just ended another life. They taught you in the military not to think about it. It was just part of the job.

* * * * *

Caleb studied his face in the mirror when the emergency department was done with him. He looked scary. A swollen, bruised nose—not broken—and eight stitches along the lower part of his left eye, just above the bone. *Almost lost it. Almost lost it.* That's what everyone who looked at it told him. *You almost lost that eye.*

The guy had waved the knife all over the place when they struggled, and apparently almost took out his eye, although Caleb felt in control of the fight the whole time. Maybe he hadn't been. The police had reviewed the incident, which was available in multiple video formats thanks to the paparazzi by the hospital entrance, and concluded he'd acted in self-defense. *Almost lost that eye, too,* they told him.

He stared at the stitches, arranged in their straight, measured line. They'd taught them in the Army to always go for the eyes in a close attack. *Sink your finger in there to the knuckle,* one of his instructors had barked in a clipped Brooklyn accent. *Shut 'em down quick.* Maybe the attacker had been ex-military. Maybe that furious intensity in his eyes was combat PTSD. A lot of military folks liked Nathaniel York's action films, and maybe in this case, the wrong veteran had walked into a showing of *Fire and Fury* and gotten worked up.

They'd never know the attacker's motivation now, unless he'd left notes or letters about his intentions. Brains were delicate things, so easily messed up. Caleb had done what he had to do to protect his client, and if he'd gone a little too far, well, he'd been in defense mode and he hadn't been able to stop. If he'd shot the guy at that range, he definitely would have killed him.

If the guy had had a gun...

Caleb didn't want to think about that.

Thanks to the paparazzi footage, the attack was already all over the news. He'd seen the whole thing replayed on TV while he was in his hospital room. He'd have to call his mother later. He'd sent her a reassuring text once he was stitched up and showered off, but she'd be beside herself with worry. He'd texted Jenna, too. *Eight stitches. I look like hell but feel okay. Going to meet with Ironclad boss and get back to work soon.*

Tough guy, getting back to work, but he wanted to be sure she was okay. A couple minutes later, his boss was at the door.

"Running up the company's insurance bill, I see." Hector forced a wry smile through his worried expression, then squinted at the stitches. "You almost lost that eye, man. Too close for comfort."

"I didn't even feel it."

Hector laid a set of clothes on the bed, to replace the bloodied ones the police had taken. "You were in client protection mode. Good work eliminating the threat. She was unharmed."

"Just scared," said Caleb, remembering her stricken expression.

"Well, I would have been scared too. These nutjobs running around... If they'd give these guys the help they needed, things wouldn't go this far." He handed Caleb a copy of the police report. "Tony Dubrowski. Iraq War veteran and ex-Green Beret. They graduated him out of a treatment facility a few months ago, but lost track of him. No record of him refilling his meds. Poor fucker."

Guilt prodded Caleb. He felt ashamed. "I didn't have to kill him, Hector. I don't think... I don't think I really had to."

"When you're in a situation like that, you can't always think as much as you'd like. You protected the client and you protected yourself." He surveyed his bruised eye and nose. "Well, mostly. Don't beat yourself up about it. Police feel it's a clear case of self-defense, and so do we. Once you file your report on the incident, we'll consider the whole thing closed." He paused, studying Caleb. "So...do you want to stay on this detail?"

The question surprised him. "Why wouldn't I?"

"Sometimes people don't, after an attack like this happens."

The idea flabbergasted him. "It's more important than ever to watch my client. If one crazy guy tries this, others might be emboldened."

"Hey, I know. Just wanted to give you a choice. We can get someone in there in a couple of hours, so you can recuperate. Let us know in a week if you feel ready to—"

"I don't need anyone to fill in. I can go back tonight."

Hector studied him even more closely. "Tonight? Are you sure that's a good idea?"

"I... I just need to be there. The biggest period of risk is right after an unsuccessful attack. I know what's going on in the house, know where the flash points are."

"You've got stitches in your face right now."

"I'll put a bandage over them."

"If you're still trying to prove yourself as a bodyguard, you could probably stand down. Your heroism today—"

"Heroism is getting back to the job when you're needed."

Even as he said it, Caleb knew he sounded over the top. Hector thought he should take a break, but he wasn't going to, and maybe that made him seem a little less stable overall. *I'm stable. Really. I just need to protect her.*

Because I love her.
Which I know is against the rules.

"You know," said Hector, "one thing we talk about in bodyguarding is not making yourself indispensable. Not making the client believe you're indispensable. If someone else had to go in to protect her, everything would be fine. You know that, right?"

"Yes, sir. Of course."

"And she should know that, too. Close protection can be a hell of a thing. Over time, you get attached to the client. You know them, they know you, to the point where you start to feel like you have to be there, that you're the only one who can do the job, you're the only one who can keep them safe. But we've got plenty of agents who can guard her, right? If you have to be away?"

He was being conversational, but there was a message, and that message was, *don't get too attached.*

"Of course, sir," he said again. "You're absolutely right. If you think I should take some time off, I will."

"You don't have to take time off. Just watch the messages you're sending to the client, especially after an incident like this. She should be able to feel safe with anyone, not just you."

"Yes, sir. I'll make sure she knows that." *And try to convince myself of that, but I'm not holding my breath.*

Hector's dark eyes studied him another moment or two, and Caleb knew he was being measured and monitored.

"I really am fine," he said, trying to lighten the mood. "My brothers and I would do this to each other's faces all the time back in Texas. I've almost lost many an eye, and I've had stitches at least a dozen times."

He raised a brow. "Broken bones too, I guess?"

"Never any of the important ones."

Hector laughed. "I was young and invulnerable once. I miss those days. All right, Mr. Winchell. File an incident report with Ironclad by tonight, and get back on duty. We'll take things day by day."

"Yes, sir. Thank you."

"Thank you for protecting your client. That's what we're here for."

Caleb's stitches throbbed as a flush rose in his cheeks. *Yes, we're here to protect*, Hector meant, not fall for married Hollywood wives.

8.
LIFE AND DEATH

Caleb crept through the York house, hoping against hope he wouldn't see Gladys on the way to Jenna's wing. She didn't pop out at him, blinking and talking, so she must have already gone home for the night. The whole place was quiet as death.

It might be quiet now, but he was sure there'd be hell to pay tomorrow. With the story of Jenna's attack all over the news, Nate might decide to fire him for creating negative press. Ironclad might decide to move him to another protectee, even another city until the story died down. Killing someone on assignment wasn't illegal if it was warranted, but it wasn't desirable either.

None of it mattered. If he could go back in time and do everything over, he was pretty sure he'd still twist the knife.

He let himself into Jenna's outer room and heard her TV on the other side of the double doors. She was watching her favorite cartoon, an obnoxious screen-vomit of shrill voices and colors.

He knocked on the door as always before he entered. By the time he swiped his key, Jenna was waiting on the other side, her hair a mess, her eyes red from crying. She threw herself into his arms, pressing her face into the curve of his neck. He felt tears against his skin.

"Hey, it's okay," he said. "Don't cry. I'm fine and you're safe. Everything worked out."

She pulled away and scanned the bruised mess that made up his face. "Oh, Caleb, you're so busted up. Your eye must hurt."

"I'll live. I've had worse injuries."

She couldn't seem to let go of him, and he didn't make her. "I've been crying for hours now, just thinking I could have died, or you could have died." She gazed at him, her eyes wide with emotion. "You saved my life."

"I was happy to do it."

She took his chin to get a closer look at the bruise under his eye, and the stitches. His left eye was half-swollen shut. "It hardly hurts at all," he lied. "Don't worry about it. How are you?"

"Freaked out. Angry. Still kind of scared."

"You don't have to be scared. There are lots of people looking out for you, and cops outside to keep the surge of paparazzi away. Heard from Nate yet?"

"He and Gladys are in a meeting with the PR team. There's this whole freaking deal now, how to handle this in conjunction with the new movie release. I refused to go."

"Good for you," he said. Crazy fuckers, more worried about PR fallout than the actual attack on Jenna. "Have you had dinner?"

"I made some eggs. Would you like some? I know it's not morning, but breakfasts are all I can cook."

He hadn't been hungry a moment ago, but her offer was so endearing that he wanted eggs like crazy. "I'm starving. Eggs would be great."

He went to his bedroom to change into his own clothes, then returned to sit at the counter while she made an excellent plate of scrambled eggs, cheese, and bacon. Comfort food, not just for him, but for her too. He could see she needed to do something busy and mindless right now. Perhaps cooking for him, giving him milk and toast and a napkin allowed her to repay him in some way for what he'd done. He'd killed someone for her. *The scary thing, Jenna, is that I would do it again without a second thought. I'd do it three times a day, every day, to keep you happy and secure.*

Of course, that wouldn't be necessary. As he ate, he emphasized how rare it was for an assailant to charge with a knife, that a security agent might deal with one or two such events over an entire career. He talked about evasive actions she could take in future situations, like running in the opposite direction, or escaping through the other side of the car. It was all to calm her down, and to fight the emotion that ricocheted between them. After a while, the silences grew deeper and the eye contact more prolonged. He wanted to say things that he couldn't. When she sat beside him and reached to touch his bruised face, he flinched.

"I'm sorry," she said quickly.

"It's okay."

"I just want to—"

"Jenna, it's really okay."

She ran her thumb so lightly and gently beneath his eye, it felt like a whisper on his skin. He didn't flinch this time, just went very still.

"I keep thinking about what would have happened if you hadn't been there," she said. "Or if he'd overpowered you…" She swallowed hard. "When I saw the blood all over the front of you, I was afraid you were hurt, that you might die."

"I'm not easy to kill," he reassured her. "But if something happened to me, you'd be okay. You'd get another bodyguard who was just as skilled as me."

"Maybe." Her eyes held his. "But they wouldn't be the same as you. I've never known anyone like you."

If any other woman were saying these things to him, it would be a come-on, a flirtation. With Jenna, the words sounded like a prayer. *I've never known anyone like you.* He felt exhilarated. He felt afraid. He shook his head, trying to deny the energy flowing from her fingertips to his bruised face, but then he stopped shaking his head, because there was really no denying it. When she bit her lip, uncertain, he dropped his gaze to her mouth and dipped his head.

A moment later, their lips touched. Their first kiss was slow and tentative, a gentle transgression as each waited for the other to draw away. Neither of them did.

His plate lay on the counter between them, forgotten. He traced her features with the same cautious lightness, running his fingertips along her jaw and tilting her face up to his. They kissed more deeply the second time, still afraid, but that only made it more exciting, like walking along a knife's edge of desire. She tasted so sweet, so lovely and beautiful. He released her when she drew away, drinking in her soft, amazed sigh that echoed how he felt.

"Jenna," he whispered. "We shouldn't. I can't."

"I know." But she still kissed him again.

He tightened his hands on her waist and held her when he should have been pushing her away. "It's not real, what you're feeling," he said against her velvet-soft lips. "It's because of what happened today."

She drew back, her gaze immediately focused and intent. "That's not true. You know that's not true. I felt this way before today. I—I—" A fiery blush rose in her cheeks, further challenging his self-control. "Caleb, I've wanted to kiss you since the night of that storm. I dropped my mug on the counter and you told me to..." She could barely get the words out in her emotional state. "You told me to watch for glass. Do you remember?"

He nodded. He couldn't speak at all, couldn't stop his arms from tightening to pull her closer. Her fingers curled around his shoulders, over his tense muscles. He wished they were skin to skin.

"We shouldn't," he said again. *But oh, I want you.* He pulled her in between his legs, grasped her close, and kissed her harder and deeper still, because *shouldn't* wasn't the same as *wouldn't*. He'd fallen for her over days and weeks, fallen for her courage and beauty, and that part of her that appreciated his integrity.

So much for integrity. Romancing clients wasn't okay, but he couldn't stop kissing her and tasting her, and running his hands over her curves. She felt a thousand times more vital and sexy than she'd ever felt in his dreams, and when she pressed against his front, he didn't bother hiding the evidence of his arousal.

As they kissed, some wilder, more basic connection bloomed between them, perhaps because he'd saved her life, perhaps because they'd wanted this for so long. When she reached down to stroke him through his pants, he should have said no. Instead, he lifted her so she was straddling him, and ground his rigid cock against her, kissing her so hard his bruised nose hurt.

"I know we shouldn't." She was sobbing as she said it. He could feel her tears against his ear. "But Caleb, please, I want you so badly, all of you. Everything. I feel like I'll die if we don't go to bed right now."

It was life or death with them, at this point. Why not celebrate cheating death with a carnal glorification of life?

"I won't tell," she pleaded, stroking his hair, kissing the straining tendons in his neck. "I won't tell anyone, ever. No one has to know."

She was begging, like he might deny her, but he was far past the point of no return. He carried her to his room, because he knew there were condoms in his toiletry bag, and because he wanted her to be able to walk out if she changed her mind.

"If you want this..." he said, laying her on his bed. She looked up at him, tearful and hopeful and vulnerable. "If you want this, I want it too, Jenna. God, I *really* want it. But if you don't want it, that's okay. Or if you just want it once, tonight, because our emotions are running high—"

"Please shut up." She reached for him.

He held her hands, making her listen. "If you just want to cuddle, or touch each other—"

"No. I need—everything. I haven't had sex I actually wanted in ten years."

His mind stumbled on the words "sex I actually wanted," but then she was kissing him again and pulling at his shirt, and he decided to ask what she meant later. For now, he helped her strip off his clothes until he was naked in front of her, his cock hard as granite. She stared like he was a God in the flesh, which only made him harder.

"You're even more beautiful than him," she said, and he knew she meant Nate. "You should be the movie star."

Her mention of Nate made him pause. Jenna was his wife, even if she was a fake wife. She saw him falter and responded by taking his face between her hands. "Don't you dare stop now. I didn't mean to bring him up. He doesn't matter anyway."

Caleb kissed her, his way of agreeing, and stripped off her nightshirt and camisole. He knew all the shirts and camis she slept in, saw them when he checked on her before bed, and now he got to see the gorgeous breasts and curves underneath, all her tan-bronze skin bared to his gaze. He meant to be gentle, he ought to be gentle, but he found himself squeezing her breasts with the same possessive impulses that drove him earlier. *Mine. Mine to protect, mine to have.* When his force seemed to please her, he yanked off her panties with the same intensity.

That was when he realized he might have miscalculated. He'd thought they only wanted to sleep together. Now that they were in bed, they wanted to devour each other, or hurt themselves trying. He pushed her back, shoving aside the sheets and blankets, wanting only her naked body, her straining arms, her luscious legs. She clung to him, her nails sinking into his shoulders and arms. The last four weeks had been foreplay, and now he wanted to shove himself inside her, as deep as he could go...

"Protection," he said, forcing himself to get up. "Don't move."

He went in the bathroom and got a rubber, and put it on while he was walking back to the bed, because he couldn't wait much longer to get inside her. His bruised face, his nearly-lost eye, all of it was forgotten. "Are you sure about this?" he asked, moving into her beckoning arms.

"I'm sure. Please. Now, Caleb. Before I die."

* * * * *

His muscular, magnificent body took her breath away. He probably thought she was exaggerating about the dying, but she wasn't. If he didn't come inside her and fulfill the longing that had taken over her, she'd curl up into a wisp of devastation and blow away.

Some part of her was ashamed at the way she wanted him. He was so young, so virile and powerful in his twenty-five year old physique. Maybe he kept asking if she was sure because he didn't really want her. Maybe he was only mollifying her. Maybe he pitied her.

She jerked back from his embrace. He instantly went still, blinking down at her. "What's wrong?"

"Do you want this? Really want this?" She repeated the question he'd asked her several times. Her voice sounded close to breaking, but she didn't care. She had to know. "Do you really want me, or are you just doing it for—"

For me. Because you pity me.

"Does it seem like I want you?" He nudged his huge cock between her legs, making desire flare alongside her fear. "We shouldn't be doing this, but I can't stop myself. I'm putting aside my honor for you. Is that enough to convince you?"

He was a little scared too, or angry. Hell, he'd killed a man today, for her, and now he was naked, arching over her with his teeth gritted and his arms tense. It made her wild for him, because he had more honor in his little finger than she'd had in her entire life.

"I'm sorry." She didn't know what she was apologizing for. She didn't know why she couldn't stop trembling, or why tears squeezed from her eyes. Maybe it was because she wanted this so badly, and she was finally getting something she wanted. Maybe it was the intent way he looked at her as he started entering her inch by halting inch.

He was big. She didn't remember other guys' cocks—it had been *forever*—but he was bigger than average. He took his time penetrating her, taking care not to hurt her even as her nerves jumped beneath her skin. She was going to come just from the sensation of being entered, being prodded and caressed and taken. "Oh my God, I can't," she murmured.

"What?"

"Don't...stop..." She grasped his arms, trying to catch the breath he was displacing with his size and nearness. "If...you...stop..." She didn't finish the threat, because he was all the way inside her now and pressing deeper still. Her legs gripped his hips, her ankles hooking together as she squeezed on the unfamiliar girth inside her.

"Jesus, Jenna." He let out his breath in a gasp. "You'll kill me."

"No."

"This feels too good."

"Please don't...don't stop..."

He pressed a kiss against her lips, then shoved his tongue inside as his cock drove inside her too. "You don't have to keep saying that, sweetheart. Now that I'm here, I'm not going to stop anytime soon."

Sweetheart. The old-fashioned endearment sounded horny and dirty in his Texas accent, his drawl exaggerated in the midst of sex. The closer he got, the harder they held each other, and the more she wanted. He moved in her like a dream, as if he'd known her needs his entire life. He licked her skin and bit her nipples hard enough to shock her, making her buck in erotic torment. She came suddenly, hard and fast, far too soon, long before she wanted their connection to end. Her walls gripped him, the pleasurable waves almost too much to bear.

"No, don't stop," she begged, before she even finished climaxing. "Please, more."

"Greedy, aren't we?" he teased in his sex drawl. "You want more?"

"Please!"

He caressed her from release to desperation all over again, and made her wait longer for her orgasm this time, pulling his cock out to torment her, grinning when she grasped at his shoulders and hips to draw him back in. He felt so good inside her, it was almost unbearable. He touched every part of her that evinced a reaction, following her cues with some instinctive sense. Well, he was good at being a bodyguard. He was good at protecting her. Why wouldn't he be good at this, too?

"I can't anymore." She stared into his eyes, which were stitched and bruised but still so expressive. "Please let me come."

"Are you sure?" His lips quirked at the corners. "You've had enough?"

"For now. Only for now. Please make me come."

She could make herself come, of course, had been doing that for many years. She'd become an expert at masturbation, but to orgasm from his passion and power, his hard, girthy cock rubbing over her clit as he surged inside her...that was delectable, and that was what she wanted right now.

He spread a hand over her ass, bracing her for his strengthening thrusts. He couldn't fuck her hard enough. Each time he filled her up with his cock and muscles and presence, she was astounded and awed, going blissfully insane.

"Yes, yes, please," she whispered, until he smothered her words with another vigorous kiss. Her second orgasm was greater than the first: longer, stronger, more satisfying. The clenching pleasure was one aspect, but their connectedness was something else. She could feel when Caleb stopped worrying about her satisfaction and unleashed his own animal impulses. His growls grew a little more feral-sounding, and his muscles tensed with effort. Even now, when he must feel as wild as her, he was holding back a little so he wouldn't hurt her.

She wondered what he was like when he didn't hold back. The idea scared her, but it excited her too. She wrapped her arms around his neck to ground him as he climaxed inside her, groaning and thrusting hard, pushing her legs back with the effort. These boys from Texas could be a little crazy. They definitely knew how to fuck.

No, not just fuck. Whether it was his Texas breeding or not, Caleb knew how to take care of a woman in bed. He'd gotten her so worked up that she hadn't had time to obsess over her cougar ways or how he might perceive her horniness.

Now that it was over, though, she didn't know how things would go. She'd always been bad at this part, the after-sex, when people were meant to be tender, because she'd learned to use sex for other things. Reward, attention, or revenge. When Caleb pulled out of her, she avoided his gaze, afraid of what she might see. While he got rid of the condom, she lay where he'd left her, afraid to break the spell he'd cast. What would he do now? Would he hold her? Would he want her to leave?

"Why does your face look like that?" he asked when he returned. He stood beside the bed, a work of art and bruises, his cock still a little hard. "Is everything okay?"

"What do you mean? What does my face look like?"

"Like you might vomit, or cry. It wasn't that bad, was it?" He climbed in next to her, pulling her into his arms.

"What do you mean? I don't look like that."

He pretended to analyze her face again. "You look a little less stressed than you did a few seconds ago." His regard turned serious. "Really, though, is everything okay?"

"Everything is…too okay." She snuggled close against him, hiding her face in his chest. "Do you know how long it's been for me?"

"I have an idea." He chuckled. "It created a little pressure on my side, but we seemed to do okay."

"Oh my God." That was all she could say. It was kind of a swear, kind of a prayer. She took a deep breath of his scent, faint cologne or deodorant, and the subtle musk of a post-sex male. It had been a crazy day, and tomorrow would be crazier, but she wasn't going to think about that.

"Can I sleep here with you?" she asked. "I don't want to be alone tonight."

"Of course you can sleep here, if you don't mind me crowding you."

"I want you to crowd me."

She stumbled to her bathroom to get ready for bed, then hurried back to his room, not bothering to put on any clothes. He hadn't bothered either.

Both of them had weathered a trauma; both of them had things to forget. As it turned out, they didn't settle in to sleep until a couple more beautiful hours had gone by.

9.
REALLY WANTED

"Jenna." She felt fingertips along her cheek, and someone brushing back her hair. "Baby? You should probably get up."

It was Caleb's voice, as gentle and sexy as it had sounded in her dream. Waking was a long, strenuous trip to the surface, one she didn't want to make. For the second time, she'd slept like a log in Caleb's bed because of his smell and closeness.

And last night...

Oh God, last night. He'd been everything she'd never had in a lover—gentle and rough, protective and feral, driven and generous, all the mind-blowing things. He was everything in bed, and she'd taken advantage to the fullest, because she'd never had a chance to sleep with someone like him until now. She opened her eyes and blinked at him, remembering so many things, wanting him to look happy today, as happy as she felt.

He gazed back at her, not super happy, but not cold either. If he'd gone cold on her the morning after, she would have died. He sat beside her on his bed, fully dressed, already on duty. His eyes looked a little better today, a little less swollen.

"Why are you always in a suit?" she asked.

"To remind myself I'm a professional." He paused with a slight frown. "It's especially necessary after what happened last night."

"Please don't get weird about it, Caleb. Oh God, I don't care if it was unprofessional. If you say you have to quit because you slept with me, or that we can't do it again—"

"Hold up." He leaned over her, silencing her with a kiss and his body's weight. "I'm not leaving, and we'll do it again. We'll do it over and over..." Another kiss. "And over and over." More kisses, hard and lovely, before he drew back. "But we'll have to be careful. Discreet. I'd be fired if Ironclad knew." He arched a brow. "And how do you think Nate would feel about it?"

She didn't want to wake up like this, thinking about realities. She wanted the escapist fantasy of last night, always, forever. "I won't tell Nate. He and Tom stay away from me now that you're here."

"They didn't stay away this morning."

She could feel the color bleed from her cheeks. "What do you mean? They were here?"

"Nate knocked on the living room door about an hour ago. Tom was with him. Nate said he needed to talk to you, but I told him you were still asleep, that you'd had a difficult night because of the attack."

"Thank God they can't get in on their own. If they'd found us in bed together..."

"I know. He's already worked up about what happened yesterday." Jenna saw a shadow pass over his bruised features. Yesterday had been hard for her to process, but how much harder for him? He'd *killed* somebody, and taken a beating to the face in the process.

"I'm sorry." She didn't know what else to say. "I'm sorry all this has happened."

"It's not your fault. Ironclad communicated with Nate's people about the police report, that no charges were being filed, but he looked pretty grim when he saw me, and he said he needed to talk to you. It might be better to get up and face him now, before he decides..."

"Decides what? He's not getting rid of you. He's not fucking firing you." The last vestiges of sleepiness were gone. She felt ready to chew through nails on Caleb's behalf.

"I've been arguing with myself all morning," he said. "Maybe it would be better for you to have a bodyguard whose mind is only on protection." His gaze traveled over her body, ending with a kiss and caress. "At the same time, I don't think I could leave you. I couldn't trust your safety to anyone else."

She melted at those words, snuggling forward into his arms when he opened them. She wanted to rip off his ever-present suit and pull him into bed, but knew she couldn't. Caleb was right, she had to face Nate before he got too wound up.

"I'll be right there with you," he said, reading the anxiety in her expression.

"Nate won't let you be there."

"Then I'll be waiting as close as I can."

* * * * *

Jenna met with Nate by the pool. Caleb sat near the edge of the patio, far enough away that he couldn't hear, but close enough that she could see him if she moved her gaze to the right. Of course, Nate brought Tom with him, because whenever he was upset, he needed his true love beside him.

"Jenna." Her husband greeted her with a hug. "How are you feeling? I was worried yesterday."

"Were you?" *Because I didn't so much as see your face.*

"Of course I was worried. That's all we talked about yesterday, ways to keep you safer than you are now." He glanced toward Caleb as they sat down. "I think we should probably start with a personnel change."

"You're not changing anything."

"A new bodyguard, Jen. Someone better."

"Someone better? Caleb saved my life yesterday. You should be giving him a raise."

"A raise for what? Causing a media furor?" He leaned closer and spoke through his teeth. "I just had a movie come out, and all anyone's talking about is how your bodyguard killed someone. He *murdered* someone."

"It's not murder if he was defending me. He was just doing his job."

"But he literally gutted him. Have you watched the videos of what happened?" He turned to Tom. "Have you ever gutted someone, babe?"

"No."

Jenna pursed her lips. "That's because he's not a real bodyguard."

Nate's controlled veneer bled away. "I didn't ask you out here so you could be a salty bitch to my boyfriend. What are we going to do about this? Everyone wants to know who your bodyguard is, and why he stabbed a veteran in front of a children's hospital. Papers are running stories."

"I know. One hundred percent of the stories say that Caleb was heroic, that he saved my life." *Unlike your bodyguard, who's only ever ruined lives.* "I would think you'd be grateful to him. Did you even tell him thank you?"

"No, cause I'm fucking scared of the guy. Where'd the knife come from?"

"The attacker."

"I asked his agency. Caleb has some crazy gun clearances."

She rolled her eyes. "All bodyguards are licensed to carry guns, and he's ex-military."

"Ex-military's even worse. Look at his face, those stitches. He seems, I don't know..."

"Dangerous," Tom provided.

"Of course he's dangerous. It's a damn good thing he is, or I might have been sliced into a bunch of pieces in the back of that car, not that you'd care. What are you upset about?" She swallowed down anger, hating that everything between them was a fight. "Maybe you're upset that I survived. Maybe you wish I'd died yesterday. It would have been so easy for you two then. You could have played the grieving husband forever, never remarried, just soldiered through life with your trusty 'bodyguard' by your side."

They both frowned at her air quotes. "You're talking shit," said Nate. "No one wants you to die. I don't want you to die."

Tom stayed silent. He definitely wanted her to die.

"What do you want?" she said to Nate. "You want me to give up my personal bodyguard? The one who *just* saved my life?"

"Maybe, babes. He's possibly crazy."

"He's the only sane person I know." Her voice rose with her temper. "You're the crazy one if you think we should get rid of him. How would that look to the rest of the world? I was just attacked. He saved me. Oh, yeah, let's fire him and hire someone else."

"I'm just saying, it was a traumatic experience for you to live through. Maybe Caleb's an unwanted reminder of what happened."

"Caleb's the only reason I can get up in the morning and not want to kill myself."

"You're awfully passionate about Caleb," Tom cut in. "Something going on between you two?"

"Nothing's going on," she said too quickly. "I've just...come to depend on him. He's honest and trustworthy, unlike everyone else in my cursed existence."

"Cursed?" Nate lowered his voice to a mutter. "I give you everything, you little bitch, and you think you're cursed? You have all the money you want, all the fame, all the pretty dresses and jewels and people kissing your ass—"

"I don't want the fame. I don't want stupid jewels and dresses." She took a deep breath. "Sometimes I get tired of pretending we're in love and everything's okay."

"Because you're an ungrateful cunt," said Tom.

Nate held up a hand. "Don't get that way. Let's not turn this into another..." He swallowed the rest of the sentence and turned back to Jenna. "Talk to me, babes. What's so wrong with your life? Are you lonely? We can try to make another kid."

"No. Fuck you." Tears filled her eyes. She'd never get over the baby she lost. "Another baby won't solve anything. Nate, look, I'm not trying to sound ungrateful."

"That's weird, cause you really sound ungrateful. You signed an agreement, and you knew the terms from the beginning. Do you want out?"

What would he do if she flat-out asked to get out of their marriage? His hard, calculating glare made her afraid to respond. "I don't want out. I don't have anywhere to go anyway."

"You should fucking remember that," Tom snapped.

Nate turned on him. "Tom, please. Let us talk."

"I'm done talking," said Jenna. "I'm tired, I'm confused. And yeah, I'm getting a little burnt out with my life. I don't know if I can go to another premiere and paste a smile on my face."

"Well, that's too bad, because you're going to the premieres. Someone has to fix the damage that Murder McBodyguard's actions have caused. You're going to go and you're going to smile, and you're going to move the story on. That's what you agreed to do, support my career."

"Really? I was almost killed, and all you care about is the effect on your fucking career?" She buried her face in her hands. "I need a break. You can have your PR people use the attack as my excuse for not being there."

Nate's hard voice turned angry. "Look, I'm sorry you were attacked, but you survived, right? Now you have a job, and that job is standing beside me when I'm in the spotlight. That's what all of this is for." He swept an arm around the patio, across the glistening, still pool water, and the gorgeous Hollywood Hills view.

"Maybe if I'm not there, the 'story' will move on faster. Maybe if I disappeared for a while…"

"Disappeared? That's even more of a story. You're coming to those premieres, Jenna, and if you're catching too many complicated feelings about this marriage from that sweet, trustworthy bodyguard, then he's got to go."

"He's not going anywhere." Her voice cracked with stress. "Why does it matter so much, to have me with you, hanging on your arm? All the crowds want is you, not me, and when you're behind closed doors, you have your boy toy to keep you happy," she said, flicking a hand toward Tom.

"Boy toy?" Tom bristled. "Don't talk to me that way. I'm more masculine than your pretty bodyguard. Wouldn't count too much on him being hetero."

"She's probably already tried to sleep with him," said Nate.

"Wouldn't be the first time someone in this house slept with a bodyguard, would it?" she shot back. "Unfortunately, you picked a guy who's fifty times crazier than Caleb." She turned to Tom. "If only Caleb had been around with his knife when *you* attacked me."

Tom's eyes darkened as he leaned forward on the table. "Listen here, you rancid little slut. If it wasn't for me—"

"Tom, chill out," Nate said sharply.

"No. I'm tired of her uppity shit. You pathetic little whore, living off Nate's money. He would do anything for you. He has done everything for you."

"For you too, asshole."

"And if it wasn't for me," he said, talking over her, "you wouldn't have had a chance at your first little baby. Yeah, the one you killed because you're such a rampaging, self-hating alcoholic."

"Shut the fuck up," Nate said, not because his lover was crossing a line, but because Caleb had stood and was moving toward their table. "Pull your fucking shit together. He's coming over."

"I'm leaving," said Jenna.

"You can't leave until we talk about the premieres."

"You don't have to talk about it," said Tom. "She's going. All this is bullshit." He turned to Caleb as he reached their chairs. "The Yorks are having a private conversation. This is none of your business."

He ignored Tom and looked directly at her. "Everything okay, Jenna?"

"Yes. I think I'm ready for lunch."

"Will you be eating with your husband?" he asked with absolute sincerity.

"No, I'd rather go out."

Nate faked a concerned smile as Tom fumed beside him. "Are you sure that's a good idea after yesterday, Jen?"

"If I'm with Caleb, I'll be safe."

"I think you should stay in tonight," Nate persisted. "With media interest so high." When she didn't respond, he pulled her close and whispered in her ear. "Don't you dare humiliate me. You're supposed to be at home recovering in my loving arms, not out at some restaurant with your 20-year-old, murderous—"

"Fine."

She stood and moved toward Caleb. It was all she could do not to throw herself into his arms, but she restrained herself and shot a scathing look at Tom instead. She hated him so much, more than words could ever explain or feelings could ever feel. She hated Nate right now too, and the idea of going to his stupid premieres. As for Caleb...

She loved him to the point of fear. She'd never survive if Nate took him away.

* * * * *

Caleb worried about her. Not just because he'd grown close to her, and been inside her three times the previous night. No, he worried because she got a look on her face sometimes that was utterly hopeless.

"What would you like to order for lunch?" he asked.

"I don't want lunch."

"Dalton and Wilma are ordering too."

"I'm not hungry." She covered her face, leaning against the counter. "I need a drink. Can I have a margarita or three?"

"Sweetheart. No." He hugged her from behind, pulling her hands from her eyes. She turned and laid her head against his heart.

"Take me away from here," she said softly.

"I can't do that. And I'm not letting you drink, but we can order some food and..." He ran a hand up her back. "Maybe find other ways to relax. What do you want to eat? Something wonderful and full of calories so you can't fit into your premiere wardrobe?"

To his relief, she cracked a smile. A small one, but still. She ordered three tacos and a burrito supreme from their favorite Mexican place, and Caleb ordered even more, in case she wanted leftovers later. It was all on Nate's dime anyway.

After they ate, they sprawled on the couch, full and drowsy from lack of sleep the night before. He took off his jacket and holster and pulled her into his arms, wanting her again. She already felt so natural in his arms, which was dangerous for his job, but necessary for his soul.

"Jenna." There were four words he couldn't stop thinking about. "Can I talk to you about something you said yesterday?"

"Something I said?"

"Last night, when we were undressing and deciding whether to..." He stroked her back, a reassuring touch. "What did you mean by 'sex I actually wanted'?"

He wished he could look in her eyes, but she didn't look up at him, only pressed her cheek into his chest.

"Jenna?"

She gave a small, forced laugh. "You know my situation. Ideal sex isn't easy to find."

"That's all you meant by it?"

She pulled back and finally met his gaze. There was more to say. He could see it in the turmoil behind her eyes. He knew a lot of her secrets, but he didn't know all of them, and the secrets he didn't know were probably the worst. "Sex I actually wanted" sounded like she'd been compelled to have sex she didn't want. Then there was Nate's comment about her being a punching bag...

"Jenna, was I hired to protect you from Tom?"

The direct question made her look away. Maybe she considered lying, but by the time she turned back, he could tell she'd decided to be honest with him.

"Yes. Pretty much."

"Why? What happened? Was there some...incident?"

"He didn't attack me sexually, if that's what you think. We had a fight, one really bad fight when he was wasted, and Nate hired you after that so Tom would stay away from me. Tom's always hated me. I mean, of course he does. I'm living the life he wants."

"He wants this life?" Caleb tried to keep the contempt out of his voice—contempt for Tom and Nate—but he couldn't quite do it. "He wants to hide away in a house with a full-time bodyguard, with no ability to have a real relationship and live a normal, truthful life?"

She shied away from his words. "Am I that pathetic?"

"Don't make this into a fight between us. I worry about you. I wonder what's really going on between you, Nate, and Tom, and I'm afraid for you to be around them when I'm not there."

"You probably should be."

She fell silent, her dark eyes going dim, her thoughts far away. He didn't know where to take the conversation next. He didn't want to push her too hard, but he needed to know just how abusive Tom had gotten with her. As he struggled for what to say, she started to talk without prompting.

"Things got really crazy a few years ago," she said. "Really crazy."

"Crazy in what way?"

"It was kind of like now. I was starting to regret marrying Nate, starting to get angsty from the isolation and fakeness. I was drinking a lot, which was causing tension between Nate and me, and even then, Tom and I didn't get along. Things were starting to fall apart, and none of us knew how to handle it. But Tom..." She rested her head back against the couch and let out a long breath. "Tom decided he had the perfect idea.

He started talking about Nate and I having a baby, about how good it would be for the optics." She gave a bitter laugh. "The damn optics."

"Did you want a baby?"

"I never thought about it." She shrugged, her lips trembling. "I figured with the nature of our marriage, it wasn't something that would ever happen. Nate hadn't considered it either. I mean, he's so wrapped up in his fame thing and his ego, he had no desire to be a dad. It was a step too far, you know? Too far into the fake marriage. But Tom has always had this force of personality. It's how he keeps Nate in check, even though Nate has all the money and power."

She paused, her fingers moving across the cushions. He thought of her pregnant, holding a baby. He'd tried to eavesdrop on the patio, just to know Jenna was okay, but all he'd heard through the mutters and whispers had been Tom's deep, rough voice saying *If not for me* and something about a baby.

"Well, the more Tom pushed the idea of a baby," she continued, "the more I thought it might solve my problems. I could put my energy into motherhood, and Nate would have walking, talking proof he was a real, heterosexual husband. I thought I might even be able to leave him one day, that having a kid would be enough cover for his straightness, and I could take my daughter or son and disappear while Nate played the lonely single dad with occasional custody. It started to seem like the answer at a time I was really searching for answers."

"That's understandable."

"And I really wanted a baby. In the end, I really, genuinely wanted to be a mother."

Caleb couldn't help looking past her at the end table, where she piled the handmade baby caps she made for her trips to the hospital. "What happened?" he asked.

"I got sober. I took really good care of myself, prenatal vitamins, fresh air, yoga, everything. Nate's people started looking into procedures, you know, IVF and surrogate pregnancy, but Hollywood is such a small town for someone like him." She clasped her hands in her lap, kneading her knuckles one by one. "It was Tom's idea to keep it in the family. It was his decision, really." She looked up at Caleb as she said this, before her eyes darted away.

"Keep it in the family?"

"He said Nate could get me pregnant, that he would help. But it didn't work. We tried twice, with Nate drunk and high and Tom there beside us trying to move things along. When I say twice, I mean, it was two months of cycles, but physiologically, it wasn't happening. If Nate was drunk enough to try it, he was too drunk to perform. So then Tom..."

She stopped, pressing her lips together. Caleb wasn't sure he could take any more of this disturbing confession in her soft, hurt voice, but he also sensed she'd never told anyone else, not until this moment. These secrets had twisted and rotted inside her, like the twist and rot of Tom Maxon's soul.

"Did he rape you?" Caleb asked, trying to sound matter of fact about it, even though he wanted to kill Tom, and Nate too.

"No. I told you, it wasn't like that. He asked Nate if...if he wanted him to try. He tried to present it like, well, that this baby could be the link between all of us, that we could finally be a legitimate, connected family because Nate's child would really be his wife and his lover's child. Nate ate that right up. He wanted to raise Tom's child, because that's the hold Tom has on him. And I wanted a baby, you know? I wanted to get pregnant and start a new life without waiting for Nate to accomplish it, or waiting to do IVF treatments in some far-flung, secret clinic. I wanted it to be over with, so I said fine, that I would sleep with Tom. So we did it again. The two of them drank champagne, and Nate and Tom got aroused together, and then..."

"Oh, Jenna."

"No, I was okay with it. I consented. That's how much I wanted a baby."

She didn't talk for a long moment, and Caleb didn't talk either. There was a dread in the air, something left untold. He pulled her back to him and held her against his body. She rested her face against his shoulder. Her hands stayed in her lap, clenched into fists.

"I'd had sex before," she said when she finally continued. "Good sex and mediocre sex. Stupid teenager sex. But I'd never had sex with someone who hated me." She closed her eyes on the last two words.

He held her as she trembled. "I'm so sorry."

"But I wanted it, you know? I agreed to sleep with him. It was my fault."

"None of this is your fault."

"All of it's my fault." She tried to sit up with her harsh exclamation, but he wouldn't let her go.

"Shh." He smoothed his hands over her hair, giving her all the comfort he could, wishing he could have comforted her then. "It's not your fault."

"It was a mistake, then. That's what it was. I shouldn't have said yes. The things he said to me in that bed…the things both of them said…and the way he fucked me…"

Caleb's shooting fingers twitched. It was all he could do not to set her on her feet, grab his gun, and crash through every door until he found the two men on the other side of the house.

"Not technically rape," she said, still trying to drive that point home. "I never told him to stop. Anyway, I got a baby. We timed the…the encounter with ovulation tests and I got pregnant the first time around, which was good, because I never could have tried again." She let out a sigh. "I was so happy, so relieved. And I was so careful, so well-behaved the whole pregnancy. I didn't drink, I didn't smoke or hang out with anyone who smoked."

Caleb had never heard about any baby—and it would have been big news if Nathaniel York had a baby. Which meant something had happened, something he was afraid to hear.

"I made it through the first trimester," she said. "I was tired and miserable and sick, but the baby did great. We found out we were having a girl. I wanted her so badly, even though she was half Tom's. I thought of names, I made clothes because Nate wouldn't let me buy any yet. No one could know I was pregnant until the PR team said it was okay. It was going to be a big surprise, a big reveal with money involved, but not too early in the pregnancy, or people would lose media interest before the birth. It was this whole plan, you know?"

"Seems like it's always a plan with Nate."

She sniffled, sighed, and finally broke. For the first time, she cried, really wept as she told him the rest. Her eyes stormed with emotion now that her wall of secrecy had crumbled. "They told me to come up with a list of names," she said, "and Nate and his team were going to pick. All of this was happening as I started to feel her move inside me, tiny little flutters. I had endless names picked out. Hayley Rose, Melinda Jane, Katherine Louise." She choked back a sob. "For Katherine Louise, I would have called her Katie Lou. But before they could decide on the final name, I started seeing blood. I started having cramps."

He held her. That was all he could do. "I'm so sorry, sweetheart. So sorry."

"They had the whole plan set to go. They had deals with a certain magazine, six figure deals for the scoop and the ultrasound photos, and for the...the first pictures after her birth. The name reveal, all of it. All they had to do was decide on a name."

She could barely get out the words. Grief poured off her body, in tears and shudders. "I think she would have been so beautiful. I really wanted her. I don't care if it was all a deal, a PR stunt. I loved her so much. But I started bleeding and there weren't flutters anymore, and a doctor came to the house to take care of things so it wouldn't be in the papers. And after that, I didn't want to live. I didn't want to be here with Nate and Tom, but I didn't know how to get out. I started to drink again, and I thought about taking pills, but Gladys..."

She laughed and sniffled at the same time.

"Crazy fucking Gladys realized I was suicidal. She wouldn't leave me alone. She helped me get sober and started trotting me out to those charity hospital events, and over time, those sick, struggling babies became my lost baby, and the sad, suffering children became my baby all grown up. I used to think that losing her was a punishment for this life I've chosen, for being weak and stupid and drinking to chase away the pain, but now I think it's something that happened to teach me how to love. My baby's not here now, but she was the first person I ever truly loved."

"Did you have any ceremony for her?" he asked after a moment. "Any burial?"

"No. They decided it was better for Nate's image to keep things secret. Action stars who have kids lose a little of their edgy appeal."

"How did you feel about that? Keeping it a secret?"

"I didn't like it, but I didn't really have a choice." She took a shaky breath and looked up at him. "It's not a secret anymore. I've told you."

"Did you end up choosing a name for her?"

She nodded, almost shyly. "I decided on Katie Lou."

"Katie Lou. That's a good Texas name."

So many thoughts crowded his head. So many things he wanted to do, so many things he wanted to fix for her, so many acts he wanted to revenge. In the end, he could only say one thing.

"You need to leave this marriage, Jenna. Somehow, you have to get yourself out of it."

"I know."

"I mean, tomorrow. Today. Now. You need to call a lawyer and find out your options."

She was already sitting up, shaking her head through tears. "I don't have a lawyer, and no one would represent me anyway, with Nate there to pay them off. I don't have anything of my own to barter with. He's set things up that way as a deterrent. His lawyers have made it impossible for me to have a life without him."

"They've told you that, but it's a false narrative. Do you know what that is? He's made you believe his threats because it suits his purposes, but life doesn't work that way. I could help you. There are so many people who could help you."

"And so many people who would take his side, because he's got the money. He's got the influence in this town. He'd ruin me. You don't understand."

He did understand, but he didn't want to push her right now, while she was grieving and trembling. He understood that she was too emotionally beaten down to see her situation as it was. She was so used to being a captive that freedom was the last thing she wanted. He understood how comfortable it could be to hole up and hide.

They sat together awhile longer, until she calmed down. He didn't know what she was thinking, but he could only think of one thing: getting her away from Hollywood and her fucked up marriage.

"What if you got away for a while?" he said. "Took a vacation away from Nate and Tom and this house, just long enough to get some air? You have a good excuse for the PR people—someone just tried to kill you."

"I tried to use that excuse to get out of attending the other premieres, but Nate shut that down."

"So what? Reopen the conversation. You're his wife, not his child. You have power in this arrangement, more power than you know. Tell him what you want. Negotiate. Go through his PR people if you have to. Maybe Gladys could help you again."

"Gladys." She said it with disdain, because neither of them enjoyed being in her company, but if she'd helped Jenna once, she might help her again. "What should I ask her? Where would we go?"

We. He and Jenna. Was he suggesting a getaway so they could be together, far away from this place where they might get caught carrying on together? Was he being more selfish than altruistic?

Possibly.

Probably.

"There are a lot of places celebrities go to recuperate," he said. "Gladys might have some ideas."

She gazed into his eyes, tearing up again. He cupped her face. "What is it, sweetheart?"

"I like when you call me sweetheart. I like you."

"I like you, too."

"No, I scary like you. I like you too much. I've never told anyone about Katie, but I'm glad you know." She wiped away her tears before they could fall. "I don't want to cry. I'm actually feeling better. Secrets aren't such a burden when you don't have to carry them alone."

"So you don't want a drink anymore?"

She shook her head. "I don't want to cry anymore either."

She pressed closer to him, tracing the planes of his face, skirting gingerly around his bruises. She took a few moments to work up to kissing him, but he didn't mind the wait. She'd had a lot of emotions to process. So many difficult days and nights, and if he could make them better in any way... He wrapped gentle fingers in her hair, returning her tentative kiss that tasted too much like tears.

"I know something that's a lot more fun than crying," he said. "Something I'd love to do with you."

"Please," she whispered against his lips. "Let's go do it right now."

10.
AN ESCAPE

There was an art to making love to a tearful woman. You needed tenderness and patience, and a willingness to accept whatever emotions followed the tears. You needed to make it easy to let go.

"Come here," he said as soon as they were undressed. He let her know with lingering kisses that he was there for her, for whatever she wanted. He could think about everything she'd told him later, after he comforted her and made the bad things go away.

They lay side by side, connected by trust and the crazy situation that had brought them into each other's lives. She stared in his eyes, and he showed her she was safe. She let out a small breath, tracing the lines of his shoulders, running her fingers across his pecs. Last night, too, she'd spent a great deal of time looking at his body. He was flattered, and happy his physique aroused her. He stayed fit because his job demanded it, but he was glad it excited her, too. His cock was hard as fuck, but he kept himself in check as she pressed her fingertips against the ladder of his abs.

"How do you get this strong?" she asked.

"Running and weights. Fight training."

He stopped there. Why bring up fight training? Here, in bed? She was stroking him everywhere, tracing all his muscles as if measuring his virility, and it made him want to ravish her. She touched his cock and he drew in a breath. *Control. Control yourself.*

He pushed her back on the bed beneath him. If she enjoyed looking at him, let her look, but he would show her how gorgeous *she* was before they were through. His cock fell against her soft, curved belly as he brushed back her hair. Her tearful secret-telling had left her emotionally open, pliable and needful and maybe a little reckless.

He wanted to have all those emotions. He kissed her eyes and forehead, all the lines and tense spots, taking on what she felt. He licked her cheeks and bit her earlobe, before burying his head against hers and opening his teeth against her neck. He didn't bite her, even though she moaned and arched against him. He nipped her instead, then kissed his way to the hollow at the base of her throat.

He held her in the circle of his arms and dipped his head to kiss her breasts next, paying particular attention to her nipples. He was rewarded with more squirming, and an indrawn gasp of pleasure. To him, it seemed as if she was finding her body again, learning what felt good. He was desperate to teach her everything, so he could heal any damage Tom might have left behind.

Tom, the fucking asshole. He'd have to stay away from him, or he might accidentally eviscerate him as he'd done to Jenna's assailant. This was a new thing, a woman driving him to murderous thoughts. He refocused that intensity on Jenna, caressing, kissing, stroking until she was shivering with erotic anticipation.

"Please," she said. "Please take me."

Beneath her exhausted expression, under her turned-inside-out fatigue, the wildness was rising. When he sheathed himself and nudged his cock against her opening, she grasped his shoulders, the nails digging in a little. When he started to press inside, all hell broke loose. She'd been urging him forward with a low croon, but now it rose to a moan of demand.

"Oh God, you feel so good." She clasped her legs around him. "How do you feel that good?"

She was so wet, so eager for him to possess her. He figured it was partly the long, slow, teasing caresses he'd begun with, and partly the chemistry that sparked between them whenever they touched. He vibrated from that chemistry too, and had to steel himself not to go too fast and too hard. He was glad it felt good to her, even if her reactions were making it difficult to stay in control. She deserved to feel good. He drew out every thrust, making her ride the sensation from tip to root. She responded with delicious fervor, squeezing him and bucking her hips. He kissed her, teasingly, to try to calm her, but she bit his tongue.

He finally gave in to her need for wildness. He didn't want to be too rough, the way he imagined Tom had been, but there was a roughness that felt satisfying and not hateful, and that was his favorite way to fuck. He held her down, squeezing her neck just enough to excite her. He kissed her when she moaned and pounded his body against hers.

"Yes, yes, yes." Her lustful pleas had given way to breathless wonder. "Yes, yes, please, Caleb. I'm so close."

"Come for me, sweetheart. I want to feel it."

She grasped his shoulders, shuddering through an orgasm that felt like angels dancing on his cock. He gazed down at her dark hair strewn across his pillow, her eyes squeezed shut, her lips trembling as she sighed in ecstasy. *I love her*, he thought. *I love this woman. This married woman.*

The married part didn't matter, not in this case, but the love...

He clenched his teeth as he climaxed inside her, the knowledge burning in his brain. He loved her. Or maybe he just wanted to help her. Maybe their sexual connection was making him feel more for her than he should. Maybe he should cool it with the sex...

No. There was no ending this thing they'd started. She clung to him, her eyes opening to reflect the same love and connection he felt. It had to be okay, didn't it?

"You're amazing," she said softly. "That felt so good."

"It felt better to me, because you're smiling again."

He rose to take off the condom, and returned to find Jenna deep in thought, her features pensive.

"How do you think this ends?" she asked. "You and me?"

"With you safe and happy," he replied without thinking. It was the only answer. Whatever it took to make that happen, that was the only direction he could go.

* * * * *

It was easier for Jenna to email Gladys while she was still lying next to Caleb. He gave her strength. He wouldn't come up with the demands for her, or tell her how to word them. No, she'd asked him to handle it and he'd refused, but he gave her the encouragement she needed to write the email herself.

Dear Gladys,

I know you've done a lot of planning for Nate's overseas premieres, but I'm going to have to bow out this time. I'm still recovering from the attack, as is my bodyguard. I might slip up and say or do something damaging to Nate's career when I'm suffering this kind of emotional distress.
I'm sure I'll be fine in a few weeks, if I can stay out of the spotlight for a while and find my footing. Please confer with Nate and his PR team to find an appropriate locale for me to convalesce with the help of my security team. I appreciate your assistance and understanding.

Jenna

It was short, sweet, and subtly threatening, and it did the trick. It took a few days for the PR folks to work everything out, and a couple heated arguments with Nate to come to a compromise, but when she showed Caleb the abridged plans a few days later over breakfast, she felt proud.

"You were right," she said. "They listened to me more than I thought they would."

"Because you know more secrets than they want you to. You could ruin Nate just as easily as he could ruin you."

Caleb had become so much more than a bodyguard to her in such a short time, which kind of scared her. She wasn't sure she should have revealed so much about her life to him. He wasn't supposed to know about anything—about Nate and Tom, or the reasons for the tension between them. The contract she'd signed with Nate forbade the disclosure of "private information" without his prior agreement. She told Caleb he couldn't scowl at Tom the way he'd been doing, because it might give too much away. They were trapped in a circle of secrets now, and they all had to play the game.

"I'll enjoy going to London," he said, looking over the new itinerary. "I know you hate premieres, but it's just one appearance, which is way better than six. Then we're off to..." His brows rose. "Taos, New Mexico?"

"That was the PR firm's suggestion. New Age-y enough to be a healing place, but trendy enough to protect Nate's brand. We'll have to make the best of it."

He flipped open a pamphlet tucked into the packet. "*Lama Vista Retreat and Visioning Center.* Sounds like revenge for skipping the other premieres."

She shrugged. "I like llamas. They're cute."

"I don't think it's that kind of llama. See. There's one l, like the guru meaning of the word." She gave him a blank look. "Like the Dalai Lama, Jenna."

"Shit."

He laughed and added some milk to his coffee. "Maybe the Lama Vista Retreat is a cult."

"Even if it's a cult, it's better than flying all over the planet with Nate and his bodyguard bottom."

Caleb tilted his head. "You really think Tom is the bottom in that relationship?"

"Outside the bedroom, yes. In bed..." She gestured the imagery away. "I don't want to think about it." She wouldn't have to think about it, not for a while. A flood of happiness rushed over her, warming her soul. "I can't believe we get to go away. Three weeks in New Mexico."

"You asked for a month."

"A month would be too long. It might be long enough for me to realize there's more to life, and refuse to come back and play his wife anymore."

Caleb started to speak, then stopped. She knew what he was going to say. *You could refuse anytime. You don't have to be here. You're a free human being. This isn't your prison.* She'd finally pleaded with him to stop lecturing her about it. He didn't understand the enormity of Nate's fame, the tidal wave of his life that drew all of them along. Even with the security, the staff, the armored sedans, the crazy crowds, the unhinged ex-military attackers, he didn't get it.

But she did think about leaving Nate more often now, more than she'd ever allowed herself in the past. She'd think through a step or two of a legal separation or divorce and then stop, cowed by the consequences. It was easier to slog through the days playing the dutiful Hollywood wife, and spend the nights in Caleb's arms.

* * * * *

Nate was a jerk all through the London premiere. The limo ride from the hotel to the red carpet was so brittle and angsty that Jenna felt suffocated. It wasn't just Nate's anger about her escape to Lama Vista, which he expressed in silent, cutting looks. It was also Caleb's barely suppressed hatred for Tom.

Caleb tried to hide it—she'd begged him not to confront Tom, especially in front of Nate, because that would be the final impetus Nate needed to fire him. Instead, Caleb's fury simmered under the surface, beneath his carefully neutral expression and slick, tailored suit. She felt it in the way he moved his head whenever Tom moved, and the way he pressed his fingers together when he was trying not to make a fist.

She hadn't known this side of her bodyguard before. She'd known he was pure and kind, the model of integrity, but she hadn't realized he could harbor fierce rage too. Of course, he'd killed someone to defend her, so he could be fierce when he needed to be.

He was the same in bed. Kind and honorable to an extent, but also dangerous when they were caught up in mounting passion. She knew he'd never go too far—he was too attentive to her to let that happen—but he took more from her sometimes than she thought she had the ability to give. He showed her no deference between the sheets, even though he worked for her and was almost ten years younger. His commanding bedroom manners probably came naturally, from his time in the military and the abilities he needed as a bodyguard.

Mmm. She got so caught up daydreaming about him that she almost took his hand in the limo, picked it up from where it lay on the seat between them. She wanted to smooth away the tension in his big fingers, bring them to her lips to kiss or suck them.

No, not possible. Not now in front of Nate and his "bodyguard," but when Caleb took her to New Mexico for her much-needed retreat, they could pretend to be a couple for a few stolen weeks, at least behind closed doors and darkened windows, when no paparazzi were around. Nate had given her a talk about that, privately. "Don't you fucking embarrass me," he'd said. "Don't do something that ends up in the news, or you'll be sorry."

When they arrived at the manic London theater for the premiere, he held her hand extra hard on the red carpet like he was still warning her that he held the power. He unleashed his signature megawatt smile while she did her best to look like the wan survivor of a recent attack. It had to make sense when she flew off to Lama Vista and skipped the other premieres. It would help if the media were already reporting that she looked strained and tired on her loving husband's arm.

"I hate doing these walks," he muttered in her ear during one of their down moments. "It's not fair that you're leaving me to do this alone."

"You're a grown up," she'd muttered back. "You chose this career."

That went down like a ton of bricks. In the beginning, he'd called it *their* career, *their* collaboration. Now she wasn't holding up her end.

"Would you smile, damn it?" He pressed a secret, fake kiss beneath her ear as he scolded her. "Just a little?"

"I'm not supposed to. That guy told me not to look too chipper." She gestured to the PR suit leading them down the line of reporters. Chet, or Rhett? Nate squeezed her fingers to the point of pain.

"A little smile's not going to make a difference. Don't look unhappy. There's a difference between unhappy and tired."

"Jesus, you're the actor."

But she forced a weak smile because if he gripped her hand any tighter her fingers were going to break off, and her bazillion-caret diamond wedding set would tumble onto the carpet and possibly be lost. She wasn't ever allowed to take off her wedding rings.

"Stop hurting me," she said through smiling, gritted teeth. "A real husband would have sympathy for all I've been through."

His snort wasn't audible to the bank of flashing cameras and reporters, but she heard it. If he got his wish, another knife-wielding crazy person would rush her right now and finish her off. She was sure Tom had wet dreams about it. If her attacker hadn't already been a known threat by security, she would have suspected Tom of setting up the attempted stabbing himself.

She resisted the urge to look back and see where her nemesis was. She probably couldn't have seen him anyway, because Caleb had a habit of positioning himself between her and Tom. He'd done it even before he knew the grotesque details of their relationship, but now he stood a little closer. She met his eyes for a moment, a mere second of relief. That was all she dared with the cameras everywhere.

God, she couldn't wait for this red carpet to end. Her sequined gown was too revealing and too itchy, and her shoes pinched her toes. More revenge? She could imagine Malik conspiring with Nate to punish her. Ugh, if she could just get through the screening and the stupid, excruciating party afterward, she could get away and maybe find herself again, get in touch with her real emotions.

Well, if there were any real emotions left inside her to find.

Just smile, Jenna. Wave and look tired. You'll be in New Mexico soon enough.

11.
LAMA VISTA

Caleb stood outside a humming private jet at Heathrow. It was early, too early for Jenna to be fully awake, but he was on guard, ready to shield her from any paps who'd followed them from the hotel. Even if photographers weren't visible, they could be using telephoto lenses from thousands of yards away.

Inside the jet, their four-man security team was checking for recording devices, weapons, and stowaways. The bomb dogs had already been through. It was business as usual, these security checks and rechecks; as thorough as they were, they still hadn't been able to head off the attack on Jenna. Crazies had a way of getting through. If Nate had been flying to some resort in New Mexico, there would be ten or twelve security guys coming along, but Jenna drew less attention, and they were going to try to stay under the radar as long as they could.

"Are they done?" she asked.

"Almost."

She yawned. "When will we get there?"

"They're seven hours behind us, so we'll get there sometime around noon. You should try to sleep on the plane."

She nodded, but he doubted she'd manage to sleep. She wasn't a relaxed flyer, and once they were in the air, the excitement of escape would set in. They hadn't been able to spend last night together because their rooms had been part of Nate's presidential suite. Nate didn't go so far as to sleep with Jenna in his room for appearances. The snoring, he joked before he went to bed. No, they'd all gone off to separate rooms, two secret couples keeping up appearances on the top floor of a luxury London hotel. Jesus, Caleb needed a getaway too.

"Ready?" he asked Jenna as the security guys waved them in.

"Yeah."

"Let me help with your bag."

"No, it's okay."

Their luggage was already loaded, so she only carried a small travel bag with a few books and electronics for the trip. On the plane, the security team moved to the back, while Caleb took the seat across from Jenna. He was expected to sit near her, since he was close security, a different echelon from the operations guys. Even at the house, they didn't cross paths too often. In Taos, they'd be doing their jobs if Jenna didn't even know they were there.

"Comfortable?" he asked.

"Yes. This is a nice plane."

It wasn't as big as Nate's personal plane, the one that would continue to the other premieres with Nate's salaried pilot at the controls, but it was luxurious. The tan leather interior was sleek and spotless, and he could see a kitchen and a couple bedrooms in the back. His brother had doubtless been on planes like this when he worked for Jeremy Gray, but the rest of his family wouldn't have a clue that private jets like this existed. His great-grandma would wrinkle her nose and refuse to board. She'd never been on a plane.

He missed his family, simple and Texan as they were. From what he could gather, Jenna didn't have much family to lean on when things got stressful. He'd called his mother and talked to her about killing the man last week, and received the only absolution that mattered. Did Jenna have anyone to call when she was sad or conflicted? He remembered her face when she'd shattered her bathroom mirror with the towel rack. No. Probably not.

The bathroom would be back to normal when they returned. Gladys had arranged for renovators to update her whole wing while they were away. Why not, when you had endless money to blow? When was the last time his parents had renovated their farmhouse in Spur? Still, he'd always feel more comfortable there.

"What are you thinking about?" she asked.

Caleb glanced out the window as the jet pulled away from the gate. "Nothing. Home," he admitted. "Wondering what my parents would think of this plane."

"Are you close to them?"

"We're all close. We grew up on top of each other."

"Is that why you joined the Army so young?"

"I didn't think I was that young when I joined." He paused, reluctant to reveal too much about his military years. "I wanted to see the world, and get out of my parents' hair. I felt up to it."

She stretched her legs, then drew them back with a laugh. "I got a job at a grocery store after high school, and some days that seemed impossibly hard." She sobered. "But you're stronger than me."

He propped his head on his hand and gave her a stern bodyguard look. "You're stronger than you think. You stood up to Nate, right? Now you're getting the break you deserve."

The plane was accelerating, lifting into the air with a gentle roar of engines. The pressurization system filled the cabin with calming white noise. One of the security guys in the back was already sleeping. Jenna rested her head on the back of the seat.

"Tired?" he asked.

"A little."

"You should take a nap." He handed her one of the large velour blankets stowed nearby. "The crew'll make lunch in a few hours."

"What part of the Army were you in? I mean, what did you do?"

Her question surprised him. There was an edge to it, a curiosity that put him on guard.

"I did general Army stuff," he fibbed. "Infantry. Ground troops, I guess they're called."

"I was just wondering, because that guy...the one who attacked me..."

He waited, wishing she didn't want to talk about this. He'd been doing everything he could to put it out of his mind, to let it fade as his bruises faded.

"I watched those videos online," she said. "I couldn't help watching, you know? I had to see what happened, and the way you engaged him was like...really intense. Like you didn't even think, you just acted. I wondered if that came from your military experience."

"Probably. We trained in hand-to-hand combat. That was a big part of what got me the bodyguard job."

"You can use guns, too."

"Yeah."

"You're pretty lethal for someone who's so nice. I guess, being in the Army, that guy wasn't the first person you've killed?"

He fought back a pang of irritation. She wanted to know this thing about him, perhaps to process those videos she'd watched. He could deny that he'd ever killed anyone else, but that would be lying. He could ask if they could change the topic, but she'd been so open with him about her past.

"Jenna, I went into war zones. I went on missions where I had to defend myself and my team. I've killed other people."

"Oh."

"Does that bother you? I was doing my job."

"Of course it doesn't bother me. I'm grateful for your service."

Her voice was mild. She wasn't attacking him, but he still felt attacked.

"I don't kill people for fun." He chewed a nail, a weak, nervous gesture he'd excised from his habits long ago.

"Do you miss being in the military?" she asked. "Why did you leave? I bet they didn't want you to go."

"Oh, they wanted me to go." He felt the truth pushing up from places he'd buried it. "I didn't leave. I was asked to go."

"You were? Why?"

"Because I shot my mouth off when they wanted me to be a quiet, obedient grunt. I saw things in the military that weren't right. Justice is big to me. You know when things aren't legit, and at some point I couldn't…" He let out a breath. "I couldn't keep my mouth shut."

He clasped his hand into a fist so he couldn't bite that damn nail again.

"What kinds of things did you see?" she asked, staring at that fist. "You can tell me. I won't tell anyone else."

She was giving him a chance to unload his soul, the way he'd urged her to tell her story while they sat on her couch. And he wanted to unload, but what would it change?

"People are dishonest," he said, too quietly for the guards in the back to hear. "People lie and give away their honor." He snapped his fingers. "Just like that, without a second thought."

"Yes, they do."

"Some lies are harmless. Some lies are convenient, like Nate drawing you into his life. Some lies are just shitty cowardice and refusing to admit what you did wrong, and I can't stand those kinds of lies." He felt himself drawing back in time, saw his buddy Jared with his buck teeth and black curls. "I had a good friend in Speci—in the Army. His name was Jared Nichols, and he was killed by friendly fire. Do you know what that is?"

"Yes. Oh, that's sad."

"And the guy who did it, this asshole in our group, he was a great fighter, but he didn't have a soul. This guy—let's call him Asshole. Major Asshole. He was our group leader, because in addition to having no soul, he had no fear. He got us involved in a firefight that we could have won if we'd waited for the right time, but he didn't want to wait. In the smoke and confusion, Asshole fucked up and shot Jared, thinking he was one of the insurgents."

It was still so vivid in his mind. The reckless shot, the red bud blooming on Jared's forehead, erasing his smile, his personality, his life, his military career. Fighters bore down on them, yelling in Arabic, gunshots, fire, and the smell…

"I'm sorry, Caleb. That must have been awful."

"Friendly fire happens. It is awful, but people make mistakes. What I couldn't get past was…" He closed his eyes. "We never leave people behind. If it's humanly possible, we don't leave people behind, but Asshole ordered us to leave Jared and retreat. In his report, he claimed Jared was killed by enemy fire. Without a body, without forensics, no one could dispute him. We left him behind and…"

He wouldn't tell her the rest, the way the enemy had desecrated his friend's body and dragged it around the area's enemy camps to rile their troops, all because Major Lloyd couldn't own his mistake. Weakness. Dishonor. Soulless cowardice. Later, he reasoned that some of the fault was his, that he should have defied his leader and brought Jared home for his family, and spared them the grief of learning his grisly fate.

But he'd been too shocked. He'd been gobsmacked that someone in command would sink so low. It was understood that Special Ops played by their own rules, but those rules still had to be honorable. Didn't they?

When he requested a hearing with his command coordinator and asked that question, the man refused to answer. When he demanded a hearing with the Committee in Charge of Special Operations, they told him to shut up and return to duty, and keep his damn mouth shut. When he protested and asked for a third time if honor didn't matter, they escorted him from the room and stripped him of his security credentials, and his job.

"I still think about Jared," he said, summing up what he'd never be able to sum up. "He was a great guy. A Texan, like me."

"What happened to Major Asshole?"

"Nothing. That's why I left the Army. Without honor, all of it's useless. I couldn't be part of the system anymore. I've talked to you about false narratives, about the spin your husband and his lover put on everything. In my corner of military operations, there was a lot of fucked-up shit going on, but that…" He shook his head. "That was the lowest of the low."

He let his voice trail off. His missions had been top secret, confidential. He couldn't tell her about the goriness and rape in the war zones, or the innocent people who were killed. He couldn't tell her he'd worked for five years as a glorified assassin, earning medals and promotions to make it seem okay.

"I'm not saying there aren't great people in the military," he said, backtracking to more solid ground. "Ninety-nine point nine percent of soldiers are paragons of selflessness and humanity, but the tiny percentage who aren't somehow end up in power. I'll never figure that out."

He forced his body to relax. He'd done what he could to avenge his friend's death, by speaking against his group leader, even though he lost his job. "It's complicated," he said, when his voice felt less strained. "Sometimes you get into situations that aren't ideal, even though you meant to do a good thing."

"Yeah. I know about that." Her dark eyes were mournful. "I'm sorry about your friend, and that you were punished for seeking justice. Sometimes I think you're too good and honorable for this world. I worry for you."

"You don't have to. You have enough things on your mind." He shifted in his chair, leaned forward, and took in a steadying breath. "Can I get you something to drink? Anything to make you more comfortable?"

"I'm good." She studied him, tucking her blanket closer around her. "But I do have one more question. How'd you become so honorable? Where does that come from?"

"I'm not honorable." He flicked a gaze toward the back of the plane, to be sure no one was eavesdropping. "I'm sleeping with a married woman. That's as far from honorable as you can get."

"I'm not really married, though. Nate and I knew there wouldn't be fidelity between us. We've never operated that way. Don't try to distract from my point. You're so, so honorable. You've never cheated on anyone, have you?"

He shook his head. "Never."

"And you never would. I mean, is it easy or hard to live that way?"

"It's easy most of the time." He returned her gaze, wishing he could take her hand and hold it across the center aisle between them. "Life's easier in general if you stick to honor and truth."

"Did you learn that in church?"

"I learned it in my soul. I know what feels right, but like anyone else, I'm not one hundred percent good."

As their eyes held, he recalled silent memories, stolen kisses and sultry hours in bed. She bit her lip, and he knew she was recalling the same things.

"You're ninety-nine point nine percent good," she said softly, hugging the blanket around her. "Probably even a couple decimal points more."

* * * * *

They arrived at Lama Vista in blazing sun and heat. To Caleb, the resort looked a lot like the mansion in Hollywood Hills, except there were no hills and the exterior was adobe-brown. But inside, the expanses of white, the fine furnishings, the sterile luxuriousness was all the same.

While the security team walked the facility and inspected their private "casita," he accompanied Jenna to a meeting with her wellness guide, Lauren, a tanned older woman with curly brown hair. She was the New

Mexico version of Gladys—too perky, too fake, too effusive. Caleb sat to Jenna's right as Lauren slid her a glossy portfolio.

"We're so happy you've chosen Lama Vista as your destination to refuel your soul," she began. "We offer an award-winning slate of amenities and therapies for getting your life back on track."

He and Jenna exchanged looks. "Amenities and therapies" sounded so involved.

"We offer horseback riding, hot rock therapy, tantra lessons, past life readings, and rectal irrigation treatments," their guide continued.

"Wow," Jenna said in a voice that almost made him crack.

"That's not all. We've also got a therapeutic yoga garden, an herb tent, a mineral water immersion chamber, and a nature-based gym facility."

"What does that mean, nature based?" asked Caleb.

"It means that instead of lifting weights, you'll chop wood for our kitchens, and instead of using a treadmill, you'll hike the mesas that surround us. We immerse ourselves in nature here."

Jenna didn't look happy about that. She was the most indoorsy person he knew.

"In addition to all these amenities, Mrs. York," said Lauren, "you'll meet daily with one of our resident lamas, or gurus, in a sacred and sage-cleansed teepee, and receive three hours of meditation and counseling."

Jenna leafed through the folder of papers in front of her. "I don't remember reading about that in the brochure I received."

"Not all our clients access the lamas, but your particular plan calls for—"

"My plan? What plan?"

Lauren blinked at her. "The arrangements were made through your husband's contact last week. Gladys, I think? She was determined that you'd have access to all the resort has to offer. And you'll be happy to know that everything on your schedule is included in the cost of your stay," Lauren said, curls bouncing. "As for food, we offer a five-star menu of nutritionally balanced, locally sourced vegetarian meals to be delivered to your casita every day. You put in your order in the morning and voila, everything's taken care of."

"I'm not a vegetarian," Jenna pointed out. Lauren's only reply was her continued, cloying smile. Caleb watched Jenna, both amused and concerned for her. Three hours in a teepee with a lama? And what was an herb tent? Around here, it probably involved smoking pot.

"Do you have any llamas here?" Jenna asked. "The animal kind?"

"No, but we can try to arrange an outing for you to a llama farm."

Jenna shook her head. "You don't have to arrange anything. We'll go exploring on our own, won't we, Caleb?"

Lauren peered down at the activities Gladys had arranged for Jenna, studying it with comic gravity. "There isn't much time built into your schedule for exploring, I'm afraid."

"No one consulted me about this schedule." Jenna glanced at him, peeved, and he returned a look of solidarity, along with a subtle nod in Lauren's direction. *Tell her no. You're an adult woman.*

Jenna looked back at Lauren. "I'm not..." Her voice gained strength. "I'm not sure I want to stick to a schedule, actually. That wasn't the type of getaway I had in mind."

"Mrs. York, you'll get more out of your experience if you take advantage of everything we have to offer." Lauren's voice dropped a little, as she spoke with manufactured sympathy. "We heard about the attack on your personal space." *Personal space?* "It can't be easy dealing with the perils of fame, and the stress of being Nathaniel York's wife. We want to help you."

"The kind of help I need is to relax," said Jenna.

"Exactly. There's nothing more relaxing than pampering yourself and working on your sacred core."

He saw Jenna's jaw tense, and gave her an encouraging look. *You're doing great. Don't let up.* He could have stepped in as her bodyguard and put a stop to this silliness, but it was better for her to advocate for what she wanted. Little by little, in front of his eyes, a new, stronger Jenna was emerging.

"I have my own ways of working on my soul." As she said it, he thought of their bedroom sessions, their talks over Chinese takeout, even the baby hats she knitted while she binge-watched cartoons. *Good girl. You tell her.* Jenna kept her eyes on Lauren's, and her voice level. "I'll certainly look at the schedule you've set up, and do the activities I'm in the mood for, but I might also hang out in the casita a lot."

"Hmm." Lauren looked bereft. "That's your prerogative, of course, but I wish you'd reconsider." She gestured to the schedule. "It's all been arranged."

"It'll have to be unarranged. To be honest, Lauren, I'm mostly here to relax and get away from cameras and reporters for a while. My security guys have a car, and I have a full time bodyguard." She gestured toward him. "So I may come and go, and miss some of the activities you've set up for me. You can go ahead and un-schedule the rectal irrigation stuff right now, because I'm definitely not doing that."

"It sounds daunting, Mrs. York, but you won't believe the benefits of a good colon cleansing."

"Definitely not doing that," she repeated.

Caleb bit the inside of his cheek so he wouldn't laugh. He was the bodyguard, invisible to Lauren, only here to serve his client. His behavior reflected on Jenna, so he couldn't throw back his head and laugh his ass off the way he wanted to.

But when they got to the casita, they looked at each other and let it all out. "It's all been arranged," he said, imitating Lauren's voice as he shrugged off his jacket. "First you'll do some smoking in the herb tent, then go for your mineral water immersion. In other words, swimming."

She giggled as he took off his holster and set it aside. "Instead of lifting weights, you'll chop wood so we don't have to," she said, pointing at him.

He pointed back. "All our teepees have been sage-cleansed."

"I forgot to ask about making pottery," Jenna said, picking up her portfolio. "That's got to be a thing at this place."

"Look through your schedule. Maybe that's what you do while you're meditating with your guru."

"Oh, yeah." She laughed harder. "It'll be like that scene in *Ghost*." She shook her head, throwing the portfolio down again. "I don't believe Gladys scheduled me into all that stuff. How stupid. I'm here to relax. They're probably charging extra for all that shit too."

They settled down, looking around the white, crystal-and-fern accented living room of their casita. The white was definitely calming. There was no TV, although a top-scale sound system offered various New Age and Native American selections to be piped through the rooms. Near the kitchen, a couple rustic weavings brightened the space.

They explored the bedroom suites next. There were two of them connected by a hallway, similar to the layout in Hollywood Hills. The beds were wide and white, with faux fur coverlets in mottled brown, and a few muted paintings of soaring silver birds. The security guys would be housed in the two adjacent casitas, not connected to theirs, but on either side of it. Aside from the scheduling, it was a nice resort, a perfect set up for relaxing. Even their locally sourced lunch wasn't that bad. The vegetables were fresh and the flavors were appealing.

Jenna turned to him when they finished eating and took a deep breath. "Well, here we are."

"Here we are," he agreed. "The adventure begins."

"I'm going to take a nap."

Why not? She was free to do anything she wanted. They'd put her charity appearances on hold back home because of the attack at the hospital, and Nate was on his way to a far-flung premiere she didn't have to attend.

"I think you should take tons of naps while you're here," he said. "And spend lots of time in bed."

"Only if you're with me."

"Oh, I'll be with you. But first..."

"But first...?" she repeated, raising her eyebrows.

"But first, it's time for your rectal irrigation."

She shrieked out a laugh as he swept her into his arms, carrying her back toward the bedrooms.

"I told you, I'm definitely not doing that! Why don't *you* try a little irrigation while you're here?"

"Nope."

He dumped her on the first bed they reached. They hadn't divvied up the rooms yet, but it didn't matter. They'd only use one bed. "Speaking of definitely not doing that," he said, pulling her against him, "you should feel proud of the way you stood up for yourself."

"I did pretty well, huh? I'm getting better at it."

He nodded, soaking in her flirtatious gaze as he pushed up her gauzy, resort-appropriate shirt. He tossed it off the bed, and ran his fingertips along the cups of her bra. She reached down to stroke the front of his pants.

"You're standing up for yourself too," she joked, finding his cock's outline. "Why don't you ever wear things with easier access?" She tugged at his waistband. "Are you going to wear a suit the whole time you're here?"

"Yes, I'm your bodyguard." He slid his burgeoning erection against her hand, then sat up to unbutton his shirt. "But I won't wear it in bed."

He took off her linen shorts with his teeth, teasing her with his scratchy goatee. She was fun to tease and torment, so he did it often. She'd built up so much sexual energy over her years of chastity that she had an incredible lust drive, and he was young and healthy enough to help her burn it off. When she reached for his cock to hurry him with the condom, he held her wrist and made her wait.

"Be a good girl," he said.

"I'm never a good girl."

"You were today." He made sure the condom was secure, then rubbed his stiff length across her clit. "You should always ask for what you want."

She squirmed against him, lifting her chin. "What if I don't get it?"

"You'll almost always get it." He teased over her clit again. "What do you want, sweetheart?"

"You know what I want." Her hips rose against his. "Please."

"You have to say it. Use your words, like you did with Lauren."

She made a frustrated sound. "I want you to fuck me. It's been so long."

He chuckled. "It's been, like, three days. I love that you're so insatiable."

"I have to take you while I have you." Her words were reckless and sexy, but also a little sad. *While I have you.* They hadn't talked yet about their future, if they could even have a future. All of it was up in the air, distant and vague.

He slid inside her, feeling her shudder at the strength of his possession. *Yes, I'm inside you. I have you and I'm going to fuck you. You're mine right now.* That was all they had to work with for the moment. Right now. It gave their lovemaking a heightened note, a desperate, frenetic energy that had its own appeal. They'd tried doing it doggy style, or spooning back to front, but they always ended up in some position where they could keep their eyes on each other. *I have you now. Right now. I don't want you to disappear.*

He rolled over so she was on top of him, bracing against his chest. "You're so deep," she moaned as she worked herself on his shaft. "You're so deep inside me."

He squeezed her breasts and tweaked her nipples, the way he'd come to learn turned her on the most. Her walls grasped him, letting him know he was doing it right. He didn't bother to think about the future at times like these. He could only think about her now, wild and beautiful, her intent eyes focused as she sought an orgasm.

"Kiss me," he growled, pulling her down to him, fastening his lips to hers. He wanted her to come that way, kissing his lips and biting and licking his jaw. He held her hips, making her ride him as he bucked up to meet her.

"Oh God, oh God," she cried into his mouth. "Oh God."

Oh God, he thought, and he wasn't much of one for praying. *Oh God, how did the two of us find each other, and make this connection? I don't know where we're going, but I'm so grateful we're here.*

12.
FLIGHT

It took about a week for Jenna to lose her patience with the ultra-healthy food, and a few days after that for her to lose her privacy. The paparazzi tracked her to New Mexico when she didn't show up at Nate's premieres, and set up camp by the gate to Lama Vista. It was bound to happen, since the staff and other visitors knew she was there. She was just surprised it had taken so long for someone to tip off the media.

"Cell phone at two o'clock," Caleb told her as they had lunch at a downtown Taos cafe. He nodded to one of the two security guys who'd accompanied them, and he glared at the offender from the adjacent table until Jenna saw the woman tuck her cell phone away. The women stalkers didn't bother her as much as the men. They didn't remind her of the guy who'd charged the car outside Mercy Hospital, but it was still an invasion of privacy. She prayed the woman wouldn't come over to say hi.

First world movie star wife problems, she thought. *I'm a spoiled asshole.*

Then came the guilt and remorse, the endless cycle. To her relief, the woman kept her distance and turned her attention back to her kids. Other people watched her too, glancing at her often. She had three security agents with her, so she kind of stuck out, even to the one percent of people in Taos who hadn't heard of her famous husband.

"I wish everyone would stop staring." She brushed her hair back, needing to feel the sun. "I don't want to hide inside, though."

"You shouldn't have to hide inside," said Caleb. "It's beautiful here."

"Beautiful, and crawling with paps." She spotted a paparazzo across the street, and angled herself away from Caleb so the two of them wouldn't look too cozy in the photos he was snapping. "They're everywhere. What's that saying you have? Like fleas on a dog."

He noticed the pap too, and frowned in his direction. "They follow us every time we go out now. I don't know how to prevent that, because Lama Vista only has one exit gate. I guess we could crawl over the fence."

She made a face and pushed away the roast beef sandwich she wouldn't have been allowed to eat within Lama Vista's walls. "This isn't how I imagined my private getaway."

"Taos is a celebrity place. I imagine Nate's PR folks knew that. If they didn't want you to be recognized, they would have sent you somewhere off the Hollywood map."

"They want everyone to know that Nate York's wife only recuperates with the best."

"Something like that, I'm sure."

"Would it have killed them to give me a break?" She poked her ice water with a straw. "Why can't they take the screws out of me for one freaking three-week vacation? Ugh." She buried her face in her hands. "Listen to me. Why am I such a privileged whiner? I'm at a New Mexico resort with every luxury and perk in the world, and I'm not happy."

"I know, right? There's an herb tent here, for God's sake."

She lifted her head and scowled at him. "It's not funny. Something's really wrong with me. I'm supposed to be getting better out here, but I feel worse than ever."

"Okay, calm down. Why don't you contact Gladys and tell her what's going on, and see if she can book you another place?"

"I tried. She said it would be too complicated to change things now. They want me here, I told you. They're punishing me. I'm sure they knew what a bullshit resort this was when they signed me up, and they probably like this extra press." She waved a hand around at God knew how many reporters who were hiding out and recording them.

"You're giving them a great show right now," he reminded her. "You're doing a perfect job of looking upset."

"Because I am upset."

But he was right to remind her that the more emotion she showed, the more likely they'd run stories on the entertainment shows and gossip columns. She composed herself and stared at the ground while the security head paid the bill.

"I know what'll cheer you up," Caleb said in the car on the way back. "Two words: Spongebob binge."

"You know me so well."

He'd become an expert at calming her down. She wished she could relax against his broad chest as they rode back to the resort, but of course, that wasn't possible. They couldn't be themselves anywhere except behind closed and locked doors. Story of her life.

Back at their casita, Caleb took off his jacket and holster while she searched her tablet for a good Spongebob episode. As soon as Caleb sat on the couch, she crawled onto his lap, and he held the tablet propped against her legs as the rollicking theme song came on.

"I'd die without Spongebob," she murmured.

"I know."

She moved her hand up his chest and rested it against his heart. "I'd die without you."

He pressed a kiss against the top of her head. "Don't say that. You're stronger than you think."

He always said that. *You're stronger than you think.* If only she could bring herself to believe him. If only she could do something that was actually brave and strong.

"Caleb?"

He moved his arms so she could turn to face him.

"What do you think would happen if we just left here?" she asked. "Ran away someplace without the security guards?"

"Shh. I'm watching this."

"I'm serious." She put her hand over the screen. "What if we took off for a week without them and went somewhere no one could find us?"

She could read his face well by now. She could see his amusement that she'd think of such a scheme, and the sympathy that he couldn't allow her to do it. "It wouldn't be safe for you to run off."

"I'd be safe with you. You would be enough protection."

"Sweetheart."

She held his gaze as Spongebob's maniacal laughter sounded in the background. "What if I just told you we were leaving, right now? That we were taking off somewhere without them? You'd have to comply. You work for me."

"I officially work for Nate, unfortunately." He touched her hair, his expression communicating regret. "I'm sorry. It's a nice daydream, but if you think through the details, it wouldn't work." He paused, running a hand down her back to soothe her. "But God, wouldn't it be fun?"

They watched the cartoon a few more minutes, silent, thinking their own thoughts.

"You know what's weird?" she said. "I haven't been on my own, really on my own, in ten years. It's been ten years since I've gone anywhere without a security team around me."

"There's a reason for that. You need security."

"But you could keep me safe." How could he doubt that? He'd killed the one man who'd come at her within a matter of seconds. "I wish we could escape somewhere. Just us, you and me, away from this stupidity. I want it so badly. It's like..." She clasped her hands against her stomach. "It's like this frenzied desire in my soul."

"Such a flare for the dramatic." He stroked her face and kissed her, once, twice, lightly on the lips. "I shouldn't even tell you this..."

"Tell me what?" She sat up straighter. "What?"

Caleb shifted against her, his features creased in thought. "I know a place you'd be pretty safe, at least for a few days. It's about a seven hour drive from here."

"Where?"

He paused a moment, then shook his head. "No. I don't even know why I'm thinking of this. It's not a good idea. I don't want to be accused of kidnapping, especially Nathaniel York's wife. He's got more lawyers than God can count."

She ripped the tablet out of his hands, forgetting the video. "If you have a place to take me, a safe, private place, we have to go. I don't care where it is."

"It's in Texas." He met her gaze, his blue eyes glinting with possibility. "It's my hometown, Spur. We could stay at my parents' place to avoid using hotels, and no one there is going to know you. Caressa Gallo came to visit with my brother and no one had a clue who she was."

"*The* Caressa Gallo?" She was one of the most famous cellists in the world, right up there with Yo Yo Ma. "How did Caressa know your brother? Was he her bodyguard?"

"And assistant, yes."

"Spur, Texas," she mused. "It sounds like a great place to go on the *spur* of the moment."

"You're very punny."

She hopped off his lap, bouncing on the couch. "We have to start packing, right now! We could rent a car tonight. Sneak out and start driving, and be there by morning."

He rolled his eyes. "How about we drive during the day? We can just as easily sneak out in the morning by saying we're going to one of the teepees for breakfast, and meeting your guru afterward. That'll give us a couple hours to play with before they realize we're gone." He rubbed his eyes, a nervous gesture he could do again now that his stitches had healed. "Wait. What the hell am I saying? Why are we talking about this? Nate'll lose his mind if you take off on your own without telling him and Gladys first."

"Nate will have an aneurysm," she agreed. "But they'll never agree to it if I ask. We just have to go and tell them about it later. If they freak out—"

"Which they will."

"If they freak out, I'll tell them it was all my idea, and that you had to come with me or abandon your client." She squeezed his arm. "Come on! It'll be fun, like being on the lam, but not really. I mean, I'm a grown woman. What are they going to do? Call the police on me? Can't I go where I want?"

"The jury is out on that. The same jury that will possibly convict me of kidnapping."

"You're not kidnapping me. That's ridiculous. I just want to see the town where you grew up. I want to see the place that turned you into such a kind, generous, honorable man."

He sighed and rested his head back on the couch. She could tell he was conflicted. He wanted to make her happy and get her away from this Taos nightmare, but yeah, Nate would really be pissed.

"If we keep a low enough profile, it won't even be in the news," she pleaded. "That's the only thing that would bother Nate...if I went someplace with you, and the paps started a bunch of rumors about some inappropriate relationship."

"Which we do have."

"Which no one needs to know. They won't find us if we stay at your parents' house. If it doesn't get out, why would he even care?"

"He would care." Caleb sighed. "But I've been missing home, and this weekend's the Fourth of July. My family does a huge reunion and barbeque every year, so I could catch up with everyone at once, and they'd respect your privacy, because that's the Texas way."

"The Texas way." She repeated it with his subtle drawl. "This is crazy and perfect. I want to go to Texas. I want to meet your family."

He snorted. "My family's gargantuan. I have three brothers and two sisters, ten nieces and nephews, and more cousins than you could meet in a month's time. Then there's Great-Grandma Winchell. She's one of a kind."

The more he talked, the more she knew she had to go. This was the getaway she needed, to visit a real place with real people—and the fact that they were Caleb's people made it even better. Lama Vista wasn't a getaway, it was Hollywood in the desert, with more patchouli and pot. "Spur's not a Hollywood kind of place, is it?"

He laughed again. "Spur is the exact opposite of Hollywood. Honestly, it's deep-fried country, if that would bother you."

"It won't bother me. And if you're there..."

He rubbed his eyes again before bending his head for her excited kiss. "We're going to do this, aren't we?" He shook his head, defeated. "Okay. We'll have to pack light and hope the guys don't catch us on the way out. Have you ever dumped the security people before?"

"No, but I've wanted to so many times. I've never been brave enough."

Caleb made her feel brave. He was changing her, healing her far more than rectal irrigation and gurus ever could.

"This won't be a getaway from reality," he warned her, stroking her face. "I wish we could get away from reality, but we'll have to visit Spur as client and bodyguard, even in front of my family."

"I know. We're a big secret. I'm used to keeping big secrets."

"You are, aren't you?"

He kissed her in that gentle, lingering way that said he understood, that he felt for her. It made her love him even more, which was an increasingly dangerous thing.

* * * * *

They set out just before ten the next morning, in an unremarkable sedan Caleb had rented under his own name rather than through Ironclad. Because his client wasn't one to ditch her security team, none of the men were keeping close tabs as they drove away from the casita. Since they never went to lunch until one or so, there weren't any paparazzi waiting at the gate with cameras.

"You can come out," he said when they turned onto the main road. "No one seems to care that we're leaving."

She popped up from under the blanket in the back seat. "That's no fun."

"I know. We may have overestimated the need for stealth, but if it makes you feel better, you can stay hidden back there until we're out of Taos."

She let out a sigh—a delighted sigh—and Caleb was relieved there hadn't been any mess or confrontations with the security team. He'd text them in a couple hours to let them know they were taking a side trip into Texas, but after that, he wasn't sure how things would shake out. Surely his client had a right to go wherever she wanted, and he had a duty to accompany her. If Nate York was unhappy about that...

Well, he'd let Nate and Jenna sort it out, and hope there wasn't any blowback from Ironclad. As for his family, he'd texted his mother the night before.

Coming to visit tomorrow, and bringing a client. Is that okay?

She'd texted back *that's wonderful*, with no hesitation. He missed his mom.

She's trying to keep a low profile, so if you could not tell anyone she's coming, that would be great.

Is it that sweet little musical star?

He'd smothered a laugh, thinking of his previous rave-queen client as a "sweet little musical star." *No, it's someone new*, he texted. *Nathaniel York's wife. Do you know Nate York? Big action star?*

Hmm. Not that into action movies, you know. So much violence and shooting. Maybe if I saw his face?

Anyway, we'll at least stay through the Fourth of July. Maybe longer? I'm excited to see you, mom.

I can't wait to see you too, honey. A moment later, *What is your client's name?*

Jenna.

Oh, how nice. Will Jenna mind sleeping in the living room? The other rooms are already set for your brothers and sisters.

He rolled his eyes. His mom continued typing.

We'll blow up the air mattress for you. She can have the big couch. The kids are camping on the porch.

One thing about Spur...there weren't many hotels nearby. Luckily, Jenna wasn't the type to complain about sleeping on a couch, although his back ached already, thinking about the air mattress.

I'm sure she'll be flexible, mom, thanks. Sorry for the late notice.

I love you. When will you be in?

Tomorrow evening. I'll let you know if any plans change.

He debated whether to tell Jenna she'd have to sleep on the couch, but why bother? Nothing would have dissuaded her by that point. Now that they were on the road, he put all his worries away. They stopped at a gas station a few miles outside town to load up on snacks and drinks, and Jenna moved to the front seat, wearing her big designer glasses to disguise her and protect her from the glare.

"We're like Thelma and Louise," she said, playing with the car radio.

"Do you remember how that movie ended?"

She made a dismissive gesture and settled on a classic rock station. Soon they were on the interstate, heading south toward the Texas border and his home. "We can stop in Las Vegas for lunch," he said, checking the clock.

"Las Vegas?"

"Las Vegas, New Mexico," he said with a smile. "Not as big and flashy as the other one. Speaking of which, Vegas is always an option. Sure you wouldn't rather escape there? You could gamble a little, maybe see a show?"

She shook her head. "Spur or bust."

They drove south, through whole stretches of country without a sign of life. After a while, Jenna slept, her head bobbing against the window, until he finally nudged her and told her to recline the seat. She did, sleepily. He had selfish reasons for going to Spur, but he thought, somehow, the small Texas town might be good for her too.

They stopped in Lubbock to eat, even though they were just an hour from Spur at that point. No one noticed them, and no one cared as they hunkered over their plates at the Sit 'n' Bull diner. He told her about his family, his tree-surgeon father and homemaker mother, his grandparents and gruff Great-Grandma Winchell, who was almost a hundred years old. He told her his brothers' and sisters' names, and how many kids they had, although he still couldn't keep the kids' ages straight.

"You don't have to remember all this," he told her. "They won't expect you to know their names."

"I'll try." He could see some nerves starting to show. "I'm not used to being around a lot of people. I mean, you know, *real* people. How long's it been since you've been home?"

"Since Christmas. I try to get to Spur a couple times a year." He noticed the tension lines around her mouth, the stressed look in her eyes. "We don't have to go if you're having second thoughts," he told her. "We could drive back to Taos right now."

"I don't want to go back. It's too late now, anyway." She blew out a breath. "The security guys will be pissed."

"They're a little pissed. I texted them a while back."

"I haven't heard from Nate yet," she said, checking her phone.

"I think they'll wait as long as possible to tell him you've left, in case you come back."

"Not going back."

As nervous as she was, she clearly intended to see this adventure out. It was a declaration of independence, and as Jenna's bodyguard, charged with her protection, he knew it was a good thing. Let Nate see that she'd survive on her own if she had to.

Not on her own. With you.

But she's not yours, remember? Not by a long shot.

He silenced the voice that accused him of ulterior motives, because there wasn't time to rethink things now. When they arrived at his parents' five-acre property in Spur, he watched Jenna enjoy her first taste of Texas hospitality as his family welcomed her. His mother, God bless her, even gave her a hug. There were kids everywhere, wound up on the sugary cola cake his mother had served for dessert. She cut slices for Jenna and him too, and they ate in the living room with Great-Grandma Winchell smiling from the corner, and the deflated air mattress spread out in the middle of the floor.

"I didn't know if you'd be tired as soon as you got here," his mother explained. "You had a long drive."

"It wasn't that long." He grinned at Jenna. "I forgot to tell you: I'm sleeping on the air mattress, and you're on the couch."

His parents' tan and black mixed-breed puppy sidled up, his wagging tail beating the side of Caleb's chair. "How big is this critter going to get?" he asked, rubbing the dog's floppy ears.

"Big enough," said his dad. "Name's Jethro. He'll keep the raccoons from the trash."

Jenna giggled, and Caleb smiled too. He'd told her they were going to the country, and that included raccoons and hounds named Jethro, along with snakes, possum, coyotes, spiders, and feral cats. There was a little daylight left, and the temperatures dropped to bearable on Texas evenings, so they took a walk outside, around the flat, expansive backyard. His sisters waved to them from the porch, one of them rocking his nephew to sleep, while the older kids played pick-up football with some of his cousins in the yard.

"This is nice," she said. "Reminds me of home, a little."

He guessed she meant her Florida home, where she'd grown up, but her voice didn't invite further conversation on that topic. Maybe she was talking about the humid heat.

"Sorry we have to sleep in the living room," he said later, when they were sprawled under light quilts on their temporary beds. "There are four bedrooms upstairs, but they're taken up with the out-of-town folks. I think mom's even put a couple cousins in the laundry room."

"A little more privacy would have been nice." She gave him a look that fell somewhere between sultry and flirty, but he could see she was tired after the long drive.

"There are private places around," he said, in a voice that promised some very private activities. "Maybe we can hunt one down tomorrow. That'll be our last chance before everyone arrives for the barbeque. Yes, even more people," he said in response to her wide-eyed look. He stretched, so the air mattress made a groaning sound. "So much for your quiet getaway."

"I like it here. It's quiet enough. Sure you don't want the couch?" she asked.

"Too short for me. I'm comfortable. I'm fine."

It was true. Finally, here, he'd taken off the suit in favor of jeans and a tee shirt. His guns were locked in the rental car's trunk. If he needed a gun, there were plenty in the family's safe downstairs.

"Are you comfortable?" he asked.

She closed her eyes, taking in a deep, slow breath. "It's like another world here, another existence, in a good way. It smells different."

"Like humidity."

"No, like nature and flowers. And cake."

Caleb couldn't help but wonder what was happening in Jenna's other real world, away from flowers and cake. Had she silenced angry messages and texts from Nate? She hadn't looked at her phone once since they'd arrived. He'd ask her in the morning, after he filed his Ironclad report. *Side trip with client to Spur, Texas. The environment is secure.*

Jenna closed her eyes, and he watched as she drifted to sleep. She held out her hand when she was almost there, and Caleb took it, rubbing his thumb over the back.

"Thanks," she said, so faintly he almost couldn't hear.

"You're welcome, sweetheart," he said just as softly. "Pleasant dreams."

13.
WHAT WE ARE

Jenna woke the next morning to a barrage of messages from her husband.

Call me, right now.
Call me.
Call me, Jen.
CALL ME, DAMMIT.

As she was scrolling through the texts, the phone rang, flashing his name.

"Okay, okay," she answered. "Let me find a place to talk."

She couldn't have this conversation in the living room, with his mother banging pots in the kitchen, and kids sleeping on the adjacent porch. She went in the quaint, floral-papered powder room near the back door and locked herself in. "I was going to call you," she said, sitting on the padded toilet seat. "I just woke up."

"Sorry you just woke up," he said in a voice that sounded like *fuck you, bitch*. "I've been up all night wondering what the freak is going on. Who are you with? Where are you sleeping? Why did you leave the security team? Are you running away from me?"

His voice pitched higher as he spoke, tight with tension. He thought she was leaving him, that everything in his carefully curated life was about to unravel. She knew from experience the terror and anger that possibility unleashed.

"Don't freak out, Nate. Calm down, take a breath. I'm not running away, I'm just lying low for a few days, a week or so, through the Fourth of July. I'm in a small town in Texas called Spur."

"I know where you are. Your bodyguard files reports every day." His hissing voice sounded close on the phone, even though he was half a world away, getting ready for the Sydney premiere. "What the hell are you doing in Texas? Why aren't you in Taos where you're fucking supposed to be?"

"Because it was horrible there. I needed a getaway from my getaway, which is Gladys' fault. Did you realize what a celebrity trap that place was?"

"All right. Fine. You decided to go somewhere else, but why did you leave the security team behind? You're the one who's always complaining about your safety." He said the word "safety" in a high, mocking tone. Was that how she sounded to him?

"I left the security team because I don't need them, and they make it hard to move under the radar."

"You think you'll stay under the radar just because you don't have your bodyguards with you? Jenna, Jesus Christ—"

"I do have a bodyguard," she said, cutting him off. "Caleb came with me. He knew this place would be safe because it's where he grew up."

"Oh, how wonderful." His voice dripped sarcasm.

"It is wonderful. I don't need security here, because this place is so weirdly wholesome. It's in the country, in the middle of nowhere, this charming little rural village. The whole place has a population of, like, under a thousand people, and most of them are Caleb's extended family."

There wasn't any sound for a moment, just the silence of Nate fuming. She didn't say anything, because she was afraid the more she talked, the more guilty she'd come across.

"What does it matter?" she asked, to deflect any more questions. "Who cares if I'm here?"

"Everyone cares. All the tabloids will care."

"For all they know, I'm still taking a break in New Mexico. No one's going to notice me here because nobody knows who I am. They don't have a supermarket in this town, much less a tabloid section."

"Well, they know who *I* am," he said in an insulted tone.

"Of course they do, Nate. Everyone knows who you are. They just don't care about me." She sighed as dramatically as him, because two could play at that game. "I only want a few days, okay? There were paps all over Taos, and it started driving me crazy. The resort was full of tourists and staffed by pot-addled hippies, and the food was so earthy and healthy I couldn't eat it anymore."

"You're fucking your bodyguard, aren't you?" he cut in. "That's why you ran away with him. You're going at it twenty-four seven with your boy-toy bodyguard's stunt cock."

"Nate, come on."

"Ironclad told me you're staying at his house."

"It's his family's house," she said, "and we're not a couple, for God's sake. We're staying here because it's secure. It's safe."

"How old is he, Jen? Twenty? Twenty-one? Not a good look for you."

"You're an asshole," she said. "Don't talk to me about boy-toy bodyguards, considering your 'life partner.' You have no idea how honorable Caleb is."

"Honorable? When he's fucking my wife?"

"You don't know what you're talking about," she snapped, which wasn't an outright lie. "I'm not going to continue this conversation with you. I have to go."

"Oh yeah? Well, he's gone, too. When you come back, you'll have a new bodyguard sleeping in your wing of the house, someone old and grouchy and ugly as fuck."

Her heart pounded as she stared at the faded flowers on the wall. "Fuck that. If you try to fire him, Nate, I won't come back. I'll stay here and tour all over Texas with Caleb on my arm, posing for the paps. Is that what you want?"

More silence. More fuming. "I told you you could have a fuck buddy," he said. "But it can't be your bodyguard. If you're that hard up, we'll work something out for you."

"With one of your bisexual minions? Sorry, no thanks. And I'm not fucking Caleb." Okay, that was an outright lie. "I have to get off the phone, Nate. I'm hiding in the bathroom so no one hears this fucked up conversation. Don't call again, please. I'll see you when we get back to L.A."

"When? When are you coming back?"

"Around the time you get back. We'll go out on a fake date or something, okay? *Nathaniel York's wife is smiling again, all healed after her attack.* That'll be a good headline."

"If anyone finds you there, you come home at once. Do you understand me? Here's the headline I don't want to see: *Nathaniel York's wife goes to Texas to meet bodyguard's family.* I'll fucking destroy you if that happens. Don't think I won't."

"Goodbye, Nate."

She hung up the phone, threw it on the counter, and buried her head in her hands. *Don't cry. Don't get upset. He's not worth it.*

Nothing to do with him is worth it.

She heard a soft knock, and Caleb's voice. "Jenna? Everything all right?"

"Yes. I'll be out in a minute. Everything's fine."

She rinsed her face and brushed her teeth, and deleted Nate's wall of texts so she wouldn't have to look at them again. Then she opened the door to Caleb's concerned expression and waved a hand.

"I talked to Nate, so that's over with. Long story short, everything's going to be fine." She forced a smile. "I told him we'd get back to L.A. after the Fourth of July weekend. As long as we stay out of the spotlight, he's okay with this trip."

"There are no spotlights here," he said, his soft drawl a comfort after Nate's snarling. "Come on and get some breakfast before the kids eat it all."

* * * * *

The kids were more fun than Jenna could have imagined, running around, playing and yelling outside, or huddling over the video game system in the living room. She didn't mind giving up her bed—the couch—during the day. After a couple days, she knew most of the names in Caleb's family, and was even trusted to rock the youngest baby on the porch while his sister stole a quick nap.

She'd done a lot of charity work with babies over the past year. Caleb told everyone about her charities with a clear note of pride in his voice, but to hold a fat, sweet, slightly sweaty baby on the porch in a Texas summer was different. It was *pure*. That word came to her repeatedly to describe the way of life around her. There were no agendas, no sadness, no posturing. Even Caleb's great-grandma, who was cranky, old, and infirm, smiled and joked with the rest of the family several times a day.

It made her love Caleb more, always more. It wasn't like they could do anything about it, without a private bedroom to retreat to. But it wasn't only the sex that made her love him. This trip home showcased his caring side, his family side, which, combined with his capability as a protector and bodyguard, made him damn near one of the most perfect men alive.

And rocking his little baby nephew made her think about having a baby with him, and a real marriage with love and caring. Which was nonsense, of course. She couldn't have that life now, even if she could get away from her fake marriage with Nate. Caleb was young, she was a few years away from forty. He had his whole life and career ahead of him, as well as this huge, loving family, and she had... Well, she had nothing to bring to the table family-wise.

July Fourth arrived, brimming with cowboy hats, American flags, and summer heat. Amid the flurry of preparations, the already crowded homestead seemed to burst at the seams. Driving-distance family arrived from Lubbock, Dickens, and Paducah. Some cousins showed up from Peacock, Texas, and others from as far away as Dallas. The backyard tables groaned with food from family and neighbors, and the party was in full swing by noon.

Jenna was introduced as a "guest," rather than Caleb's client. If people had questions about her, or recognized her as a movie star's wife, no one said anything. For a while, she was on guard for cameras and cell phones, but no one had them out. This party was about catching up, talking and interacting, sharing stories and laughing out loud. He'd told her she wouldn't have to worry about her privacy, and she believed now that he was right.

After that, she felt more comfortable. Caleb introduced her to dozens of friends, and everyone treated her like a real person, not a Hollywood interloper. In late afternoon, when everyone was stuffed to the gills with food, the dancing started. There wasn't a band or DJ, like at a Hollywood party. No, people brought out their instruments, guitars, fiddles, horns, saxes, tambourines, and harmonicas, sat beside a clearing, and played whatever songs people called out. It was beautiful. Amazing.

Pure.

Caleb sought her out so they could sit by the dance floor together, at a weathered picnic table in the shade.

"Having fun?" he asked.

She just stared at him, grinning, not knowing how to explain how fun this really was. Just people being genuine and kind, sharing their talents in the most beautiful, natural surroundings. It made her want to cry.

"We can dance if you want," he said, reading the emotion in her gaze. "Nobody cares about technique here."

"That's the best part about it." She looked past the cowboy-booted dancers to the casually assembled band. "I've never heard music like this. It's so...alive."

He laughed. "The band grows every year. Someday they'll put up a stage."

"Oh God." Jenna squinted, not believing her eyes. She pointed to a petite woman with a head of brunette curls. "That's Caressa Gallo, isn't it? She's back again."

"Yeah. She comes here a lot. She lives and works out of Dallas, but she started an orchestra program at the local school here in Spur, and funds a foundation to keep them in instructors and instruments. It's pretty amazing."

"Look at that little girl beside her. She's adorable. I didn't know they made cellos so small."

"They had it specially made for her. That's Caressa's daughter." He paused, rubbing the back of his neck. "My niece."

Caressa's daughter was his niece? It took a minute for her to put things together. "Caressa Gallo is married to your brother? The one who worked for Ironclad?"

"Works for Ironclad, yes. He still takes assignments in Dallas sometimes."

"So..." She bit the inside of her cheek. "They met that way? He was her bodyguard, and they ended up getting married?"

"Yes."

She stared at Caressa, and remembered meeting the brother, Kyle, earlier. "You didn't tell me that before. You just said Caressa was his client."

"Yeah."

"Why didn't you tell me they got married?"

He stared at her, his blue eyes guileless, even though his cheeks flushed. "I just thought..."

"That it was none of my business?"

"No."

"You were worried I might get ideas? That I might want to marry you, too? Don't flatter yourself."

"Jenna."

"I'm already married, if you didn't notice."

The look on his face, the embarrassment and regret, made her feel worse. She stood from the picnic bench and started toward the house. He was behind her a moment later, impeding her progress. He corralled her in the shadows where no one could see, trapping her back against his front.

"I'm sorry. I didn't tell you because..."

He clearly didn't know the because, or couldn't admit it to himself. When he pressed his cheek to hers, she pulled away.

"I know why you didn't tell me, Caleb. Because there's no hope of a future for us." She struggled as he held her in an embrace. "I have no idea what we're doing. Where we're going."

"I don't know, either."

The taut angst in his voice quieted her as he held her against his chest. When he nudged her face up, she couldn't meet his gaze.

"I don't know where we're going," he said. "But I care about you all the same. I'm afraid of planning anything for the future, or giving you false hope. Yes, my brother married his client. They fell in love. I'm falling in love with you too, Jenna, but I don't know how that ends up."

She was going to cry, hard. She was going to weep with the devastation of coming up against these boundaries, and she wanted to cry alone, away from lucky Caressa and her ex-bodyguard husband, and her beautiful, cello-playing daughter. She wanted to do it away from the rollicking party that surrounded her, that happiness she could never have.

"Where are you going?"

"To be alone," she said. "Please."

"Are you okay?"

"I will be."

And she would. She'd pull herself together and smile again, eventually. That was her job. She wasn't going to shatter any mirrors in the Winchell household, but she was going to cry for a while in the little floral bathroom, because she wanted something she couldn't have, something that so many of the revelers around her took for granted.

"Please," she said, holding the tears back long enough to convince him she wasn't going to do any mirror smashing. He let her go, dropping her hand when she pulled away.

* * * * *

"Hey, Caleb," Kyle said as he joined him on the porch. Caleb was waiting there because it was the closest place he could give Jenna space, but still be there if she needed help. His older brother's eyes communicated concern. "I saw Jenna head inside. Is she all right?"

"Yeah." As close as he and Kyle were, he couldn't tell him what they'd just fought about. There was the matter of Jenna's privacy. *She's upset because you married Caressa, and I can't ever marry her.* "She gets antsy in crowds," he said instead. "I don't know what I was thinking, bringing her here."

His brother sat in the chair next to him, looking out at the noisy party from their shaded outlook.

"I have an idea what you were thinking," he said after a moment. "She's a beautiful woman."

"That's not it, Kyle. It's not that kind of thing. She needed to get away for a while, from Hollywood and crowds and crazy knife-wielding attackers."

"I heard about that. You doing okay?"

"I'm feeling better. I did what had to be done. It happened so fast, I was glad for the military training. Things just kicked into gear."

"Before you know it, Ironclad will be putting you on diplomatic assignments in war-torn hotspots. Makes me glad I have more of a personal assistant skill set."

"If someone came for Caressa, you'd do something about it." Caleb shrugged. "You don't think. You just act."

"Is she your Caressa?" Kyle asked, too astute.

"No. She's my client. My protectee. Anyway, she's married."

"Oh, that's right. Nathaniel York." His silence told Caleb his brother suspected what a lot of other people in the security world suspected. "They've been together a while, for a Hollywood couple. They must have a pretty tight relationship."

"A pretty tight contractual agreement," he said, because he could trust Kyle. He'd worked with an A-lister for a while, and knew the value of discretion.

"Ah." His brother didn't sound surprised. "So it *is* like that."

"It is like that," Caleb repeated. "And it's starting to grate on her pretty bad."

They sat a moment longer, watching the sun move closer to the horizon. Maybe Kyle was waiting for him to confess his true feelings for Jenna, how his job protecting her had turned into something so much more than a security assignment.

"Your heart's involved," Kyle said, breaking the silence.

Well, that was a simple way to express what he felt. All he could do was agree in a quiet voice. "Yeah, my heart's involved. Watching her struggle, knowing her disappointment... There's so much more to it than I could have imagined."

"There always is, in those kinds of marriages. It's tough to stay out of it."

"I haven't stayed out of it."

"Obviously. I saw you holding her while I was pissing in the woods."

He waited to hear what Kyle would say about that. His brother wouldn't judge him, considering he'd fallen in love with his own client. Of course, Caressa hadn't been married at the time.

"Is it new, this forbidden romance?" his brother asked.

"Not that new. It developed over time."

"Does Nathaniel care?"

Caleb rubbed his forehead with a low growl of distress. "He cares as much as it affects his image, and his fake marriage's image. We don't dare express anything in public, or in front of him and his boyfriend."

"The bodyguard, yes? The one that's always shadowing him a little too close?"

"Yeah." He lifted his head, anger flattening his lips in a line. "They're both such assholes. They're awful to her. She and the boyfriend..." He didn't dare go there, didn't trust himself to describe to his brother how deep the animosity went. "Let me put it this way. I was hired to protect her from him. The whole situation is fucked up, and it's a fucking miserable way for her to live."

"So you're providing, what? Temporary relief? A shoulder to cry on?"

Caleb sighed.

"You're sleeping with her?"

"It sounds sleazy, I know. I only meant to comfort her, but one thing led to another... We have this chemistry."

"It shows, probably more than the two of you think, and the cameras are always watching."

"I know." Jesus, he knew about being on guard. He'd spent far too much of his youth in active war zones, and now he felt like an old, tired man. "I don't know what to do. I don't want to hurt her, or cause her problems, but we're kind of fucked either way."

"Would she leave Nathaniel?"

"She thinks she can't, that she *legally* can't, which is bullshit. He's kept her isolated for so long, surrounded by his people, playing his game and performing at his appearances, she doesn't remember how real life works. Being here is like a jail break for her, and she's having fun, but there's always that tension under the surface, the pressure to play this role she doesn't want anymore, and I don't know what to do about that." He leaned his head back, staring at the awning above them. "I feel powerless to help her, really help her, and that's a shitty feeling."

"Ironclad tells you not to get emotionally involved with clients, but sometimes you can't help it. I know, I've been there, obviously. The things that make you a good protector also leave you open to catching feelings."

"Catching feelings." Caleb snorted. "Like some kind of disease."

"It's not a disease, it's a real thing. When I met Caressa, she was a hot mess. I wanted to run in the other direction, but some part of me also knew she was barely surviving. I couldn't abandon her. Helping turned to caring, and caring turned to loving. I don't regret it."

He said the last sentence with slow gravity, as if to imprint the words in Caleb's brain. *I don't regret it.* One short sentence with so much to say. If Caleb didn't help Jenna in some way, if he walked away from her situation when the assignment was through, he'd regret it forever. But to disrupt her life and encourage her to leave her marriage... Where was the integrity there? The morality?

"It's a tough situation," he said, his voice tightening with emotion. "I'll have to figure out what to do."

"She's the one who needs to figure out what to do," his brother corrected. "Your job is to be there to protect her, whatever she decides." They watched the dancers make a line for some good old Texas stomping. "Hey, have you taken Jenna out to Burger's Pond?"

"Jesus." Caleb blinked at his brother. "I'd almost forgotten about Burger's Pond."

"How could you forget about it, man? When's the last time you went?"

"Before the Army. I haven't thought to go since then."

"That's half your problem there. Take Jenna out to Burger's and see what she thinks of it. They don't have views like that in Hollywood, or anywhere I've seen."

"You're right. I'm sure she'll love it. I should probably go in and check on her."

"Yeah, you probably should." He looked at his watch. "It's only an hour or so until dusk."

14.
BURGER'S POND

"Where the hell are you taking me?" asked Jenna as Caleb led her through dry, knee-high patches of grass. "Where are we?"

"Somewhere near the edge of Mr. Burger's property. Don't worry, he doesn't mind."

"Are you going to murder me out here?"

"I'm supposed to protect you, not murder you. Trust me. You're going to love this."

His fingers tightened around hers with a reassuring squeeze. Even though they'd hiked at least a mile from the party, strains of jovial country music still drifted to them on the occasional soft breeze.

"Over here," he said, leading her down a rise and under a canopy of trees. They followed a well-worn path down to a small, still pond surrounded by bushes and low hanging branches. One side was edged by a rock ledge, like a small country quarry.

"This is so pretty. How'd you know this was here?"

"Everyone knows this is here." He put down the blanket he'd brought from the house, spreading it on the ground near the shore. "Have a seat. The show starts soon."

"Fireworks?"

"Not fireworks. Not yet." He pulled her down with him onto the blanket. "Just watch."

Dusk was deepening. The sunlight that had seen them here was setting, casting shadows across their lush green surroundings. "There's so much *nature* in Texas," she said. She was trying to be more pleasant company after her meltdown over Caressa. Kyle and Caressa were an adorable, loving couple, and her getting salty at Caleb served no purpose at all. "There's so much green everywhere, even with the heat and dust."

"Yeah, Texas is a lively place. We have our problems though, with hurricanes and droughts, and the redneck contingent trying to secede."

"Secede?"

"From the United States. They think Texas should go back to being its own sovereign nation." He said this in an exaggerated drawl that made Jenna laugh. A moment later, a bug lit up a few feet in front of them.

"Look!" She pointed it out to Caleb. "A firefly. I haven't seen one in an eternity." As she said it, another lit up, and another. Her gaze darted around and she saw, suddenly, dozens more blinking over the water and in the trees. "Oh my word," she said softly, an expression picked up from his mother over the past few days. "Oh my word. Look."

He smiled and gazed out across the water. Every moment, there were more fireflies, more blinking lights, until fairy-like sparkles spread around the whole pond.

"The people here call it nature's fireworks," he explained, reaching out to capture one of the drifting bugs. "There's some weird aggregation of fireflies, just around this pond."

She watched in awe, seeing a wonder of nature she'd never seen before, and would probably never see again. "It's like another world," she whispered. "It's otherworldly. If I lived here, I would sleep here every night."

"The bugs don't light up all night, just an hour or so. Longer in high summer when they're breeding." He laughed. "If my parents weren't having a party, we might have run across another couple here. It's a popular makeout place."

She was so used to him in suits, the consummate professional, but she could also see him here as a local kid, before the military, before Hollywood. "Did *you* bring girls here?" she asked, raising a brow.

"Not me," he replied, the picture of innocence. "My high school girlfriend was terrified of bugs."

"These aren't bugs." She reached out, and a firefly landed on her finger. "They're magical creatures, because they sparkle."

She rose to walk closer to the pond, and Caleb followed. They ended up on a boulder overlooking the water, with the fireflies' lights dancing above them, as well as below, reflected in the pond.

"We can jump in if you want," he said, nodding to the bug-lit surface. "People swim here all the time."

She inched closer to him, leaning against his side. "I've tried a lot of new things here in Texas, but jumping into a dark pond might be my limit."

"You have tried a lot of new things." He put a finger under her chin, tilting her head up for a kiss. As they parted, a bug flew between them, lighting up their intimate world.

"This is so real," she said, resting her cheek against his. "Thank you for showing me this."

"My pleasure."

"Not just this pond, but everything. Your family, your town, the conversations and the food..." She sighed. "So much food. This is real life." She didn't know how to make him understand what she was trying to explain. "It's so real it almost hurts my heart. I'm not used to this. It makes me realize..." She paused, swallowing hard. Was she going to cry? "It makes me realize how much I'm missing out on, with the life I chose. You told me once that I had to leave my marriage, and I know I do, I just..." She sat back from him. "I just don't know how to do it."

"I've been thinking about this a lot, Jenna." His eyes held hers, the familiar blue glinting in the dusky surroundings. "And I think you'll know how to do things when the time's right."

"So I just wait?"

"Not just wait. Prepare. Be ready for anything, so when the time comes, you can act. I've told you before, you're stronger than you think."

"Prepare? Be ready for anything? Sounds like something they taught you in the Army." She leaned into him again. "Maybe I can never be happy. I was at that luxury place in Taos and I couldn't be happy, I live in a Hollywood mansion and I can't be happy, now I'm here and I can't be happy either. Even if you and I..." A blush heated her cheeks. "Even if you and I could be together, I still might not be happy."

He held her close, running a hand up and down her arm. "The thing about happy, sweetheart, is that it has to come from within. Haven't you ever heard that saying about making your own happiness? And as much as I adore you..." He tilted her head up, kissing her in the humid Texas night. "As much as I'd love to marry you like my brother married Caressa, falling in love with your bodyguard isn't the only way to fix your life. You have options."

"Falling in love worked out for them, didn't it? And you're more than my bodyguard."

His gaze didn't falter, even though she was whining at him. "I'm sorry," she said. "I don't know why I'm poking at you. Why would you want to marry me anyway? You're so young."

"It has nothing to do with age. And some would say marriage has nothing to do with love."

"That doesn't sound very Texas of you. I thought you had old fashioned values."

"I do." He grinned, lacing his fingers into her hair. "That's why all of this is so difficult."

He kissed her again, harder, maybe to shut her up, maybe because they hadn't been able to sleep together for days now. She closed her eyes, giving herself up to his possessive kiss. Behind her lids, fireflies still blinked in her imagination. *Be ready for anything*, he said. *Be ready...*

He always made her feel ready for anything. When they peeled themselves away from each other, he went for the blanket and spread it out in a more secluded part of the clearing. They lay together, half-kissing, half-undressing while they watched the fireflies blink out, then they turned their attention to each other. She pressed her body to his in the dark, thrilling to his touch. He stroked a hand down her back, easing down her jeans to cup her ass.

"I haven't had enough time alone with you," he said. His lips against her neck made her shiver in anticipation. And nerves.

"What if someone comes?"

He growled softly. "No one's going to come with the barbeque going on, and even if they did, they wouldn't see us in the dark."

"What about coyotes? Or bears?"

"They prefer barbeque too. Let's take this off."

Her shirt had already been tossed to the bottom of the blanket. Her bra was next, then her jeans. "What if bugs crawl on us?" she whispered.

"What if you stop worrying?" His wandering hands stroked down to her pussy and hovered over her clit. "Maybe I can make you forget about bugs for a while."

"Maybe," she said, already going weak. She squirmed against his solid physique. "Please touch me."

"Are you going to stop worrying?"

"Oh, yes. I'm going to try."

He held her gaze as he stroked her with practiced dexterity, first over her panties, then on her bare, wet cleft. While he drove her crazy, she traced his cock's outline through his jeans. She didn't miss his suit at all. When they went back to Hollywood, he'd have to wear the suit again, and she'd be back in the world she hated, the fake, unnatural world that was nothing like a Texas barbeque and a still country pond.

"I wish we could be like this forever," she said, unbuttoning his jeans and working at his zipper. "I know that sounds stupid and dreamy."

"It sounds wonderful." He smothered the rest of her musings in a hard kiss as she gripped his rigid, velvety length.

"Oh no." She broke away, coming up for air. "We don't have a condom."

He held up a hand, a rubber cinched between two fingers. "I came prepared."

She clung to his shoulders while he put it on, hungry for his intensity and force. She spread her legs, her clit aching for him to come into her, but when she tried to pull him forward, he held back.

"No." His thick cock nestled between her legs, teasing her. "I want you to be on top."

She would have argued if she didn't so desperately want him inside. She would have asked, *Why? I'd rather be safe and protected underneath you, especially here, where bears and coyotes could be lurking around.*

But as soon as he positioned her straddling his hips, her complaints faded away, replaced by the delicious sensation of his cock easing inside her and stretching her walls. She could look down at his spectacular body and watch his abs working as he thrust into her. His shoulders were tense and he gritted his teeth whenever she squeezed around him. She liked doing that to him. It gave her such a feeling of power.

"Jesus, Jenna," he said, gripping her hips. "You're too beautiful for words."

No one had ever said anything like that to her before, and she would have said it back to him, but her heart felt too full to talk. Or maybe her pussy was too full. It was probably a combination of both. Maybe she needed to stop trying to find words for the thing going on between them. Tryst, relationship, affair, none of them sufficed. What they had was too beautiful for words.

She would just experience Caleb's love and care, and appreciate it in her soul. She arched her shoulders back as he anchored her hips, working to bring her to orgasm. She spread her arms up into the darkness as her pleasure mounted, an impulsive gesture that felt daring and wonderful. Cooler evening air blew across her sensitized skin, and her nipples tightened under Caleb's regard. Maybe the fireflies were watching them now, just as she and Caleb had watched their light show. But no paparazzi or gawkers were watching, which gave her the freedom to let go.

"Yes, baby." His fingers tightened on her hips. "That's right. Yes, sweetheart."

"You're killing me," she said, but what she meant was, "You're giving me such a wonderful gift." Her orgasm bloomed, starting at the place they were connected, then taking over her whole body as she shuddered beneath the dark shelter of the trees. Caleb tensed beneath her as she gasped through her climax. When she opened her eyes to look down at him and watch him come, she saw a stray spark of light in her peripheral vision. Oh God, a camera?

No, it was the first firework of the evening, barely visible through the branches. It raced into the sky and exploded in a cascade of color, complete with accompanying boom.

"You're too beautiful for words," she whispered in Caleb's ear, but she wasn't sure he heard her over his rasping breath. Either way, he rewarded her with another deep, possessive kiss as more fireworks went off in the moonless sky.

The booms rolled across the Texas plains as they lay back in each other's arms, exhausted and replete, watching the light show that marked the party's high point. Occasionally, the fireworks were bright enough to shine through the trees' cover, lighting up Caleb's face with pastel colors of pink, blue, or green.

They might not know where they were going, but this moment was something she'd always treasure, no matter where they ended up.

15.
CONSEQUENCES

"I'm not ready for this," Jenna said, holding Caleb's arm. "I'm not ready for the confrontation."

"I know." He did what he could to soothe her, but he didn't feel ready either. As soon as they'd arrived at the York mansion, Gladys was knocking at the door, inviting Jenna to have dinner with Nate. "Just the two of you," she'd said, eyeing Caleb in the background. "Nate can't wait to reconnect. He's missed you so much."

Gladys didn't ask how Jenna had enjoyed her travels, or whether she was feeling better than when she'd left. Based on Gladys' saccharine invitation and rapidly blinking eyes, Jenna wasn't going to enjoy this meeting, and Caleb couldn't be in the room with her to offer support.

"Remember what we talked about," he said. "You're stronger than you think. You have power in this relationship too."

"You keep saying that, but I'm not feeling it."

Caleb wanted to punch Nate's lights out for doing this to Jenna. All the work he'd done to build her up and find her some respite outside her toxic marriage, and Nate had undone it with one "invitation to dinner" that wasn't even delivered in person.

"What if Tom's there too?" she fretted.

"Insist to Nate that you want to talk in private. 'Just the two of you,' that's what Gladys said."

"Gladys is a liar and so are the other assholes." She couldn't seem to bring herself to say their names. "I want to run away again already. I want to go back to Spur."

"I wish you could, but you need to face him and set him straight about what you're feeling. He's your husband, whether it's a real thing or not. Maybe you can make him see that things need to change, *really* change, or else..."

Or else you'll leave him. Caleb needed her to realize that was an option, not just for her own sanity, but because it would pave the way for them to be together. Selfish motive, but he was getting to the point he didn't care.

"I'll be right outside the door," he reassured her. "If things get bad, yell for me. If he starts shouting threats or gets physical with you—"

"You'll beat him up?"

"Damn straight I will."

He wasn't lying. He'd beat the shit out of Nate, and Tom too, if they ever gave him a legally permissible reason to do so. He wished he could do it right now. He wished he could do it every fucking minute of every day, from the time he woke up until the time he fell asleep. At Ironclad, they'd call that being "overinvolved." They'd point to the way he lived in Jenna's wing even when he wasn't working, when the other security guys were looking after her. They'd ask if he needed a transfer, if he was in too deep.

He was in really fucking deep, but in no sense was he ready to get out. It was an effort not to hold her hand as Gladys escorted them to Nate's side of the house, to his fancy dining room where they'd "reconnect."

You're strong. He'd said it to her so many times by now. He hoped she'd call on that strength when Nate started trying to manipulate her.

Because that self-obsessed bastard definitely would.

* * * * *

To Jenna's relief, it was just the two of them, and Nate's eyes weren't flashing with fire and brimstone the way she'd expected. No, something else was afoot. As Nate's personal sushi chef served their food, Jenna wondered if he'd go the poisoning route, and feed her some fugu disguised as a tuna roll.

"You probably thought I'd be mad," he said, tapping his chopsticks on the table, "And I am mad, but I'm mad at myself. I had no idea you were so desperate to get away from the spotlight. I appreciate that you and Caleb went somewhere you wouldn't be seen together. Where was it? Stirrup? Burlap?"

"Spur," she said.

"Oh, yeah. I knew it was something country like that. I guess you felt right at home."

Ah, there was the dig. She'd known he was only pretending to be nice. He always alluded to her white-trash roots when he really wanted to hurt her.

"I'm sorry I bolted without warning you," she said. "We were careful, though. If we'd taken the whole security team, we would have been followed."

"Yes, because I'm a notable person, arguably the most famous movie star in the world."

Did he want her to lift her glass in a toast? She poked a maki roll, nudging it across her plate. "I know you're famous, Nate. That's why we were so careful."

He worked his jaw as he stared at the table, then gazed back at her, his eyes wet with tears. "I just wasn't ready for this, you know? I wasn't ready to lose your allegiance so soon. We've been through so much together, and this...this behavior of yours has come out of nowhere. Well, not nowhere. I guess it's the bodyguard. This all started when he came."

She gritted her teeth so she wouldn't lash out at him. Fake tears, really? She hated how manipulative he was, especially when he was perfectly aware she knew him well enough to see through his melodramatic crap.

"It started before the bodyguard," she said, keeping her voice level. "Remember? We hired the bodyguard because of Tom, because your lover couldn't keep his crazy shit in check. And that wasn't my fault."

"It was partly your fault," he said, then wiped away a tear, remember his victim act. "I don't know, Jen, I just feel like everything's falling to pieces and I don't know how to stop it. What do we do? I don't want to lose you. We've been together so long."

"There's one thing you could do, but it's impossible."

"Impossible?"

"You could get rid of Tom."

"Jenna, I'm trying to have a realistic conversation. I'm sure you don't mean what you just said."

"You asked and I answered you. If you broke up with Tom, maybe we could find a way to make things work."

Even as she said it, she knew it was a lie. Getting rid of Tom would make her life easier, and Nate's life healthier, but things would never revert to some easy, fake marriage arrangement again. She was still in love with her bodyguard, and still desperate to live an honest, truthful life.

"Tom's my partner," Nate said. "The other half of me. You don't understand our relationship, our thing. You never have."

"He's not good for you," she cut in before he could get going. "He controls you. He drinks and cokes and needs an anger management counselor—"

"You're one to talk about drinking."

Jenna scowled. "You know I don't drink anymore, mainly because I don't want to end up like him. He takes advantage of your trust and money, and treats your wife like shit. If he wanted to make you happy, he'd try to get along with me."

There were no more tears. Nate was getting worked up as he pushed his plate away. "Tom's mine, don't you get that? You don't get a say in our relationship."

"He's toxic. He's a substance-abusing bomb ready to explode, and that's way more dangerous than me running off to Texas for a few days."

There was a commotion outside the door, raised male voices. Tom came striding into the room with Caleb at his heels.

"Has he been listening to our conversation?" Jenna asked, indignant. "Oh, poor Tommy. He must be angry." Caleb's presence emboldened her as she stood and turned on Tom. "Did I say too many mean things about you? Too many true things that hit close to home?"

"Why can't you control your wife?" Tom said to Nate, his narrowed eyes flashing. "I shouldn't have left the two of you alone."

Nate looked past Tom to Caleb, his jaw tense. "Get out, please, Caleb. This is a private conversation."

Caleb stayed where he was, planted between her and Tom. "If he's here," he said, pointing to Tom, "I'm going to stay."

"Mr. York told you to leave, and this is his house," said Tom in a hard voice.

"And I said I wouldn't leave my client's side as long as you're in the room."

Tom squared his shoulders, taking an aggressive step in Caleb's direction. "What the fuck do you mean by that?"

Jenna shivered at the way Caleb's features hardened. Nate's voice rose as he tried again. "Tom, let's have some sushi in the kitchen. Let Jen go with her bodyguard. You know I'd never leave you, so who cares what she says? Who fucking cares?"

"I care." He pointed at her. "These are our lives, you little bitch. Why are you always messing with us? Why can't you just smile and pose and hold up your fucking end of the deal? It's not that hard. If Nate won't hold you to it, I will."

Caleb held up a hand in Tom's direction. "I'm not going to allow you to speak abusively to my client. Lower your voice or leave the room."

"Leave the room?" Tom forced a laugh. "You can kiss your job goodbye, asshole, if you keep this bullshit up. You don't order us around. You work for Mr. York."

"So do you, and he asked you to let up."

"Are you lecturing me now?" His laugh sounded more like a growl. "Now that you're fucking her, you think you're untouchable? You can still be fired."

"You can't fire him," Jenna said. "I have some power in this relationship. As much as you hate it, I have more power than you."

When she spoke up for herself, it drove Tom over the edge. Maybe she used the strident voice because she knew it would make him lose it. Nate said, "No, Tom, no," as his lover launched himself at her, hands extended to hit, punch, slap. When Caleb caught him and pushed him back, Tom tried to go around him, considering he probably outweighed Caleb by fifty pounds.

But Caleb was strong, soldier-strong. They only grappled a moment before Caleb had him in a headlock. He subdued him so quickly Jenna barely had time to smother a scream. Tom's legs kicked and his hands flailed back, trying to attack Caleb, but he couldn't breathe.

"Let him go," Nate shouted, his voice pitched high in panic. "You're killing him."

Yes, Jenna thought. *He might kill him.* He had the same focused, intent look he'd worn in those videos of her attack, the ones she'd watched with morbid curiosity. "Caleb," she said softly, as Tom gasped for air.

His eyes met hers, and she saw he was still there, however angry and focused he was. He dropped Tom, releasing him from the headlock and pushing him forward to gasp and flail on the dining room floor.

Nate rushed to his side, like he could help him regain his breath. "Easy, baby. Breathe deep, in and out. It's okay." He looked up at Caleb. "You maniac. You fucking menace. You're going to jail for this. Jenna, call the police."

"I'm not calling the police." Jenna stood over them, partly to keep Caleb from attacking again. His hands were still in fists. "Tom went after me first. I'll tell them the truth."

"They won't believe you, they'll believe me," Nate yelled. Tom blinked, moving his lips, but no sound came out. "Your psycho bodyguard has already killed someone else."

"Between the two of us, who's more afraid of an investigation?" she yelled back. "And what might the police discover if I had to tell the truth, the whole truth, and nothing but the fucking truth? You think truth is a movie, Nate, a script you can edit at will, but the police will demand the *actual truth*."

Nate looked between her and Caleb. Her hands were in fists, ready to take on Tom herself if she had to. Caleb stood beside her, dead calm and composed.

"Get your maniac bodyguard out of here," he said as Tom started to come around. "And if you don't want me to call the police on that fucking psychopath, get him and all his shit out of my house now. You're fired," he said, turning his wrath to Caleb. "If you set foot in this house again, I'm reporting you for attempted murder. That's not a threat, it's a promise. Where's the fucking security around here?" Nate was losing it. "Where's the fucking security?" he howled.

"You don't need to call security," Caleb answered in a clipped drawl. "I'll be out of your house in fifteen minutes." He glanced down at Tom for a moment of scathing hatred. "Maybe less."

* * * * *

"Shit," he said, as he locked them into her wing of the house. "That felt good. That felt amazing, but I shouldn't have done it. I'm sorry, Jenna."

"Don't be sorry."

"I wanted to kill him. I think I'll kill Tom if I stay here."

His words half-pleased and half-terrified her. As much as she wanted him to remain as her bodyguard, she knew he had to go, quickly, before Tom convinced Nate to call the cops and press charges.

So she helped him pack, throwing things into suitcases. He hadn't brought much, just some books, a couple guns, and a bunch of suits. She let him handle the guns.

"I shouldn't have done that," he muttered. "I shouldn't have used that much force. I didn't have to."

"You were protecting me," she said, handing over piles of socks and undershirts.

He glanced up at her, businesslike, decisive. "You're coming with me, okay? At least for now. I can't leave you here, not with Tom and Nate all wound up."

"I'm definitely coming with you. Someone has to help you carry these suitcases to your car."

She wondered why she felt so calm. When they finished packing, they hauled his stuff to the door, where security met them to "help." As nice as some of them were, they were on Nate's side. They hovered around as she helped him put suitcases in his trunk. When she moved for the passenger door, one of them stopped her.

"Mrs. York, I'm sorry. Mr. York doesn't want you to go."

She saw Caleb freeze, and she felt a little frozen too. She wasn't a hostage here, a prisoner. "I'm just going for a while," she said. "He'll bring me home."

"You shouldn't leave the property without security."

"We're not going anywhere public," she argued. "I'm just helping him take his stuff to his place."

Caleb watched her. She knew he wanted to intervene, but she also knew he couldn't, not without worsening the situation. She opened the door and sat in the car.

"If Mr. York wants me to stay, he can come and try to make me. But I want to go out for a while."

The security agent—he had a kind face, really—put his hand on the door. He, too, was calculating how far he could intervene.

"I have the right to leave, don't I?" she asked softly. "You can't stop me if I want to go."

"We'll have to tell Mr. York."

"That's fine."

She slammed the door shut as soon as he moved his hand, and Caleb got in the driver's seat and cranked the engine. It felt like a getaway, even though his car was a very sedate, fuel-efficient sedan.

"They didn't stop me," she said, a little shaky now that the incident had passed. "I stood up to them."

"You're a badass."

The security guys stepped back as he put the car in reverse, staring after them mournfully. Hysterical giggles rose in her throat.

"You okay?" he asked.

"I don't know. For the first time in a long time..." She closed her eyes and sat back in his seat, on her own, independent. Alive. "I can feel myself coming back. It's like there's a real world again."

"Even if that real world is a little fucked up at the moment."

He was ever practical, her serious bodyguard. Yes, there would be repercussions from what had happened tonight, last week, repercussions stretching back to the first time he'd held her, the first time they'd kissed. But for the first time in a long time, she wasn't afraid of those repercussions.

"I can still visit you, right? Even if you aren't my bodyguard?" That was the main thing she was thinking about, that they couldn't lose the connection they had. "I can visit you whenever I feel like it, right?"

"Sure, but we'll have to be careful. I think you're skirting the limits of that godforsaken contract Nate hooked you into, and that he'll try to threaten you into compliance. But if you want to be with me, I won't let anyone stand in your way."

Free, so free. She looked out the window as they navigated the rolling hills. "I get to see where you live now. In all this time, I've never been to your place."

He gave her a look that made her think about the things they could do at his place, a look full of longing, exasperation, and some lingering adrenaline that made her tremble.

"It's not as nice as your mansion on the hill," he warned her.

"It's not my mansion, it's Nate's, and I don't care what your place is like, as long as you're in it."

"Oh, I'm in it," he said, stroking a hand up her leg. "For better or worse."

16.
OUT THERE

Caleb told Jenna to drop the suitcases wherever. He needed her in his bed, now, immediately. He needed her safe and aroused, all his, at least in his fantasies. He walked her down the hall to his room, stripping off her clothes as they went. "I wonder if you could join me in the bedroom, sweetheart."

"I'd be happy to," she said, tilting up her face for a kiss as he paused to molest her against the wall.

He'd been raised better. He'd been raised to respect other's marriages, and not have sex without a wedding ring on his finger. But how you were raised wasn't always how you turned out.

"Oh God, Caleb," she sighed as he filled his hands with her lush breasts. "I love it at your place." Her fingers tugged his hair as he sucked first one nipple, then the other. His cock strained against his pants.

"Undo me." He pushed her roving hands to his fly. "I need you now."

They both yanked at his belt buckle as he shrugged off his jacket, holster, and shirt. She knelt, unzipping his fly, and he leaned on the wall to steady himself as she took his cock in her hands. She gazed up at him, naked and hot, and gave the head a few teasing swipes with her tongue. Jesus Christ. Didn't she know this wasn't the time to play with him?

At his groan, she gripped him tighter and opened her lips over his cock. Small mouth, big cock. He couldn't shove inside her the way he wanted, so he groaned again as she took him as deep as she could.

"Does that feel good?" she asked.

"I'm dying. Yes."

He fucked her mouth against the wall with as much restraint as he could muster. They were both worked up from the events of the day. A few seconds later, he yanked her off her knees and picked her up so she straddled his hips.

"Are you going to give me a ride?" she asked as he finished kicking off his pants.

"The ride of your life, sweetheart. Hold tight."

He took her to his bed and laid her back, and spread her legs so he could have his turn making her crazy. He toyed with her clit, tonguing her, teasing her with his goatee. He had to hold her by the ankles or she was likely to kick him in the head, but he didn't mind a stray kick or two. He loved that she got so wild; he loved that he could make her forget everything for a while.

He clamped a hand over her mouth when she came, because she tended to be loud. It wasn't so bad in a sprawling, soundproofed mansion. In this cheap apartment, the thin walls would make the neighbors talk.

"I want more," she cried. "That felt so good."

He kissed her, caressing her own sweet-salty scent across her lips. "You're so greedy."

"Yes, and spoiled by my lover."

"I try my best."

He dug a condom out of his bedside drawer and sucked in his breath as he rolled it on. He was so hot for her, so close to losing his mind. He eased inside, reveling in her satisfied sigh. Jolts of pleasure rolled over his body as she started to move.

"You feel too good," she said, shaking her head. "Too amazingly good."

He held her close, kissing her gently, then passionately, then fucking her hard. He wanted to spend all the time he could in this moment, because he didn't know what would come next. His bed was a size smaller than the bed at the mansion, a queen rather than a king, and they kept almost falling off one side or the other as he moved her and thrust in her, and arched his body over hers.

Her second orgasm came quickly, squeezing his shaft in rhythmic pumps of ecstasy. A growl of satisfaction rose from his throat as he came too, violence and completion taking over him. Now she was the one who put her hand over his mouth, trying to muffle his groan. So gorgeous, coming together in tune with her. Pleasure arced through his body, leaving him wrung out. She sprawled under him, her arms spread in contented relaxation. Her lazy smile was his entire world.

* * * * *

His second-floor apartment had a tiny, sad balcony, but Jenna didn't seem to mind. She stood looking out at the tangle of brush behind his apartment, trees growing wild on the side of a hill. "You have a beautiful view," she said, still rumpled from the nap she'd stolen in his bed.

He thought, *beauty is in the eye of the beholder.* That wasn't just a Texas saying. People used it all over the world, in all kinds of languages. He'd seen a lot of ugly things in his life, but he'd learned to recognize beauty, and Jenna was a thing of beauty.

"I love you," he said, confiding what she must already know. He'd intended to say more, but those three words seemed enough as soon as he uttered them. He loved her, that was all that mattered. The age difference, the fact that she was married, the fact that her husband might still accuse him of attempted murder, he didn't care.

"I love you, too." She admitted it without a fuss. Their connection had been a thing for so long, why not name it now? It was love. "I don't know how I'm going to go back now," she said, putting an arm around his waist and hitching her thumb in his shorts. "I feel like I belong here with you."

They embraced, standing at his railing. "Leave Nate," he said when they parted. "Ten years is a long enough time for him to establish his fake heterosexuality, and it's more than enough time for you to put up with Tom. Ask for an exit strategy now, while he's already pissed." He brushed her hair from her eyes and kissed her, lingering over her lips. "I'm not trying to rush you, or pressure you to do anything."

"I want to leave him, I just—"

"I know." He silenced her with another kiss. "Don't think about it now."

He didn't want her to worry. He wasn't worried, not really. He'd sent his resignation letter to Ironclad Solutions while she took her nap, and that was okay. He'd figure out next steps as well as he could, and keep Jenna safe and happy, even though he wasn't on the York payroll anymore. She was what mattered, and he'd slogged his way through complicated times before.

* * * * *

Jenna thought through her situation as Caleb drove her back to Maison de Misery on the Mountain. She had to get out of her marriage to be with him. That was a given. Maybe she could lay low for a couple days, mind her own business, set up some new charity events to paint Nate in a good light, then ask him to give some kind of separation a chance.

She knew he wouldn't agree, but she had to start asking, or nothing would ever change. She crawled into her bed and fell into a restless sleep with dreams of Nate and lawyers and unknown threats, then came awake with a start. Gladys was calling through her bedroom door. She'd broken into her side of the house, and someone was with her, banging, not knocking politely, as Gladys would do.

She looked at her clock. Six-thirty a.m. "Go away," she yelled.

She heard hissing, whispered voices. Gladys said, "Nate and I need to speak to you. It's very important."

"Is Tom there?"

"No." Nate's voice now. "Let us in."

She didn't want them in her bedroom. "I'll meet you in the living room later," she yelled, her voice husky from sleep. "Like, in a couple hours."

"You'll meet us in the living room now, you whoring bitch. Someone took pictures of you last night, photos of you and your damn loverboy on his balcony. Wake the fuck up, Jen, cause shit's about to get real."

Jenna swallowed hard and crawled out of bed, feeling a weight bloom in her chest. Caleb's balcony? They'd been half-dressed, making out. It had been so quiet behind his apartments, she hadn't even thought to check for cameras, but someone had been lurking, spying, looking for the money shot.

How had they known where to find her? How had they known she'd be there with him?

"Just wait," she said, as the banging started again. "I'll be out in a minute."

She pulled her hair back in a messy bun and pulled on a robe, and brushed her teeth forever, stalling for time. Hell, fucking hell. This wasn't how she'd wanted this to go down. When she came down the hall to the living room, Nate was there with Gladys, and two men she didn't recognize, both of them in shiny suits. New bodyguards?

"Hello, Mrs. York," one of them said, gesturing to the chair. "Please join us."

Oh, great. They weren't bodyguards, they were lawyers. Possibly PR executives, or PR lawyers. In any event, this was going to be a hell of a conversation. She conjured Caleb's features in her mind and tried not to panic as she arranged herself in the seat.

"We received some bad news this morning," the other man said, kicking things off with an authoritative frown.

"Bad news." Nate snorted. "That's an understatement."

"Okay, there are photos," she said.

"Yes, babes, lots of them," said Nate. "You hugging your bodyguard, you kissing your bodyguard, you gazing off his chintzy balcony together like a couple of dreamy fucking lovebirds."

"I'm sorry." This was really bad. "We tried to be discreet."

"Do you have any idea how much money it's going to cost to buy those photos and kill the story?"

"You can still kill it?"

"Yes," said Nate, the picture of seething fury. "For twenty million dollars, we can kill the story, but what about the next story, Jen? What about the next set of photos?"

The first shiny-suit guy broke in, perhaps so Nate's brain wouldn't explode as he vented his anger. "We've bought the photos and the story already, but it came at a hefty price, and there's no way to stop the media group—in this case, Celebrity News Network—from following you around the clock, trying to get another story and more hush money. You see the situation we're in."

"I don't understand how Celebrity News knew to go to Caleb's apartment," she said. "We've kept up appearances in public. There was no reason for anyone to suspect we'd be together."

"How many people saw you in Texas?" Gladys asked, blinking convulsively. "One of them could have tried to sell the story for money. All Celebrity News needed for a bombshell was photo evidence—"

"Which anyone in Spur could have provided by taking photos of us at the Winchell's Fourth of July party. And trust me, no one in Spur understands how 'media groups' like Celebrity News work. They wouldn't have known how to sell a story, much less that someone could even do such a thing." She thought of the people she'd met, how friendly and caring they'd all been. "It wasn't someone from Spur, so who was it? Someone on the staff here who saw us leave together? One of the security guys?"

She looked at Nate when she said it, but she could see Gladys in her peripheral vision, hunched over, blinking...looking at Nate too. Not a manager's look, but the look of someone who was really, really worried, because she really, really cared.

That's when Jenna realized that Gladys had called the paparazzi to photograph her and Caleb. Her mind quickly processed the why—because Jenna was becoming a threat to her beloved employer. Also, maybe, Gladys wanted a shot at marrying Nate herself. She adored him, she always had. She was always hopped up and nervous around him.

She stared straight at Gladys, narrowing her eyes. *Bitch, I know, I know it was you.* The shiny-suit men were droning on, talking about codicils to their contractual arrangement, and the possibility of financial penalties for further photos or stories that came out.

"Are you listening?" Nate said, his voice sharp as a knife. "This can't fucking happen again. You have to snap out of this obsession with that bodyguard." He rubbed his forehead with a groan. "Why did we have to hire him? You picked him out," he snarled at Gladys. "Fuck me. What do you want, Jen? I'll get you a baby if you want that. We can use a doctor this time, something failsafe, IVF or whatever it's called. You know, with the kind of money I have, there are places that can sort things out so you can even pick a boy or a girl. Or both. Do you want twins?"

Twins. He thought twins would solve her "obsession with that bodyguard." She pressed her hands to her face, thinking over a thousand things. Caleb, first and foremost. Gladys, the sad, neurotic traitor. Tom, the psychopath, and Nate, who was such a scared, pathetic person when it came down to it. She was living his lie, but Nate was the lie. Everything about him was a lie.

What a horrible way to exist.

"Who are you?" she asked, turning to the shiny-suit brigade. "You're lawyers, right?"

They both nodded. One of them, supremely uncomfortable, licked his lips with a dry sound. She turned back to Nate and took a breath.

"I don't want a baby, not with you. I don't want twins. I want a divorce. I'm sorry, but it's time. We've been doing this long enough."

The room fell into absolute silence. Jenna wondered how hard it was for Gladys to stifle a hyper-blinking smile, or some soft sound of glee. She would be happy. Tom would be happy, even though he'd call her a faithless whore for leaving.

But Nate... He looked stricken.

"You can't... There's no... Divorce isn't an option. We have this..." He grabbed some papers from his lawyer's briefcase. "We have an agreement, a contract. Ours is the dream Hollywood marriage."

"The dream's over."

"But my career!"

"Lots of people get divorced," she countered. "Fifty percent or something, on average, and it's higher for celebrities, way higher. Maybe this will give your fans something to feel good about when their own marriages fail. 'Oh sure, my wife left me, but so did Nathaniel York's, and look at him.'"

"You can't leave me." He looked at the lawyers, his panic turned to outrage. "That's not how this would go down. You wouldn't leave me, I'd leave you. You signed a contract to uphold my image."

His anger brought out the petty, self-interested child. That was all he cared about. Number one: that no one would ever find out he was gay. Number two: that no one would ever think him anything less than the most perfect, desirable, heterosexual male in the world.

She threw up her hands in exasperation. "Whatever. Spin the breakup however you want, with whatever fucking story makes you look best. Talk to your PR people about it. But if I'm the one who's going to look bad, you need to pay me for it."

"Pay you?" He looked at the lawyers again, who flushed deeper the longer this conversation went on. "You're going to get nothing, do you understand that?" His eyes flashed with animosity as he jabbed a finger at her. "If you leave me, you get nothing. No money, no alimony, no baby, no life, not one thing I ever bought for you or provided to you. You walk out of this house with absolutely nothing."

"Mr. York," one of the lawyers began. "By California law—"

"Don't talk to me about the fucking law. Your agency wrote up those contracts. You're going to make sure, if she leaves me, that she doesn't get a cent."

"I don't want your money," she broke in. "And I am leaving you. I'm a different person than I was when I signed those papers ten years ago, and you are too." She gazed at him, appealing to his humanity. "Maybe it's time to think about living a more authentic life, Nate. Times have changed. People are more accepting of—"

"No." He cut her off cold. "Nothing changes for me. I have a persona, a career to uphold."

"You could change so many lives by being honest," she pleaded.

"You want to hear honesty?" He stood and pointed at her, and if his finger was a gun, he would have fired it. "Here's some honesty for you, Jenna York. If you divorce me, you're going to realize you made a huge mistake. You're going to drown in your regrets, and even that boy toy bodyguard of yours won't be able to cheer you up. That's a promise, so why don't you take a few days to think about what you're doing, and get your priorities straight?"

"You don't understand. I've been thinking about it for months now. For years. I can't stay here anymore."

He made an explosive sound of fury. "What do you mean, you can't stay here? You can't go out there." He slung his arm toward the views beyond the window. "I told you, they're waiting for the next photos, the next story. They're camped outside your boyfriend's shitty apartment by the dozens."

"I don't understand. Do you *want* me to stay here?"

"Yes!"

"And do what? Hide my entire life? Let me go, Nate, and find someone else to marry. Have your PR folks work up some story about how we grew apart because of your busy schedule. In a couple months, you can start dating someone new, someone who can heal your damaged soul. Maybe Gladys," she added with an acerbic glance in her direction. "She's someone you can trust."

Nate didn't get her sarcasm, and he'd never believe Gladys was the informant anyway. Everything would always be *her* fault, *her* failing. Jenna didn't care anymore.

"My PR folks will work up a story, all right," he said ominously. "And you can lawyer up as much as you want, but it won't matter. You broke the terms of our contract, and you're going to pay for it one way or another. I'll see to that."

"Why all the spite? Why does it have to be this way?"

But she knew why. It was because he was a damaged person who'd been stuffing down his true self for too long.

"If you want to leave, then go," he said, pointing at the door to her living room. "You can walk out now with the clothes on your back, with what you have right now."

"Mr. York." One of the lawyers finally interceded, pulling her fuming husband into a whispered conference. Of course, Celebrity News Network would have cameras outside their property too, just in case a dramatic breakup took place. The optics of kicking her off the property with only her pajamas and robe might be hard to manage in the press.

A moment later, Gladys was pulled into the whispered conversation. With a last searing glance, Nate stood and stormed away.

So that was that. After all her fear and worry, asking for a divorce had taken less than a quarter hour. Jenna returned to her bedroom, thinking about what she would take and wouldn't take. She'd need some shoes and clothes, just the basics. She didn't want to take any of the designer dresses or jewelry he'd bought for her, or the high-end shoes. She'd take her yarn and knitting needles, and her favorite books.

As for the rest, she didn't need or want it. She started to pack, pondering her money situation. She received a monthly clothes and food allowance that had built up in her account for a while, and she didn't think Nate could get that back, since the money was under her name. It wasn't a generous allowance by any means, but with Caleb's help she could live on it for a while, until things settled down and she could start working again.

Working again... Maybe she could work with children and babies, go to college and become a teacher, or a nurse...

She looked up at a knock. Gladys entered looking pale, her features screwed into a manufactured expression that could almost pass for "sad."

"He can get worked up, can't he?" she said. "If you'll give him some time to calm down..."

"What do you mean?"

"Surely you can't leave now? Today? His team needs time to create a story and set it in motion."

She looked right into Gladys' eyes. "You haven't already been working on a story? You wanted this, right? It was you who tipped off Celebrity News."

"What? That's ridiculous. I'd never do anything to hurt Mr. York's brand."

Jenna turned away. She'd listened to her last lie from Gladys. She continued to pack.

"If you do leave, you can't take anything valued over one hundred dollars," Gladys said quietly. "Any one item, I mean. All the luxury items have to stay."

"For his next wife? Whoever the poor woman is?"

Gladys went silent, watching her throw things into a suitcase that was probably worth more than a hundred dollars. Oh well.

"I don't understand you," Gladys said after a moment. "You could have stayed here forever, living this movie star life. You could have had anything in the world, anything your heart desired."

"Except a real marriage. Real love and a real family."

"Those aren't always what they're cracked up to be."

Jenna knew that. She'd grown up in a fucked up family, but she also knew the dream could be real. Because of Caleb, she'd realized that honesty and integrity actually existed, and that people could have selfless hearts and huge, caring, affectionate families, everyday people without money and fame and PR teams and stylists and managers.

"You'll see when you're out there," Gladys said. "You're going to realize what a mistake you made, but it'll be too late."

Jenna zipped up the few belongings she'd packed and headed to the bathroom to throw her toothbrush and toiletries in a bag. "So how does this work? Can Caleb come get me, or do I need to call a cab?"

"You can't go yet, especially to that man's place. If you leave now, you'll have to go to a hotel out of town, maybe in Pasadena or Glendale. Nate will pay for it. Jenna, honestly, if you go see Caleb again, if there are more photos..."

"Well, Nate won't have to pay hush money now, will he? The more photos, the more wronged he'll look in the divorce."

And she'd be the cheater, the bad one. Fine. She was a cheater, strictly speaking, and if that was the price she had to pay, she was happy to take the fall.

"I'll get an Uber," she told Gladys. She didn't need help carrying her stuff out. One rolling suitcase and an overnight bag, the spoils of her ten-year movie-star life. "You can tell your contact at Celebrity News that Nate and Jenna's perfect marriage is over."

Gladys gave a disapproving tsk and walked out, and Jenna shut the door after her, leaning against it for a moment.

Oh God, this was it. She was getting out and starting a real life, whatever that turned out to be. The feels overcame her and she started to cry, tears soaking her cheeks. She ran to the closet and got dressed in jeans and a light gray hoodie, leaving her cashmere pajamas on the floor.

Then she wiped her tears away and pulled her hair back into a neater twist, and got her shit together. Caleb would be so happy to hear she'd asked for the divorce. He'd be so proud of her.

Even better, for the first time in a long time, she was proud of herself.

I don't know if you're up yet, she texted him, *but things just went sideways. Nate and I are divorcing. I'll call you when I'm in a safe place.*

17.
LET ME IN

Caleb pulled up to the Economy Suites on the outskirts of Los Feliz and checked the address. He'd stopped on the way to buy flowers for Jenna, since he didn't want to tempt her sobriety with champagne. There was something good to celebrate, he hoped, though it was early in the proceedings.

He'd woken to her message—*Nate and I are divorcing*—and wondered why she hadn't come straight to his place with such momentous news. He wanted to hold her and kiss her, and congratulate her. Then he'd read the response to his Ironclad resignation, along with Hector's terse post-script. *This is a bad look for Ironclad. We can't support you in this.*

So he'd booted up his laptop and opened a news site, and realized how much could happen over five or six hours of restless sleep.

Even the big news sites were carrying the story—*NATHANIEL AND JENNA YORK: A DECADE OF ROMANCE ENDS*. Those sites stuck to the basics, showing photos of Nate and Jenna in happier times, and quoting a stilted press release asking the media for space and privacy.

With a sense of dread, he opened a celebrity gossip site. There were no journalistic regulations there, no space or privacy, just overblown headlines. *JENNA YORK SEDUCES BODYGUARD—CONTENTIOUS DIVORCE UNDERWAY*. Another site's headline read *CHEATING JENNA: BOOZE, SEX, AND LIES AS NATE GRIEVES BROKEN MARRIAGE.*

No need to look at any more. They'd all say the same thing, considering the reach of Nate's public relations influence. When the phone rang, flashing Jenna's number, he picked it up.

"Where are you?" he asked. "Do you need help? Are you okay?"

"I'm in Los Feliz, at a hotel. Take down this address, quick, in case we get cut off. I don't know if he's going to cancel my phone."

Caleb wrote the address, wishing he could leap through the phone and embrace her, and try to calm her down. "It's okay, sweetheart. Everything's going to be okay. I'm going to come to you right now."

"Be careful. Paps will try to follow you. Someone took photos of us on your balcony, that's what started this..." Her voice trembled. "Nate paid to bury the pictures, but he might leak them again, now that I've left. He's getting his PR staff to say horrible things about me."

"I know, I saw. It's okay, though. Everything's going to be okay."

She rushed on, her voice thin with stress. "I told Nate I was going to some hotel he booked in Pasadena, but I worried he'd tell the media to trail me, so I came here instead."

"That's good. That's perfect."

"If anyone follows you—"

"I'll make sure no one follows me. I want you to take some deep breaths, okay? I'll be there soon. Are you in a room? Are you settled in?"

"Yes."

"Don't let anyone in until I get there. I'm leaving now. We'll make some calls when I get there, and get everything figured out."

At least, he hoped they'd be able to figure things out. It was amazing how fast the media worked when a celebrity marriage was breaking down. There were paparazzi waiting in front of his apartment building, and more camping out back, but he used his knowledge of evasive driving to lose the ones who followed him when he left.

Now that he was here at the Economy Suites, he could help Jenna figure out her next steps. *Please, please let us figure all this out.* After one last scan of the hotel parking lot, he locked his car and carried the flowers into the hotel. The lobby smelled like burnt coffee and chlorine from the indoor pool.

He scanned the entrance's layout and sized up security. Not bad. The place was well lit. They gave out electronic cards as room keys, and the rooms were only accessible from the inside of the property. He took the stairs to the second floor and knocked on room 241.

"It's me," he said quietly. "Let me in."

She opened the door. As he'd expected, she looked like hell, but she also looked beautiful. "You're so brave," he said, enveloping her in a hug. "You left him."

"But it's awful. Everything's awful."

"For now, but things will get better."

He presented the flowers, a colorful bunch that looked pretty good for a supermarket bouquet. They hugged with them in between, the scent of mixed flowers adding to their embrace. When they parted, she led him to the sitting area of her suite, a small corner near the bed with a sofa upholstered in scratchy wool. She put the flowers on the coffee table since she didn't have a vase.

"They're lovely," she told him. "Thank you."

"I figured we had something to celebrate. Day one of your freedom, sweetheart." He looked around. "This room's pretty nice. I've never been to Los Feliz."

"Me either. Can I get you something to drink?" she asked. "I have water, and there's a vending machine down the hall if you want a Coke or something."

"I'm good."

"You're not wearing a suit." She scanned his clothes, dark jeans and a button up shirt that was missing the starch and tie. "What's happening with you right now? What did Ironclad say about the stories on the news? Did they fire you?"

"I resigned yesterday, actually, before we even went out on the balcony. Before they took those photos."

"Oh God, those photos." She dropped her head into her hands. "I can't believe someone took photos of us. I'm sorry you lost your job."

"I was already planning to quit. Hey, it's okay." He rubbed her back, trying to give her some of the strength that had built inside him since he'd sent in his resignation. It'd felt satisfying to do the right thing. "I don't think I'm cut out for the Hollywood security lifestyle anyway. Don't worry about me. How are you? How did all this happen?"

"Badly," she said, grimacing. "Everything happened badly. Nate woke me up early this morning and confronted me about the photos. He brought two lawyers with him. Two! At six-thirty in the morning."

"Good old Nate."

"Since the lawyers were there, and he was acting like an asshole, I told him I wanted a divorce. Once he realized I was serious, the threats started, but I stood my ground. I told him I had to leave, packed up my shit, and called a cab. I checked in here around ten and went to the diner in the parking lot for breakfast, and by the time I got back…"

"The stories were loose. Nate's revenge stories."

"Yeah. I saw it on the lobby TV when I walked in—NATHANIEL YORK TO DIVORCE. His PR team is already spreading dirty, untrue rumors about me. I mean, I knew it would be like this, that he'd be cruel and vindictive, but now that it's happening, I don't know what to do. It's so much more intense than I feared."

It was more intense than Caleb feared too, but he didn't say that. "You can get your own PR representation," he said. "It'll be okay. Tell your side of the story, so Nate can't control the narrative."

"I thought of that." She turned to him, tears welling in her eyes. "But… Jesus, I didn't want to cry. I wanted to be strong."

"What happened?"

"I called around looking for a PR firm to represent me, but no one will take me on. I called twenty different agencies. The good ones. The okay ones. Even the bargain basement ones wouldn't take my call."

"That's bullshit. Why?"

"I'm sure it's because Nate called them first, or his lawyers, or Gladys." Her phone buzzed. She turned it over without looking at the screen. "Reporters are calling me one after the other, leaving messages. They're not interested in my side of the story, they're just asking for comments on Nate's side of the story. And how do you think they got my number so they could harass me?" The tears in her eyes overflowed and fell. "The last one asked if I was there when you tried to kill Nate's bodyguard, so he's spreading lies about that. My charities are going to dump me over this. And what if the police come after you?"

"Honey, that's not going to happen. It's just a game Nate's playing to scare you." He embraced her, holding her tight, doing his best to calm her.

"They also asked…" Her breath hitched as she trembled against him. "They asked about my alcoholism. They had statements from people at my old AA meetings, people I thought were my friends. The reporters wanted to know if I've started drinking again, if that's what broke up the marriage." Her face crumpled into a sob. "I'm afraid Nate's going to tell them about the baby, that I lost his baby because I was drinking. He always accused me of that when we were fighting, but I was sober through the whole pregnancy. I swear I never took a drink, not for months beforehand—"

"Shh." He rocked her, stroking her hair, wiping away her tears. "You know the truth. That's all that matters."

"But it's not fair. It's not fair for him to spread those stories, to say things that aren't true. It's not fair."

"I know." He remembered how he'd felt when his group leader had lied about Jared. The outrage, the helplessness. The sense of injustice that gnawed at his soul. "People are shitty. They lie to protect themselves, because they're fucked up and scared."

"But now I'm fucked up and scared."

"No, you're not. You're going to be fine."

She pulled away from him, fear replaced by angry, rapid-fire emotions. "How can you say I'm going to be fine? Nate's putting out awful, degrading stories about me so he can play the victim, and I can't get anyone to speak for my side."

"You can speak for your side."

She threw up her hands. "But who'll listen, and who'll believe me, with Nate the Great and his empire putting out every awful byline they can think up about me? They'll drag out lurid stories from my past, about my family and the drugs, and my mom dying in jail. They'll paint this story of Nate trying to save me from myself, and how my alcoholism won out in the end. They'll talk about…Katie Lou…"

She broke again, collapsing against him. All he could do was commiserate. He didn't know how to solve this for her, because the celebrity press was a hungry monster, and Nate would be willing to feed it fucked up stories for months to hurt Jenna, and scare her into submission.

"And they must have had this already in the hoppers, waiting for the day I left." She pulled away again, went for her phone and fumbled it open, and showed him an email titled YOU GET WHAT YOU ASK FOR in all caps.

"It's the divorce settlement," she sobbed, "and it's fifty-four pages long. I only left that house a few hours ago. How did they write fifty-four pages of legal bullshit during that time?"

"It's what you said—they already had it ready. They knew this was coming, and they were getting everything ready so they could scare you right into line."

"Well, I'm scared!"

"I know, sweetheart. I know you're scared. Here, come here. Take a breath." He took the flowers from the table and tugged a rose from the bundle. "Smell this. Take a slow breath in and out."

She obeyed, half-heartedly. He plucked another rose from the bunch.

"And this one. Breathe it in."

She sniffed, burying her nose in the soft petals. He offered a daisy next, then a carnation, pulling them from the supermarket bundle. As she sniffed them, crying, wiping her eyes, he picked up the rest of the flowers and pulled Jenna toward the bed.

"Come here. Lie down with me and rest a while. Nothing will happen if we take a break for a minute. We have each other, so we'll survive this insanity. Give me your phone and let me look at this bullshit document Nate sent."

She handed it over, and he lay beside her on the hotel bed, scanning through the divorce papers. They'd been written using lofty legal language, meant to intimidate. Those fucking assholes.

While he read, Jenna huddled against him, worn out by Nate's bullying. Caleb might not be working for Ironclad anymore, but her protection was still his number one goal. He wouldn't let them frighten her back into Nate's clutches. She deserved better. She deserved kindness and honor. Maybe—if she wanted it—a life with him.

"You know, this isn't an agreement unless you agree with it," he said, when he was halfway through his perusal. Nate wasn't offering anything, from what he could see, just threatening legal action on a variety of fronts. "You can get your own lawyer."

"With what money?"

"With my money, and yours. We have enough."

Maybe. They might have enough for Jenna to stand up to Nate for a while, but not to win. Nate's resources were boundless. They both knew that.

She turned so she was facing him, her legs intertwined with his. "I love you," she said. "I love that you're trying to keep my hopes up, but Nate's going to come out on top of this disaster. It was always going to happen. He's planned for this day."

"You could call a reporter now." Caleb held her gaze, shutting the stupid divorce doc and handing back her phone. "You could put an end to everything, and just tell the truth about Nate, about your marriage, about the last ten years."

"Even if people believed me—which they won't—it would only complicate things from a legal standpoint. I'm the one who made our agreement, and I'm the one who broke it."

"But Tom… The things that man did to you, with Nate's knowledge…"

She shook her head. Caleb understood she wasn't strong enough to talk about litigating Tom right now. Maybe she never would be.

"I spent so much strength just walking out the door," she said. She picked up a rose and rolled it against her cheek. "I'm so tired now. How am I going to do this? How am I going to fight these stories? Navigate this divorce?"

He touched the rose petals, then her silky smooth skin, her nose and lips and eyelids. So tired, his beautiful, brave protectee. So exhausted by manipulation and lies. *Enough*, he thought. *For God's sake, she's been through enough.*

"What if you just left?" he asked.

Her eyes returned to his. "Left?"

"Just left without responding to Nate's messages and emails, his threatening divorce papers? What if you refused to engage?"

She looked confused. "I… What?"

"When I had enough bullshit in the Army, I left. I could have fought my discharge, I could have stayed. But at some point, you have to realize something is too big to wrangle, that it's not worth banging your head against the behemoth anymore."

She digested his words a moment, moving the rose down to rest against her throat. "But…what would happen if I left?"

"Not much, if you weren't around. You could hide where no one in the press could find you. Change your number. Refuse to communicate with Nate. What would happen?"

She thought about that. "The stories would die out, I guess. If there was no bad wife to follow around, no comments on the rumors, no showy divorce." A slow smile spread over her face. "It would drive him crazy."

"It would. Not being able to manipulate you with his media cronies? He'd be beside himself in the space of a week. Look how crazy he's already going, now that you're outside his realm of control. What if we took off to Spur and ignored all this, and hung out there until the fuss was over?"

"What about the legalities? The divorce?"

He shrugged. "You two never had a real marriage. It won't be a real divorce. Ignore the document he sent, it's stupid. Refuse to act. That'll move the pressure to his court. As for you and me..."

He'd thought about the two of them a lot over the past few weeks. He thought about how full his heart felt when she was around, and the way he loved her so much more deeply than he'd ever thought he could love. "As for you and me," he said, leaning closer to give her a kiss. "I think we could have a lot of fun in Spur while we wait things out. You deserve an old-fashioned courtship, sweetheart. You missed out on that last time."

She tilted her head so the next kiss landed on her cheek, and took his face between her hands. "You want to court me, Caleb Winchell?"

"Yes, and marry you, eventually, once your divorce comes through." He turned his face to kiss her palm. "Have children with you, with all the knitted baby caps they could ever need. Well, if you wanted that."

"You don't know what you're getting into," she said, forcing his gaze back to hers.

"I think I do. I can handle your bad guys."

"No, I mean, you're too young to get married. I was around your age when I married, and you see how that turned out."

He shook his head. "In life experience years, I'm at least ten years older, which puts me at the same age as you. And in soul years, I feel ancient. Maybe you do too."

She stared at him, and he couldn't read her expression. He wanted her to agree to this so badly. He wanted to take her away from here, take her somewhere real, somewhere safe.

"If Spur's too small a town for you, we could go somewhere else," he offered. "Anywhere else. We could hide together anywhere that's quiet and private, and make it work."

"I want Spur." Her eyes welled again. "I want an old-fashioned courtship. Maybe even a Texas wedding."

"Now I'm going to say it—you don't know what you're getting into. Texas weddings are a cultural monstrosity. Think white, sequined boots and cowboy-hat veils."

"As long as the press isn't there."

They both laughed, then settled down, lying close to each other.

"Los Feliz is nice," he said, "but this isn't the type of place you hide to get over a bad marriage. You need fresh, humid air and fireflies for that."

* * * * *

Jenna lay in a kind of shock, sheltered in Caleb's arms. She could leave. She could just *leave*. She was strong enough, and she had more power than she knew, including the power to walk away and refuse to play into Nate's mind games.

Her world, which had seemed like a prison for so long, opened suddenly into a field of dry grass and welcoming sun, flowers, butterflies, rainbows, and fireflies. She could have the freedom of those fireflies at Burger's Pond, only lighting up when she chose to.

It was simple. She could just turn her back and walk away.

Not alone, of course. Caleb would be there with her. He'd promised he'd always protect her, and she trusted him more than she'd ever trusted anyone. He'd taught her that trust was a real thing, that honor existed in truthful hearts and souls. Despite her early experiences, he'd taught her there were plenty of people who could be trusted, people who didn't have an agenda that included using her. She wanted to go live among them.

"I love you," she said, pressing against him. "I can't even explain how much I love you."

"You don't have to," he replied, reassuring as ever.

"No, I really, really love you." She took his face between her hands and traced the narrow scar beneath his eye that would always remind her of his heroism. "But are you sure you want this? That you want to stay with me, and deal with all these complications?"

"The complications are nothing, sweetheart."

He dismissed them, just like that, and she understood how he kept his soul so clean and pure. He believed in goodness, that you could always find it if you were brave and focused enough. If you were good, life would be good.

And she'd be good, now that she had this second chance. She'd find ways to give back to the community wherever they ended up, not with Nate's money and influence, but with her own caring heart. She'd look for a job she loved, not making millions, but enough.

The longer she stared into Caleb's eyes, the more sure she was. She kissed him, tracing his cheekbones, then running her fingers back into his close-cropped hair. Soft, prickly, capable, strong. "I love you," she whispered against his lips, because she could never say it enough times, not when she'd craved this kind of love for so long.

"I love you more, sweetheart."

"I want you to take me away from here," she said, reaching down to stroke his cock.

"You got it."

"I want Texas heat and fireflies."

"Yes, baby, whenever you like."

They tugged at each other's clothes, caught in a magical moment. She needed him inside her to seal this pact, this walking-away-and-finding-a-real-life pact.

"I want real love." She smiled, caressing his bare chest. "Real emotion. Real feelings. You brought that into my life. You walked into my world and just brought it all, and I..."

"Shh."

He was right, she didn't have to say anymore. Caleb knew. His cock prodded between her legs, rigid and ready, exciting her, bringing a depth of pleasure she thought she'd never know. He sheathed himself and drove inside slowly, watching her. He smiled at her indrawn breath.

"More?" he asked in his sexy drawl.

"Yes, always more. All of you."

He gave her all of him, surging to her core. The sterile economy-hotel suite fell away, replaced by the warm sensation of connection. She threw her arms out as he pushed her back on the bed and fucked her with strong snaps of his hips. He cupped her breasts, squeezing them possessively, whispering naughty things she couldn't hear in the height of her arousal. Their lovemaking intensified to the point where she felt swept away.

She was going away with him, it was that easy. No qualms, no misgivings.

"I'm almost there." She moaned, clutching his shoulders. "I'm so close, so close."

She was so close to a better life. She wouldn't look at the news again, or the celebrity sites, or even read the dumb divorce document Nate had sent. All she needed was this, to be safe in Caleb's arms.

"I've got you," he said as she trembled to a climax. "God, you're so beautiful, sexy girl."

Her orgasm bloomed, lovely piercing pleasure suffusing her body. His weight and heft centered her, bringing her back to the world as he pounded through his own climax. The scent of their bodies melded with the flowers' scent; the bouquet Caleb brought her was now strewn across the bed. He hitched his body to one side.

"I've got a stem poking my back." He reached behind him and produced the flower, a white rose that had thankfully been de-thorned. "Beautiful," he said, touching her nose with it.

But he was the beautiful one, for showing her she could live a real and beautiful life.

18.
HAPPY

Two Months Later

Caleb watched Snowy the cat rise from his blankets under the patio glider, drawn by the tempting, teasing movement of yarn.

"I'm knitting," Jenna scolded the white puffball. "We talked about this. Let go."

He chuckled as the cat wound a couple claws in the particular yarn she was using, leaving the rest of the basket alone. "He wants to learn to knit too."

His mother laughed. "Baby hats by Snowy. Finest cat hats in the South."

Jenna nudged Snowy's claws away and carried him back to his shady spot, but he left the patio instead with an indignant twitch of his tail.

"I guess he told me," Jenna said, settling back beside Caleb on the sofa. "Can I get either of you something to drink? Some water? Tea?"

"I'm fine," said his mom. "Have a seat there and enjoy the weather. I do believe the breeze is picking up."

"Feels good." Caleb lifted his head, smelling fresh air, flowers, sunshine, all the good things that surrounded them.

He and Jenna had agreed on a small house, but invested in a sprawling patio so they could spend most of their time outside when the

Texas summer ended and fall cooled the air. They'd agreed on a dog too, and a cat. And another cat who already roamed the property, and didn't mind pretending to belong to them. And yet another cat, to the dog's disgust. Bella made the most of it, like any practical country hound.

Today, his mother had stopped by to visit, joining them on the patio's sofa, her head bent beside Jenna's as they knitted baby caps. She'd brought Jethro along, since he was Bella's litter mate. The two dogs ran circles in the yard, occasionally lunging toward the cat, who ignored their antics. Snowy had already trained them not to touch him, using his very sharp claws.

"Are you watching?" Jenna nudged him, drawing his attention back to his knitting needles.

"I'm watching."

"Pay attention," she chided. "It's not that hard to do, once you get the hang of it."

"My hands are bigger than both of yours," he said in his defense.

His mother laughed again, her needles clicking away. "You've never been one to sit and do intricate things."

"No, I can learn this." He'd promised Jenna he'd try, anyway, now that they were providing baby hats to the Lubbock Area Children's Hospital twice a month. He was starting small, but he intended to learn to knit stripes and swirls, and maybe even some sports logos. Well, once he mastered the plain, pale yellow color Jenna was teaching him with.

"Push the needle through the stitch...that's right." She leaned close enough that he could smell her floral perfume. "Then loop the yarn around and pull the needle back out. It's only a small movement."

"Again—I have very big hands."

He was teasing. He was actually getting the hang of it—the basic stitch, anyway—and he was secure enough in his masculinity to learn to purl too. As for Jenna, she was learning all kinds of things about small town life in Texas, like getting to know your neighbors, watching high school football games, and getting the shopping done on Sunday before the stores closed.

Then there were the other things they were teaching each other, like how to be true and honest, and take deep breaths, and let themselves be in love with no fear or guilt. Caleb was learning to teach self-defense and Tae Kwon Do classes at the Spur community center instead of bodyguarding celebrities, and Jenna was learning that you could be country without being poor and desperate, as her family had been.

"Look at that," she said. "Now, that's a nice row. No dropped stitches the whole time."

He looked back over the lengthening tail of his beginner project, which was full of holes from dropped stitches, but yeah, he was getting better.

Bella's bark pierced the silence, and Jethro joined in, his tail beating against the patio railing. Caleb's gaze drifted over Jenna's shoulder. "Heads up, sweetheart. Looks like they found us."

She frowned, turning to look. "Darn. I gave them the worst directions I could."

"Heel, Bella," Caleb said when the pup's hackles rose. "You too, Jethro. Stay here. Trust me, you won't get past security."

He stood and patted the hounds' quivering haunches as four burly bodyguards shouldered their way through clumps of hedges and emerged from the wooded path.

"Goodness," said his mother. "Who are those men? Soldiers?"

"Nate's security army," Jenna answered, putting down her knitting. "I told him he wouldn't need them here."

Caleb shrugged. "You know how he is. He needs them even when he doesn't need them." When she stood, he rubbed her back for support. "I wasn't sure he'd show."

"Me, either."

Nate and Gladys followed behind the security guards, walking over their soft grassy lawn like it might contain active mines.

"Jenna," Nate called, stopping a hundred yards or so from the patio. "Are those good dogs?"

"The best," she claimed, over their incessant barking. "They won't bother you."

"Why don't I take the pups back to my place for a while?" his mother suggested. "You can drop by for Bella later, when she's all tuckered out."

"Thanks, Mom," said Caleb. "Might be easier with them out of the way. Quieter, anyway."

It wasn't difficult to lure the dogs to the back of her pickup, since they loved nothing more than going for a ride. By the time Caleb turned back around, Nate and Gladys had made it to the open-air porch. They stood stiffly, conversing with Jenna. He wanted to rush over and protect her, defend her, but he knew by now she was hardy enough to deal with any bullshit Nate might throw at her. And Tom...

To his surprise, Tom wasn't there.

"She'll be okay," his mom said, watching him look back toward the house.

"I know. It's just...these things they have to untangle to get free of each other."

"They made the tangle. It's good for them to work it out together. Then the two of you..." Her voice rose in a gentle hint.

"Yes, Ma. I'll make an honest woman of her."

"Be sure you do, sweetheart," she said with her generous smile. "Because she brings out the best in you." She got in her truck and waved out the window. "See y'all later. Come for dinner if you like."

"Yes, ma'am. See you soon."

When he looked back at the house, Nate, Gladys, and Jenna were headed inside, while the security guys took up positions around the perimeter.

Well, there *were* three cats running around, any one of which might hiss without provocation, or pee on Nate's shoes. He went back to the patio and sat near the open screen door, close enough if she needed him, but not underfoot.

* * * * *

Jenna led Nate and Gladys to the dining table, since the living room doubled as a bedroom. While she and Caleb loved cuddling on their sofa bed, her visitors wouldn't have felt nearly as comfortable there.

"Can I get you something to drink?" Jenna asked.

"Water," they both said. "Extra cold, with ice," Nate added.

She laughed at his woebegone expression. "It's still warm here, isn't it?"

"Hot as hell, compared to L.A."

"Did you have any trouble finding the place?"

Nate and Gladys exchanged glances, then he waved a hand toward the guys outside. "Ask them. I think we doubled back a few times."

"A few times," Gladys agreed in her excessively polite voice, blinking rapidly. "There's so much...country out here."

"Well, I would have come to you, but the paparazzi..."

Nate's brows rose. "You're sure they haven't found you here?"

She shrugged. "They don't care about me anymore, since I ducked out of town. You were always the real story. Anyway, there's nowhere for them to stay near here, aside from tents in the woods, and no one will put up with them lurking around. They're likely to get shot at. This isn't a paparazzi friendly place."

"Your house is...nice," he said, looking around. "Is this all of it?"

"It's a tiny house. Spur is the tiny house capital of Texas. We'll probably move somewhere bigger when we have kids, but this is great for now."

"You must live on top of each other." He was clearly repulsed by the idea.

"Yeah, it's great."

Strange, that she could move from such a massive, luxurious house to such a small one, and feel so much more content. She supposed it depended on who lived in the house with you.

"Where's Tom?" she asked. "He didn't come with you?"

"No." She saw a little of the old Nate in his striking hazel eyes, the nervous, confused Nate she'd met when he first proposed marriage. "Tom and I are going through a rough patch," he explained after a taut silence. "Things changed after you left. He's gotten harder to manage. He got obsessed about vilifying you in the press, but I wanted to move on when you moved on. He still talks about you and how glad he is that you're gone, like it's some power he holds over you. It just makes him look bad. Sometimes he's so petty."

He took a long sip of water, looking to Gladys for help, but she only blinked like a pleasant robot.

"We'll probably break up soon," he said. "Not because I want to get back together with you..."

"I imagine there's too much water under that bridge." The idea of them reuniting was laughable, but she was trying to be kind. "I'm sorry about Tom, but you know, I always told you you could find someone better. You deserve a partner you can depend on, someone you can trust."

"But people I can trust aren't as exciting."

She shook her head at him, and they both laughed, and it felt good to laugh with her soon-to-be ex-husband. It felt friendly, less tense than everything that had come before.

"Anyway, I brought the new divorce papers."

It was Gladys who produced the folio of documents, pushing them across the table to Jenna.

"It's shorter now, not like the last one," he said. "The lawyers stayed on me about the protection of privacy, but the fines have been taken out, and the settlement we agreed on is outlined on page..."

"Fifteen," Gladys provided.

"Page fifteen. You get an eighty-seven million payout, plus the value of your wedding rings, which are yours to keep. In return, you agree that you'll never talk about me in any way, shape, or form. No press, no interviews, no mention of me for the rest of your life."

Jenna clasped her hands in her lap. The rings had already been sold to pay for their house, and the settlement number wasn't a surprise. They'd worked it out over spreadsheets of Nate's income, figuring what percentage she deserved for sticking out their ten-year marriage. What surprised her was how sad she felt at those words, *no mention of me for the rest of your life.*

"It sounds so final," she said.

"It is final." Gladys broke in with her weirdly inappropriate smile. "Once you sign, there will be no more negotiations."

"I know. I don't want any more negotiations. You're giving me more money than I need."

Sweetheart, you earned it. Take the money. That had been Caleb's advice as they hashed through things, and he was right, she had earned it. Once she had it, she could do good things with it, and Nate would be a little more careful about contracting new wives in the future.

"Will you get married again?" she asked, signing the final set of papers.

Nate looked lost. "I don't know. Either way, you can't say anything about our marriage. You can't talk about me, or tell anyone about...you know...my private life."

"You can't talk about me either, right? That's my side of the deal. I get fifty-thousand dollars for each character assassination story your PR agency pushes into the press."

He shook his head. "My agency's done with that. No more nasty stories, I promise. I never meant to do those stories. It was just the sudden abandonment, you wanting to leave. I was so scared you'd ruin me."

"Why would I want to ruin you? What would that accomplish?"

"I don't know. I worried you'd act out of hatred or frustration, all of which you were entitled to. Just please...Jen...for the sake of what we had together, for the sake of how good things were before everything got crazy, please...please, don't ever..."

His voice broke, and for the first time in a long time, real emotion choked him up. She reached for him without thinking, because he needed someone to comfort him, because he lived with so much fear. As soon as she reached out, he clutched her close.

"I'll never say anything," she said, trying to soothe him. "I swear, Nate, my lips are sealed forever. You can trust me." She patted his hair as he clung to her, this poor, frightened A-list action star. "I'll never out you, because it's not fair that you have to live like this. It's not fair that you can't have a successful career while being yourself. You know that, right?"

He nodded, then pulled away, wiping some moisture from his eyes, real tears, for once. "You let me be myself though, babes. You hung in there so I could keep up appearances. I'll always love you for that."

"I'll always love you too."

Even Gladys was crying as they said these final words to each other, these parting words after ten long years. At least she thought Gladys was crying. No tears actually came out.

"Listen," Jenna said, turning back to Nate. "Whenever it gets to be too much in Hollywood land, whenever you need to be yourself with no prying eyes around, come visit us here in Spur. You can bring any boyfriend you like, as long as they're nice. In other words, not Tom. You need to get rid of him and find a nice partner, and when you do, you're always welcome to hide here whenever you need a break."

"But your house is so small," he joked. He was being the goofy, charming Nate that Tom always seemed to chase away.

"Yes, it's small, but we'll go stay with Caleb's parents and give you the run of the place," she said. "And we'll leave our dog to bark at anyone who comes near the house, so you can be as gay and frisky as you want the whole time you're here. I won't care. Caleb won't care. Will you care, Gladys?"

"Not at all," she said.

"And Nate..." She paused, holding his hand between both of hers. "If you ever do decide to live your real life out in the open, I'll be there for you. I know it's not possible now—and I'll never tell anyone without your permission," she repeated for the umpteenth time. "But if you make that decision, let me know, because I'll go to the press and tell them what an awesome human you are, both as a husband and a gay man."

He accepted the box of tissues she passed to him, and wiped his eyes.

"I've been so cruel to you these past few years," he said. "Why are you being so kind?"

"I guess because I'm finally happy. I hope you can be happy too, one day. Please think about the whole coming-out thing. Maybe when you have enough money socked away, or when your looks start to fade..."

He gave her a comical glare. "Don't talk about looks fading. I need this face."

"But you're not just your face, or your films, and you deserve to be happy."

He blinked at her, his eyes getting misty again. "You deserve to be happy too, Jen. I think that bodyguard really loves you."

"Caleb. His name is Caleb."

"I know. You think I don't know the name of the man who broke up my marriage? I just don't like to say it. I hope he deserves you. You'll make a really good real wife."

"Thanks."

Their inside cat, Tabby, jumped from the floor to Nate's lap. He let out a shriek and Tabby jumped off, offended. "We should get out of your hair," he said, brushing at the imaginary cat hairs on his designer jeans.

"Okay. Before you go, could I have a few words with Gladys, alone? I want to make sure she takes good care of you."

"Sure." Nate stood, shaking off the emotion that still left him a little pale. "I might walk around outside. The air smells different here."

He went out on the patio, leaving them alone. Gladys looked at her, blinking, smiling. Crazy Gladys.

"No matter what you say, I know it was you," Jenna said.

"What?"

"I know you called the paps on Caleb and me. At first I thought it was because you wanted Nate for yourself—"

The older woman erupted in laughter. "For myself? What would I do with that bundle of neuroses?"

"I know, right? I think you're too nice for him. In fact, I think you broke up our marriage as a kindness, to save both of us from ourselves. It's okay if you're nice, you can admit it."

"I'd rather not," she said.

"Here's my evidence," Jenna said. "You were the one who stepped in to help me when I really started drinking. You were the one who chose Caleb at the Ironclad offices, rather than some cranky old guy. And when things really got rough, you made a call to the paps you knew would end a really destructive marriage. I wouldn't be surprised if you had a big hand in guiding this more amicable settlement." She patted the folio and paused, impressed by Gladys' poker face. "Anyway, I can't thank you enough."

Gladys was silent a moment, her ever-present smile trembling. "There were other times I wish I'd stepped in. Maybe you'll forgive me for that."

"There's nothing to forgive. Thanks for caring when it felt like no one was caring."

"Well, you cared about Nate."

It was true. She'd always cared about Nate. When people shared secrets, it formed a bond. "Can I ask you something before you and Nate leave?" Jenna asked.

"Sure." *Blink blink*.

"What's with your blinking thing? Is it a nervous condition? Some kind of compulsive thing?"

"Oh, no, it's an inherited condition. I have insufficient tears."

Insufficient tears. If that didn't sum up Jenna's Hollywood story...

"I meant what I said about this being a shelter for Nate, a place where he can be himself," she said as the two of them stood. "Bring him here if he needs to take a breath. I've learned how to breathe out here, and everything is different. Everything is wonderful."

"I can see that you're in a better place," said Gladys with a genuine smile. "I'm glad you've found this new life."

They walked to the door. Out on the patio, Nate was playing with Snowy, rolling balls of yarn in his direction. Snowy batted them back, then ran in frenetic circles, thrilled to find someone who understood the chaotic power of yarn. Without Tom around being a dick, maybe Nate was save-able.

"Take care of him," she said to Gladys.

Blink. Smile. Nod. "Of course, Jenna. I definitely will."

19.
EVER AFTER

Whenever they ate at the Winchell home, they visited Burger's Pond afterward before they headed home. "Carry me," Jenna said, throwing out her arms. "I'm too stuffed from dinner to walk."

Caleb grinned and swept her up, sending Bella into a fit of excited barking. "There, I carried you a little," he said. "You have to walk the rest of the way."

Bella nudged her hand when Caleb set her down, checking on her. "I'm fine, sweet dog." She patted the pup's head. "Daddy's right, I'm strong enough to walk myself. I'm just really full." She turned back to Caleb. "Why does your mom always make me eat so much?"

"She thinks you're too thin. She blames it on Hollywood."

"I've always been this thin." When she was growing up, it was because money—and food—was scarce, and starving yourself in Hollywood was normal behavior. "Do you think I'm too thin?"

"I think you should be any weight that makes you happy. Although once you get up around three hundred pounds, I won't be able to pick you up without hitting the gym."

Jenna laughed, but her heart also thudded with pleasure. He'd love her at three hundred pounds, because his love wasn't based on posturing and appearances. She didn't have to be photo ready when she was with him. She hardly bothered with makeup anymore.

It was nearly dusk, and they walked faster, not wanting to miss the fireflies. Bella trotted along with them rather than dashing back and forth. She was growing up, maybe, or perhaps Jethro had tired her out.

When they reached the pond, they ducked beneath the trees and made their way to a high-backed cedar bench set within a circle of stones. Mr. Burger had welcomed their idea of installing a bench for the firefly gazers, and this bench was special: the word *Remember* was carved along the back.

Using a pen knife, they'd scratched the first two names into the wood's grain. *Katie Lou*, for the baby she'd lost, and *Jared*, for Caleb's Special Ops friend. Sometime recently, someone had carved *Roland* into the bench, as well as the name of a neighbor's much loved, recently deceased dog. In time, perhaps the bench would collect many names. They'd intended it as a community memorial, a way to honor lost family and friends in a place that already invited meditation.

"Here, Bella," Jenna said, settling the dog on the sparse grass near their feet. The fireflies were out, in less numbers than high summer, but there were enough to put on a show. She leaned into Caleb's arms, watching the interplay of light over the dark pond.

"How do you feel?" he asked, tugging a lock of her hair.

"How do I feel?"

"About the divorce being finalized soon. About life here. Is it everything you hoped?"

"It's more than I hoped." She didn't even have to think about that. "It's so much more than I thought life could be. What about you? Are you happy?"

He held her tighter, pressing a kiss to the top of her head. "I think I was trying to be happy in all those exotic jobs and locations, when I always knew I had to be here. You can see fireflies a lot of places, but not these fireflies." He tilted her head up, ignoring the light show to hold her gaze. "And having you here..."

His voice trailed off, but she was pretty sure he'd been about to say something complimentary, based on the kiss he gave her. Jenna forgot the fireflies, forgot everything as her wonderful, handsome, pure former bodyguard gave her a very un-pure going over, licking her neck, running his hands beneath her shirt's hem to trail his fingers over her skin. Their kiss deepened, their breath mingling with delectable possibility in the cool evening air.

Bella's indignant bark made both of them jump. The dog put a paw on Caleb's knee as if to say, *hey, don't forget about me.*

"Yes, we love you, too," he assured her. "But mom and dad are busy. Why don't you go see if you can find any good sticks floating in the pond?"

He stood and threw one to get her started, then laughed as she paused to lap up a quick drink at the water's edge. Caleb's laugh was everything to Jenna: low, easy, full of simple pleasure. When he turned back to her, she probably had some dumb look of adoration pasted on her face. She couldn't help it. He was such a miracle in her life.

"What?" he asked. "Do I have a bug on me?"

"No, I just want to kiss you some more."

He returned and sat beside her, and cupped her face with his palm. "Before we kiss again, I have something to tell you. Something to ask you." He searched her features so deeply it felt like being caressed. "I think I might want to put in my claim, now that this Hollywood divorce of yours is about to come through. I'm addicted to your courage and your heart, and the way you smile and walk and move. I'm addicted to that little girl inside you that's always a little worried, and that strong woman that's so fucking brave."

Tears welled in her eyes, that he'd appreciate both the scared little girl and strong woman inside her, two sides of the same coin.

"Plus, if I don't put a ring on your finger soon," he continued with a grin, "my mother's head might explode, seeing as how we're living together. Sweetheart. Jenna. I know you've barely gotten out of your last marriage, and—"

"Yes."

"And that getting married again right away might feel overwhelming—"

"Yes."

He dug in his pocket. "But I've been carrying this ring around for two weeks and— What?"

"Yes." She held out her hand, finger extended. "My answer is yes. Your claim is accepted. Please give me the ring."

He looked a little flustered that she'd agreed so quickly. "I'm supposed to kneel down and everything," he protested.

"Then do it, now, while the fireflies are still on."

He knelt beside the bench, their special *Remember* bench, and opened a ring box to reveal a simple, sparkling diamond set in white gold. "It was my great-grandma's," he said. "We can find another ring if you'd like something flashier."

"Flashier? No. Caleb, this is the most perfect ring I've ever seen."

And it was. She didn't want flashy things anymore. The fact that he loved her enough to propose with a family ring made it beautiful beyond compare.

"I had it sized to fit you," he said as he took it from the box. "And polished up a little."

"Oh my God." That was all she could say as he slipped it on her finger. "Oh my God. Oh my God."

He squeezed her hand and made her look at him through her tears. "Is everything okay?"

Is everything okay? How many times had he asked her that, especially during the first days of their acquaintance, when he was her bodyguard, and she was a defensive mess?

"Yes, everything's okay," she stammered, overcome with emotion. "It's so, so okay. It's just... I've wanted this, oh, so much. I've dreamed of a happily ever after for so long." She touched the ring, which perfectly fit her finger. "The thing with Nate was fake, but this is real, and it's happening just the way I hoped it would when I was a little girl. The sweet proposal, the beautiful surroundings, the special ring, and the perfect man. I never thought I'd have these things. I'd thought they were just pointless dreams." She grasped his shoulders and pulled him back onto the bench beside her. "Do you know how happy you're making me right now?"

"I have some idea," he said, his blue eyes glinting in the darkening night. "I never thought I'd have this either. I lived through some dark stuff and took some bad turns, to the point I thought happiness was a myth. But it's not a myth, it's something we can fight for. I watched you fight for your happiness, and I'm going to do that, too. We're going to be happy together, sweetheart."

Bella bounded back to them, considerably muddier since she'd been splashing in the water.

"Look at my ring," Jenna said to her. "Isn't it beautiful?"

Bella was more concerned with licking her mama's smiling face than checking out the ring, but that was okay. Caleb and Jenna headed back to the Winchell house to share the good news with his family, and eat some oven-fresh pie.

Then they returned to their small house in the woods and climbed into their bed that was also a sofa, and celebrated their new engagement—the start of a true, pure, happy life.

A Final Note

I hope you enjoyed this third story in my bodyguard series. Before you ask, yes, you've seen both Caleb and Kyle in other books. My Annabel Joseph readers will know Kyle from *Comfort Object*, as well as his book in that series, *Caressa's Knees*. Caleb showed up in my previous bodyguard book, *Diva*, guarding Lola, or Lady Paradise, as Ransom took a breather.

Even in the *Caressa's Knees* days, I knew I wanted to give one of Kyle's brothers a book, and I loved the emotional world that built up between Jenna and Caleb. I think it's fun for characters and families to move between books, even between my non-BDSM and BDSM books. Could Caleb be a little kinky? Deep down inside? Maybe. Probably.

Of course, my Ironclad Bodyguard books are also connected to my BDSM Ballet series, since the hero of *Waking Kiss*, Liam Wilder, owns Ironclad Solutions along with his dad. It's fun when these characters pop up here and there, and give you more stories to imagine. I have an ongoing love for bodyguards and protective men, so the Ironclad series has been a joy to write. I'm grateful for your support and I hope you'll check out my Comfort series and BDSM Ballet series if you don't mind a little kink with your romance.

Or a lot of kink. There's actually a lot of kink! You're warned, lol.

Many thanks to everyone who's supported me over the journey of this Ironclad series, with knowledge, expertise, and opinions: Audrey, Lina, Leslie, Theresa, Doris, Carol, Marisa, Lisa, Lanie, Riane, Janine, and my cover designer Kati at Bad Star Media. Thanks also to my readers, who make everything worth it. I hope you'll review *Beard* if it touched your heart, and I'll be hard at work soon on some new books for you to enjoy!

Other Books in the Ironclad Bodyguards series:

PAWN (Ironclad Bodyguards #1)

High stakes chess competition has always been a man's game—until Grace Ann Frasier topples some of the game's greatest champions and turns the chess world on its ear. Her prowess at the game is matched only by her rivals' desire to defeat her, or, worse, avenge their losses. When an international championship threatens Grace's safety, a bevy of security experts are hired to look after her, but only one is her personal, close-duty bodyguard, courtesy of Ironclad Solutions, Inc.

Sam Knight knows nothing about chess, but he knows Grace is working to achieve something important, and he vows to shelter her from those who mean her harm. When she leans on him for emotional support, attraction battles with professionalism and Sam finds his self-discipline wavering. Soon the complexity of their relationship resembles a chess board, where one questionable move can ruin everything—or win a game that could resonate around the world.

DIVA (Ironclad Bodyguards #2)

In his years at Ironclad, Ransom has built a reputation as a hardass bodyguard. He reels in the perverts, wrangles the mangled, and controls celebrities who are notoriously out of control. He's the person agents and managers turn to when a client is…difficult. Ransom doesn't put up with difficult. He brings them into line.

So when a world-famous DJ starts slipping into risky habits, he's hired to keep her on track during a multi-million-dollar tour. He figures he'll just knock the diva down a few pegs and scare her straight. Problem is, Lola isn't easily frightened, and "difficult" doesn't begin to describe their contentious relationship. The only thing more annoying than their daily fights and power struggles is their intensifying emotional connection.

Ransom's determined to save her…even if she doesn't want to be saved.

Also Available:
The Edge of the Earth by Molly Joseph

Charlotte Rowe organizes messes for a living. She's darn good at it, but her orderly and controlled life leaves her wanting more. When an aged linguist contacts her, needing her assistance to save her grandfather's dying language, Charlotte sees an opportunity for adventure. But as soon as she meets Dr. Will Mayfair, the other linguist on the project, she realizes she's in over her head. Her research partner is far younger and sexier than she'd been led to expect. As if that isn't enough to shake her up, they are forced to work in a remote Caucasus village where local political tensions are on the rise.

Charlotte and Will race to translate a rare document, but their work is stymied by the subtext of attraction whispering beneath every word they say. Then war breaks out and a tragic ordeal sends both their lives into a tailspin. Like the hero of the mythological tale they study, they are forced to battle for love and healing, and make a perilous journey back from the edge of the earth.

The BDSM Ballet series by Annabel Joseph

Waking Kiss... A stranger in the wings, a traitorous pair of toe shoes, and a traumatic turn dancing with The Great Rubio... For ballerina Ashleigh Keaton, it's been one hell of a night.

But it's not over yet. When Rubio drags her to a private party at his friend's house in the ritzy part of London, she meets Liam Wilder, a lifestyle dominant and frighteningly seductive man. Liam pursues Ashleigh, attracted by her strength and talent, but she has secrets—an abusive past and a crippling fear of intimacy that prevents her from connecting to anyone, especially a playboy reputed to be legendary in bed.

Eventually he wins her trust and sets out to heal the troubled dancer, awakening her to a world of sensual abandon in a series of BDSM "sessions" at his home. But how pure are his motives? Is he helping her or endangering her fragile soul?

***Fever Dream*…** Petra Hewitt's the top ballerina in the world, and The Great Rubio her obvious counterpart, so why does she want to strangle him whenever he's around? He's haughty, abrupt, demanding—and alarmingly sexy. Petra knows Rubio is dangerous to her heart, to her peace of mind, and worst of all, to her career, but his rough flirtation compels her. When she gets a chance to play with him at a BDSM party, their professional partnership takes a feverish left turn.

But as they enjoy their sensual games of dominance and submission, career pressures mount, and an overzealous fan brings dangerous tension to their relationship. Soon, the dream gives way to the stark reality of her vulnerability. Maybe, just maybe, some risks are too terrifying to take.

BDSM Ballet series is:
#1 *Waking Kiss* (Liam and Ashleigh's story)
#2 *Fever Dream* (Rubio and Petra's story)

The Comfort Series by Annabel Joseph

Have you ever wondered what goes on in the bedrooms of Hollywood's biggest heartthrobs? In the case of Jeremy Gray, the reality is far more depraved than anyone realizes. Brutal desires, shocking secrets, and a D/s relationship (with a hired submissive "girlfriend") that's based on a contract rather than love. It's just the beginning of a four-book saga following Jeremy and his Hollywood friends as they seek comfort in fake, manufactured relationships. Born of necessity—and public relations—these attachments come to feel more and more real. What does it take to live day-to-day with an A-list celebrity? Patience, fortitude, and a whole lot of heart. Oh, and a *very* good pain tolerance for kinky mayhem.

Comfort series is:
#1 *Comfort Object* (Jeremy's story)
#2 *Caressa's Knees* (Kyle's story)
#3 *Odalisque* (Kai's story)
#4 *Command Performance* (Mason's story)

About the Author

Molly Joseph is the "vanilla" counterpart of New York Times and USA Today bestselling BDSM romance author Annabel Joseph. Annabel and Molly both love to explore deep and complicated relationships on the pages of their books, except that Annabel's couples have BDSM dynamics, and Molly's couples don't.

You can learn more about Annabel (and Molly) by visiting annabeljoseph.com, where you can sign up for her newsletter to stay current on upcoming releases. You can also find Annabel/Molly on Facebook (Facebook.com/annabeljosephnovels), and Twitter (@annabeljoseph).

You can write to either Molly or Annabel at
Annabeljosephnovels@gmail.com.

Made in the USA
San Bernardino, CA
29 October 2018